Haley and the Yeti

Laura Langa

Also by Laura Langa

My Heart Before You

A Guarded Heart

Between Our Hearts

For Jackie, my bestie

Chapter 1

"And this, my dearest friend, is the balcony," Haley said, balancing her phone while keeping a grip on the bottle of nail polish, acetone, and bag of cotton balls. She let the camera graze over the two unexpectedly comfortable metal chairs and the tiny square coffee table between them. The phone briefly swept over her neighbor's balcony as well.

"Wait." Remmy's digitized voice halted her phone's progress to the reason Haley had brought the video call out here. "You don't have a separator between your balcony and your neighbor's?"

"No." Haley flipped the screen back to her face and sagged onto the dusty white chair cushion. "Apparently, elderly best friends had lived in these two apartments for years, and they took down the metal dividing wall against the rental agreement. The manager said the women's relationship was so endearing he didn't have the heart to enforce its reconstruction."

"Sounds like us," Remmy interjected, a frown teetering on her lips.

Haley grinned, trying to keep the mood of the conversation light. "That's the first thing I thought too." She left out that the manager also mentioned he'd rather go back into active duty than trifle with one of the former occupants.

"Are they going to put the wall back?"

"He said they would eventually, but right now, other repair jobs inside the units are taking priority."

Her eyes darted to the neighbor's balcony, which should've matched hers since these units were fully furnished carbon copies of each other. Instead of two metal chairs and a table, an oversized, beige fabric hammock was bolted to the large crossbeam that ran the length of the balcony. It was always stuffed with pillows, giving a perpetually occupied impression. A faded-green, circular woven mat rested beneath, surrounded by three waxy, viridescent aroid palms. Each sat in their own stately gray pot. Nestled beside them, smaller matching pots of succulents dotted the concrete floor.

Despite the use of monochromatic shaded earthenware, tiny dragon sculptures peeked from each pot. It was something you'd miss at first glance. The design felt contemporary on the outside, but a little bit quirky on the inside. It made her curious about the person who lovingly cared for all those vibrant plants, thriving in this arid desert.

"Are you sure you don't want to abandon this whole thing and come home?" The frown had finally won its battle with Remmy's mouth.

Haley had to stop herself from sighing and slumping further into her chair. The only thing that did stop her was her friend's observant, dark eyes watching her through her phone screen.

They'd had some variation of this conversation ever since she'd surprised Remmy on New Year's Day with the news that she'd be flying out the next morning for an eight-week traveling job in Arizona.

"You know I could probably get you out of your contract," Remmy continued, her lawyer side coming to the forefront.

"I told you. I need to do this." Haley kept her tone even. She couldn't explain how she needed to sort this out without always leaning on her best friend, because Remmy would argue with her—she was *already* arguing with her.

It was way past time for Haley to pull up her Wonder Woman undies and figure things out—by herself. As much as she'd leaned on Remmy for everything from learning to apply eyeshadow to explaining the mechanics of how to handle her first period, Haley needed to walk this craggy road alone.

"But running away from home and moving to the desert? Seriously, if I had known about this plan before you concocted it, I would have stopped you."

Haley knew that, which was why she'd omitted sharing any of her plans with her lifelong best friend. Haley's boss, Melinda, had been surprisingly understanding of her need to take a little "sabbatical." Not that phlebotomists *took* sabbaticals, but seeing that Melinda had known her since birth, she'd been willing to hold her job for her. After that conversation, Haley accepted the traveling phlebotomist position in Tucson, found a short-term rental online, bought plane tickets, and packed a bag.

"This isn't about you, Remmy. I love you. I'm not running away from you." A sigh rushed from her mouth. "I'm just trying to figure things out."

"I get that, Lee." She used Haley's childhood nickname, the one everyone from home called her. "I just don't know why we couldn't have done that together . . . like we always do." The sorrow in Remmy's voice ripped through Haley's stomach, but before she could apologize, her friend spoke again. "You're sure this sudden move has nothing to do with the fact that Zach Abrams is shooting a movie in Tucson for the next few months?"

Haley had to keep her lips from sliding up. "No."

Remmy had always poked at her choice of crushing on the unconventional-looking actor instead of a traditionally hot movie star—like any of the Chrises or Toms. Zach Abrams was more of a cross between a young John Cusack and modern-day Keanu Reeves. But even Remmy acquiesced that there was more to Zach Abrams than his *uniquely* handsome face. He was a genuinely good man—compassionate, admired, and well known for his altruistic pursuits.

Haley would never admit it, but his filming schedule might have had the slightest impact in choosing her destination. If she ran into her celebrity crush while sorting out her mess of a life, so be it.

"I thought Arizona in January would be the perfect antidote to the winter blues," Haley said.

"Uh-huh. Deny your infatuation with Zach Abrams, even though I know you'd move to the middle of the ocean if he said, 'Fancy a swim, darling?'"

The corners of Haley's mouth kicked up. Warmth rushed over her skin, relieved to be back to their normal bantering instead of wilting under the weight of Remmy's disapproval. "He's not British. That was just a character he played in that one Wes Anderson movie."

Little did Remmy know it was that specific version of Zach Abrams who often filled out Haley's loneliest days. She'd often imagine him in aching detail as she lay down to sleep—him telling her she was breathtakingly beautiful, him encouraging her to rest her head on his shoulder, his soft lips brushing her forehead as he implored her to sleep.

"Fine." Remmy rolled her eyes with a huff. "I guess I'll let you live your dream, as long as you promise to come home afterward. Or at the very least, if you do end up with Zach, I need to be the plus-one on your A-list, globe-trotting adventures."

Haley smiled. "Deal."

"Other than convincing Zach Abrams to fall in love with you and working, what's the plan for the next eight weeks?"

Haley settled the phone on the armrest of the other chair, rolled up the bottom of her scrub pants, and propped her bare foot on the table to paint her toes. "Sightsee, I guess." She tried to ignore the exasperated sigh coming through the phone and focused on painting her tiny toenails midnight blue.

Remmy waited her out, remaining quiet on the line until Haley mumbled an inkling of her plans for the next two months. "Maybe be a little more dark and stormy."

Remmy snort-laughed. "In a place with three hundred and sixty-five days of sunshine? Lee, you couldn't even be gloomy in your escapism."

She scrunched up her face, pointing the polish brush toward the phone. "I'm painting my nails dark blue right now."

"Couldn't commit to black?" Haley had to look away from the blatant affection in Remmy's eyes. "You are a fluffy bunny and always will be."

She scowled for good measure, but Remmy continued, undeterred. "Are you going to dye that natural towhead of yours black? Get a couple tattoos?"

"Maybe," she murmured, her word sounding like a juvenile protest.

"You *don't* need to run away from home, and you *don't* need to change who you are. You just need to find someone who appreciates that sunshine within you. Jason was an elitist dirtbag who didn't realize what he had."

Haley winced at her ex's name. Jason had been a crueler-than-usual tick mark on her long list of failed relationships. Since her two-year relationship with Jason had been Haley's longest and most serious, its dissolution was a lot harder to brush off.

"There's nothing wrong with you, and I'll prove it," Remmy said. "Outside of work, how many people did you say hi to and hold the door open for today?"

Haley paused in brushing the nauseating-scented paint over her pinky toenail, recalling her donut run this morning. Mondays were always better when they started off with a sweet treat, so she'd stopped by Donut King to grab a couple dozen before her shift. On the way out, Haley *might have* helped an elderly gentleman carry his pink-boxed dozen back to his car so he wouldn't have to manage it with his cane.

"That's what I thought," Remmy continued, her voice smug. "Fluffy bunny."

"I'm not a fluffy bunny," she grumbled, pushing the furniture a bit and causing the phone to slide down onto the seat.

"What you—Wait. Does your balcony have popcorn walls?"

Haley reached to right her phone. "No, that's stucco. It's everywhere here. All the buildings are covered in it."

"Gross."

She shrugged, propping her friend's image upright again.

"There's that beautiful face." Remmy grinned. "I know it's only been a day, but I already miss that face."

Haley gave an exaggerated toothy smile, and her friend laughed. Remmy's mirth bounced around the stucco-walled balcony before spilling free through the railing bars that separated Haley from the small, single-family neighborhood beyond their complex.

The sun was beginning to set beyond the horizon, lighting up each tiny—and *sharp*, Haley had learned the hard way—cactus spine in its wake. She capped the bottle of polish and stood holding her phone over the railing.

"Here. *This* is why I brought you out here."

"Whoa," Remmy breathed.

"Yeah."

Haley had never seen so many colors streaking across the sky. Sunsets in Maysville, Maryland, could have some pink and orange peppered into the blue, but looking out over Tucson, she went through ROYGBIV and could only identify green missing from the sky. Haley didn't need her vivid imagination to embellish the spectacle in front of her. It was awe-inspiring, just as it was.

"You can see all the way across," Remmy marveled.

"The trees are so tiny here you can see for miles. I swear, almost nothing is taller than two stories."

From beyond her balcony, a road curved lazily along like a long, asphalt snake. It was one of the few that weaved and turned since most of the city, she'd learned, was a grid system. Haley had selected this apartment slightly outside of the city, nestled into the base of the Santa Catalina Mountains, so she could have a view like this.

Even though her attention should have been glued to Mother Nature's impressive spectacle, her eyes snagged on her neighbor's side of their balcony.

That strange telepathy thing occurred. Because Haley had spent almost all her free time with Remmy since she'd been six years old, it happened often.

"Any news on the yeti?" Remmy asked. "Friend or foe?"

Haley had jokingly named her next-door neighbor Yeti because the one time she saw him through her peephole, the most noticeable thing about him was his excessive hair. Thick, enviable, light-brown hair had fallen in front of his black hoodie sweatshirt, dusting his collarbones, and a darker, unkept beard obscured his face. He had ascended the stairs, typing into his phone, wearing thickly padded headphones and sweatpants like he'd just come from the gym.

She hadn't meant to spy on her shaggy neighbor. Haley had been about to leave her apartment, hand on the doorknob, when she heard heavy footsteps climbing the floating cement stairs. Curiosity got the better of her as she'd watched him enter the door that stood within ten inches of hers. Last night, while she'd been at a nearby Mexican restaurant, waiting for her pickup order, Haley had filled Remmy in on her flight, her apartment, and her Yeti sighting.

"No, other than that one time, I haven't seen him." Haley settled back into a painting position, her gaze lingering on the sliding glass door beside hers. Like usual, the thick, taupe blackout curtains the complex supplied were drawn. She often left hers open during the day to let light in, but whenever she ventured outside, her neighbor's curtains were always closed. "I should just be grateful he's not blasting death metal at two a.m."

"Or using your shared wall to play handball."

"Or an amateur opera singer," she offered.

"Or practicing to be a fireman by lighting things on fire and then timing how long it takes to put them out."

Haley stopped painting. "Soooo an arsonist?"

Remmy's shoulders bounced, brushing the edges of her curly black hair. "I briefly dated a guy during law school who did that."

"What? You never told me about that. That kind of behavior is a huge, *flaming* red flag, Remmy."

She waved a hand. "You know I haven't had the best track record."

Haley pulled her attention back to her stubby toenails as that twisting sensation she'd been avoiding by impulsively taking up temporary residence hundreds of miles away from the only place she'd ever known as home streaked through her chest. "That makes two of us."

"Perhaps you're more dark and stormy than I realize," Remmy pushed on. "Sunshine Lee would have already introduced herself to her neighbor while also bringing over homemade blueberry muffins and iced tea."

She finished painting her big toe with a flourish. "See. Progress. Who's a fluffy bunny now?"

"It's not bugging you that you don't know his name?" Remmy teased, knowing exactly which buttons to push.

Haley was about to launch into a speech about how it was possible to live next to another person and not know their entire family history, like whose grandpappy was the one to come up with the family's signature barbeque dish, when a deep voice interrupted.

"I kind of like Yeti."

Chapter 2

Several things happened in quick succession.

She and Remmy screamed simultaneously, but a flinching, whole-body jump accompanied the shout tearing from Haley's throat, sending the open bottle of nail polish careening to the balcony floor.

"Crap." Frantically grabbing for the bag of cotton balls, her phone slipped from its precarious position on the edge of the chair into the spreading polish. In her haste to pick it up and wipe 'Bewitching Blue' from the back of her case, her thumb hit the red hang-up icon on her screen. "Double crap!"

A creaking resonated from the other side of the balcony as her neighbor pushed up on an elbow. The excessive folds and pillows of his oversized hammock had completely concealed him. "Need help?" A finger held his place in a tattered paperback book.

Haley stared, frozen, for half a second.

He'd heard their entire conversation. All of that embarrassing information—the flight from her hometown, the Zach Abrams infatuation, the implication of her horrendous breakup.

ALL. OF. IT.

As her insides felt like they were liquifying, it reminded her of the semi-permanent liquid that would cost Haley her rental deposit. She turned her back on him and crouched, trying to mop up the expanding color with the cotton balls. Scraping and shuffling sounded behind her, but Haley ignored it as her frenzied movements only made the mess worse.

"Here." She jolted again when he stood over her with a roll of paper towels and the same small plastic trash bin that was also in the bathroom of her apartment.

"Oh, thanks."

After using half the roll and the *entire* bottle of acetone, there was only a slight bluish tint to the concrete floor. The whole time she worked, her phone buzzed incessantly with Remmy's calls.

"Are you going to get that? She probably thinks I murdered you."

Haley swiftly rose and took a sizable step away, surveying him through a different lens. Although his eyes were a warm amber brown, he looked large enough to toss her over his shoulder and carry her deep into the desert toward a rocky, unmarked grave.

He raised his hands, palms up, seeming to understand her concern. "I'm not a murderer."

"Isn't that what a murderer would say?"

His chin dipped with an exhale, and only one word flashed through Haley's mind as his body sunk into a defeated posture—melancholic.

The word she'd seen written over her own pale-blue irises in the mirror every morning. She'd get up, make her tea, don her scrubs in preparation for work, but every time she looked at herself, Haley only saw everything Jason had eloquently detailed as *wrong*.

The worst part was that Jason had to be right.

She'd been abandoned by her mother, ignored by her father, and dumped by every man she'd dated. Something had to be wrong, and in these next eight weeks, Haley was determined to figure out what.

As her neighbor tucked his hands into the pocket of his sweatshirt—ironically, a dark shade of navy blue—Haley answered Remmy's eighty-seventh call. "I'm alive."

In the background, she registered her friend's relieved exhalations, but her attention was fixated on her neighbor's bowing shoulders.

"Remmy, hold on a sec." Haley pocketed her phone, still connected to the call, and stepped forward to gather the nearly overflowing trash bin and remaining paper towels, placing them in front of his downward gaze. "Thanks for these."

The despondency flickering in his eyes waned briefly as they linked with hers. He didn't speak, only nodded as he collected the items from her hands.

Reaching behind her, Haley slid open the sliding glass door and stepped inside. Only after she'd closed her curtain against the setting sun and pulled her phone from her scrub-pants pocket did she see the dried streak of polish on the back of her clear, glittery phone case.

She thought better of hitting the speaker button, pressing the phone to her ear. "Sorry."

"You okay?"

"Yeah." Her mind replayed her neighbor's eyes. How sorrow had occupied the slight hollows of his cheeks, peeking above his whiskered scruff. How it had almost skied down the sharp slant of his nose. "I'm okay. I think Yeti's a friend, not a foe."

"That's good, in case you need help ransacking a small mountain village or having a boulder moved."

Normally, Remmy's wit would have pulled a laugh from Haley's stomach, but it clenched instead. "Yeah. Hey, I'm going to scrounge up some dinner. I'll catch up with you tomorrow?"

"You're sure you're safe?" Remmy was going to make the best mother someday. She already had that mama-bear routine down.

"One hundred percent."

After disconnecting the call, Haley leaned against the hip-high counter that led into her galley kitchen. The idea of having to feed herself felt like such a chore, which she knew was childish because leftovers were in a to-go box in her refrigerator.

With her balcony curtains closed, her legs automatically drew her to the only other source of natural light in her apartment—her small bedroom.

It was only after Mother Nature's spectacle had been properly savored that Haley pulled out her phone and opened OnlyApp. The social media app had blown the competition out of the water years ago, boasting it was the "only app" a user would need. It seamlessly combined yet separated photo, video, and chat streams, achieving what its predecessors couldn't. Like most of America, Haley was addicted to it.

Her veins coursed with glee, seeing that Zach Abrams had posted another video of him playing guitar. When he hunched to focus on where to place his long, masculine fingers, his hair kept flopping over his eyes. Each time he ran the backs of his fingers over the neck of the guitar to change chords, the subtle vibration of his skin against the five strings sounded like an anxious inhale. Very much like the one trapped between her ribs.

She clicked on his photo page. Zach Abrams's dark, cutting eyes shadowed by his even darker brows stared back at her. She knew his boyish black locks were just above, though they weren't in the limited profile image. Beneath his razor-sharp jawline, his name sat beside that orange checkbox, letting you know you had the account of a true celebrity.

Haley remembered the apprehension that had run through her when she'd first tapped the message button months ago and typed *Hey, Zach Abrams,* in the text box. The orange *Send* button had seemed to glower at her, almost forbidding her to touch it. But then a voice inside her had whispered, *Go ahead. What's the harm?*

In the end, she'd sent the message, and exactly what she'd expected happened.

A big, fat nothing.

Toward the end of their doomed relationship, Jason had preferred she didn't "ramble" in the evenings after work. It was then that Haley started telling Zach Abrams about her day instead.

She told him how brave her four-year-old patient had been when she drew his blood, even though his mom had been in tears over her baby needing to be stuck, how she and Trudy from the Stop And Go had danced the entire "Chicken Dance" when it'd come on the radio while she'd been grabbing her morning coffee, and how the snowflakes had fallen perfectly during the first snow and were just wet enough to squeak beneath her boots and idyllic for forming into the snowman she'd made with the neighbor kids.

"You know it's not just me who feels this way. You irritate everybody." Jason's cutting words poisoned the pristine winter image in Haley's mind.

Her counter-argument that Remmy never seemed annoyed was always met with a derisive snort and the icy assurance that she was the *only* one. Over time, Jason's criticisms became like insidious spiders, creeping between the cracks in her skull and finding a home.

Toggling back to Zach Abrams's photo page to ignore the ache streaking through her chest, Haley noticed a new picture—one of the sunset she'd just shared with Remmy before wiping up an entire bottle of nail polish. The idea of the two of them witnessing the same view at the same time in the same city sent a tiny shiver down her back.

Her thumb clicked the message tab, bringing up her conversation. *Hey, Zach Abrams* flowed quickly before she froze. Haley fully understood that she was yelling into the void, that Zach Abrams would never respond to any of her messages. But each time she opened their conversation and saw her rounded bubbles of text stacked on top of each other, she felt less alone.

Her eyes quickly re-read the message she'd sent after last night's dinner.

Hey, Zach Abrams. What's your favorite type of tamale? I'm assuming (though I could be wrong), since you work in Hollywood, that you've probably had some good ones. My favorite was Mama Nena's shredded beef with red chili. She was the woman who cared for me when I was little, until my father came home from work. Mama Nena's husband had brought her out east, away from her family, and she always said she liked having a little one to fuss over. When I was old enough, I'd help her and her friends from church make dozens of tamales every winter. My job was to spread the dough across the insides of corn husks. She died when I was ten, and I still think about her.

Haley blinked away the wetness that surged over her eyes. For a short while, Mama Nena had taken the parental place her mother had deserted when Haley was a baby and that her father didn't seem to know how to occupy.

The memory of telling her father about the job in Tucson flickered through Haley's mind. Once she'd shared the news that she'd be leaving, he'd simply nodded his head, taken a sip from his can of Coors, and said her plan "sounded good."

As much as that interaction had unfolded like a tired, worn-out play, a part of her had imagined more of a response from him. Haley had known she wouldn't get an impassioned speech from her stoic father, but she'd planned to leave the small town whose streets she'd tumbled over since she could walk. She'd be leaving the only family she'd known in twenty-seven years.

Her father's apathy had only drilled Jason's words deeper into her heart.

Haley wanted to dissolve into the queen mattress of her apartment, just become one with the springs and coils, but tomorrow was her day off. Her schedule of four ten-hour shifts left every Tuesday and the weekends free. Haley needed to fill her tiny kitchen with groceries and prepare for the rest of her workweek at Tucson General's outpatient phlebotomy clinic. When she'd arrived yesterday, she'd only had enough time to pick up the owner-loaned rental car, unpack her bags, and prepare for today's shift.

The muscles of her spine tightened until his soothing lilt brushed the hair away from her temple. *"Come on, love. Wash up, and we'll get some sleep."*

Haley pushed away the rational part of her brain that told her that her fantasies were getting out of hand, and instead, nodded to herself and listened to the deep rumble of Zach Abrams's voice.

Chapter 3

Bracing his thumb at his temple, he let his fingers tap out a frantic beat on his forehead. This two-hour task should have been done hours ago. His eyes flicked from his ultra-widescreen horizontal monitor to his second vertical one, scanning the thousands of lines of code one more time. What looked to most people like a haphazard conglomeration of letters and symbols, to him, read like a storybook. Each keystroke had its own distinct purpose, its reason for lighting up his dark-mode screen. He meticulously read each line, catching it—the tiny, four-letter error in orange monospace font.

His hand raced over his hair as a frustrated exhale left his lips.

He'd typed 'yeti' into his code.

When his neighbor had called him that word last night, he'd initially thought the name to be a ribbing joke, the kind he and his friends used to pass between each other like a beach ball—feather-light and in the spirit of fun. But then, she'd been terrified by his presence, and the true meaning of the word pierced through his skin and permeated his bones.

He'd known that the beard and long hair that shielded him had gotten a little out of control, but enough to incite fear? He'd *always* been the guy women trusted. The one who looked after his little sister and her friends. The one who would watch his friends' drinks at the bar and then drive them home when they'd had too many. The fact that his neighbor had been frightened of him made acid climb up his throat and sting his tongue.

The thought bothered him so much that he'd even pulled back the corner of the black, light-weight poster board that covered the slab mirror over his bathroom sink. Only one word had come to his lips when he'd surveyed his dark brows, unkept beard, and long hair.

The same word now keeping him from finishing what was supposed to be a simple task.

Yeti.

Just another name for monster.

The pain hit his back first, an odd presentation since it usually radiated from his chest or his left shoulder. It slithered over his ribs and tightened the skin over his torso until his mouth opened with a defeated breath. The friendly glow from his backlit keyboard disappeared behind firmly pressed eyelids. He allowed the gentle hum of his computers to wash over him, grounding him in the one thing that hadn't changed in the last five years.

"Just fix it."

That was what he was good at—looking at the enigmatic puzzle in front of him and organizing it, reshaping it, making sense of something only programmers understood. He created the vital keystrokes that made the layperson's life easier by being the ghost behind their app.

Removing the word, he tested his code only to have it fail again. This time, a growl left him as he pushed back from his desk.

This whole day had been one giant bowl of suck. He'd hardly slept last night, and at this morning's virtual standup meeting, his product manager had informed the entire team that last week's work was now obsolete, and they needed to start over. That wasn't uncommon in the tech world, but layered upon last night's interaction, it made his skin itch more than normal.

He knew from experience that working in this mindset would be worthless, and instead, searched for his sneakers and headphones. It wouldn't be the first time he'd spent his lunch break at the gym. With his extensive experience and the fact that he often exceeded his workload, he had the freedom to set his own schedule. Sometimes, he'd code late into the night or start way before their morning meeting. As long as he completed his tasks by the end of the week, his manager didn't care. Too often, she'd comment that he should be running the team, but he'd remind her that he only wanted to code.

Nothing more.

He was through his front door, three stairs down, seconds from zoning out to the generic "Workout Beats" list he usually listened to, when he heard, "Oh, hi, neighbor. Got a sec?"

No was ready to bark from his lips. He'd let most of his relationships drop from his life like rain slipping through the tiny, fine leaves of a mesquite tree. But she barreled through the pause in which he should have answered before he could take another step.

"Excuse the house romper, but Tuesdays are my day off. Eventually, I'll get dressed, but it's been one of those lazy mornings. You know? Anyway, I heard you leaving and wanted to catch you."

His shoulders turned on their own. "The house romper?"

She waved a hand over her attire with a weird twist of her mouth, as if what she was wearing was the most hideous thing imaginable. His gaze unconsciously followed her hand, taking in the magenta pant-legged romper that stopped mid-calf, leaving her blue-painted toenails exposed. The sight of the polish tightened the muscles in his back. Trying to find anything else to focus on, his eyes flicked up. They caught on the thin straps over her shoulders before she adjusted her white thigh-length cardigan.

"I don't usually wear my 'home clothes' outside," she said, nodding to her attire.

"Okay," he said slowly. He couldn't find anything wrong with what she was wearing. It looked comfortable—something he strived to be as much as humanly possible.

Her gaze skirted over his black sweats and hoodie before fixing on him with an intent that unnerved him. "I wanted to say something."

Unintentionally, his abs clenched. He prepared himself for whatever version of *I never want to see you again* she'd likely dance around, too polite to say it outright. It shouldn't have mattered, since she was a complete stranger, but that barbed feeling rolled around in his chest regardless.

She opened her mouth, closed it with an exhale, and then it was like a dam broke. "I'm sorry about last night and the whole Yeti thing. I shouldn't have nicknamed you without knowing you, but I honestly didn't mean it maliciously. I meant it in a loving, messing-around kind of way. Back home, almost everyone has a nickname. Well, except for Remmy." She snorted. "But that's a story for another time."

There was a fraction of a pause as she sucked in a quick breath. "Also, I'm sure many men are envious of your beard. It's very full, which has got to be a good thing. And heck, your hair is nicer than mine." She tugged at a straight blonde strand laying on top of her cardigan. "What shampoo do you use? I'm guessing you air dry it. That's got to help."

She dropped her hand to her side. "Anyway, what I'm trying to say is, I'm sorry. Normally, when I'm new somewhere, I introduce myself, but I'm trying out something different, and apparently, I haven't got the proportions right. I didn't mean to offend you. I might need to be 'less joyous about everything because it's childish and irritating,' but I shouldn't have been rude."

In the time she'd taken to let out that word salad, he'd rotated to face her, brows furrowed. "The dark and stormy thing?"

The exhale escaping her could have cast a fleet of ships to sea. She rushed to the edge of the stairs, taking hold of the railing. "Could you do me the biggest favor in the world and pretend you didn't hear any of that? I honestly didn't know you were out there."

He straightened. "Then I should apologize to you. I thought you were aware I was in the hammock the whole time."

Her forehead pinched, and two tiny horizontal lines appeared at the top of her nose. "Why would I have talked about you knowing you were right there? That would've been graceless." She raised a pointing finger. "Also, I screamed and knocked over a brand-new bottle of nail polish. Who would do that on purpose?"

His shoulders bounced. "People do weird things sometimes."

He caught the precise moment the memories attempted to creep into his cranium. Over time, he'd learned to control them. It was better like this, when he could stop them before it felt as if someone had vacuumed the air from his lungs. Right after it happened, they would bash him across the jaw, paralyzing him.

Automatically, he deployed his favorite coping mechanism—diversion. His gaze jolted around, looking for a distraction. A deep breath pulled into his lungs when he realized he was standing on the floating concrete stairs he hated. His heartbeat kicked up several notches as the sudden desire to be anywhere else flooded him.

"I've got to go."

She didn't respond, only studied him, her faded-blue eyes occasionally snagging on his hair, shoulders, chin. The attention was too focused, too intense, as if she was already cataloging plenty of things she didn't like.

"Okay." He turned around and descended two additional steps.

"Are you from here?" Surely, he was imagining the desperation in her voice.

He paused but didn't rotate fully this time. "Yeah."

"Where's the best place to get tamales?"

Ah, not desperation. Hunger. He could understand that. His stomach had squeezed irregularly during their conversation. It'd be a good idea to pick up some takeout after his workout.

"Rosa's."

When no additional questions peppered his back, he hurried on, landing on the solid, safe, cement sidewalk.

"Yeti, wait." That same strange quality wavered her words before she cleared her throat.

When he glanced up, she'd descended one stair, her hand squeezing the stair rail like a lifeline. "What do I call you?"

His name was on the tip of his tongue, ready to plunge over the edge into the cool winter air, but it didn't fall from his lips. The noisy, repetitive call of a cactus wren punctuated the silence between them. Only when she took a step back, securing herself on the second-story landing, did he finally swallow the strange resonance vibrating in his mouth.

Every cell in his body shouted at him to turn and walk away. Every single one.

Instead, he said, "I've never had a nickname before."

It was an uneven dance, the uptick of her lips. "You sure?"

"Yeah." The slight tapping on his sternum had to be residual anxiety from the stairs.

"Okay." Her small smile grew as she turned in halting degrees, letting herself back into her apartment.

Ten minutes later, when he was halfway to the gym, he let the word out of his mouth and sent it bouncing around the interior of his car. Nicknames were things you acquired at three, not thirty, but now that he understood its meaning, Yeti didn't seem like the worst name.

It . . . kind of suited him.

Chapter 4

Haley woke at 10:12 a.m. on the following Tuesday to the pouting face of the soul she'd attached hers to shortly after they met at the orientation for first grade. Remmy's curly afro was now dotted with clumps of white, and blotches of fallen snow spotted her mauve knee-length puffer. The offending culprit of her best friend's disarray was just above her head—a freshly clean tree branch.

Sure you aren't missing this? accompanied Remmy's photo message.

Another benefit of choosing Arizona for her quarter-life crisis was that her hometown was still covered in January snow. Here, it was sunny and only in the mid-sixties. Haley had yet to put on "real shoes" since she'd exited the automated sliding doors of the airport.

Got to watch out for those attack trees. They'll get you, she texted back.

Remmy sent a sobbing emoji before, *All I wanted was turkey chili from Dave's.*

A slight pinch started on the left side of Haley's ribs and spread across her abdomen. As much as she'd been enjoying the—honestly overabundant—sunshine and the change of scenery, a part of her was already homesick.

Maybe not homesick, but friendsick.

Even during the last few years, while Remmy was attending Howard Law and living in Bethesda, she'd come home often enough. Either that or Haley would make the one-hour drive Friday after work to visit for the weekend. Eventually, Marcus, Remmy's classmate-turned-boyfriend, would join Remmy on the trips to Maysville. Seemingly trying to max out on their cute couple potential, when they graduated, they moved in together and got jobs at the same firm.

Marcus was incredible—unnecessarily handsome, smart, considerate, and funny. He was always willing to pick up Haley and Remmy if they went too hard on margarita night, and he not only made the popcorn but often shared the couch with them on rom-com nights, frequently tearing up at the mushy parts. The only problem Haley could see with Marcus—if she was forced to pick something—was that, after dating Remmy for three years, he hadn't proposed yet.

Victory at last! Remmy sent another picture, this time of the snow-covered sign to their favorite diner.

Dave's was a staple in the downtown area where Remmy and her partners held their family law offices. On the odd week when Haley would have a weekday off, she'd join her best friend there for lunch.

Yum! Get a biscuit for me.

Always, was Remmy's instant reply. *What are you up to today?*

A sagging breath left her lips before she typed out, *Haven't decided yet.*

Haley wished she was working today. Being at work gave her a new person to interact with every few minutes. Her contract with the traveling company stipulated that overtime was for "extenuating circumstances" only, so exceeding her scheduled four shifts a week was frowned upon.

Maybe she'd run into her neighbor again. Over this past week, they'd run into each other coming and going. Usually, they'd ended up either at the top or the bottom of the stairs for a few minutes, him mostly listening.

When Remmy didn't respond right away, Haley's thumb tabbed over to her conversation with Zach Abrams and the message she'd sent last night after a particularly good shift.

Hey, Zach Abrams. Have you always wanted to be an actor? I honestly didn't know what I wanted to be when I was a kid. My best friend's mom is a nurse at the only hospital in town, and when I graduated high school, she suggested I apply for their phlebotomy program. Since I couldn't afford community college, applying for a position with on-the-job training made sense. Plus, I've never been squeamish when listening to hospital stories at the Jones's dinner table. Turns out, I'm really good at it. Call me a vampire. But it's not just the weird satisfaction of finding the spongy vein underneath someone's skin; it's when you can draw their blood without causing any pain. Then, you feel like you've won the lottery. People have asked me over the years why don't I go back to school and become a nurse, and they have a hard time understanding that I'm happy doing what I do. We can't all be at the top of every professional field. But I'm not sure you can relate since you're in People *every other month.*

Remmy's message blinked over the screen. *Whatever you decide on, have fun! Miss you.*

Miss you too! Haley replied, feeling the weight of each word before she let her phone slip from her fingertips to the downy comforter.

That pulverized feeling was back. Some ill-conceived, frivolous part of her had imagined that moving to the land of perpetual sunshine would've evaporated the niggling sadness that pulled on her bones.

But she remained the same.

Which only meant one thing.

Unfortunately, it was time to put in the work.

Haley's gaze drifted to the hastily scrawled note on her nightstand. The one she'd penned after deciding that maybe Jason had been right. Her fingertips trembled, but she forced herself to pick it up and read her own tear-stained words. Even the purple pen ink and cartoon-panda stationery of her plan further validated her ex's claims.

Grow up

Watch more introspective documentaries

Appreciate serious art

Listen to classical music

Be less emotional

That last one was going to be the hardest. She often teared up at sappy commercials and always, *always* cried at weddings. Once, Remmy's youngest cousin brought Haley a tattered copy of *Love You Forever* to read at a family cookout. Haley had somehow managed to cry-read the entire book to the smallest kids but continued to hiccup for a solid hour afterward.

"You're making us late for dinner by stopping to puff dandelion seeds? This is ridiculous. No one wants to be with a child in an adult's body."

Haley's stomach wrenched at the memory of Jason's words. Immediately after their breakup, two months ago, she'd retreated from Jason's house to her father's. That action in itself felt juvenile, as if it returned Haley to some version of her younger, latchkey self. Remmy had insisted she move in with her and Marcus, but Haley hadn't wanted to stain their coupled bliss with her heartache.

A forceful sigh left her lips as Haley dragged herself from bed. After all the necessary morning things, she settled on the balcony with a steaming cup of Earl Grey tea and her phone. On the off chance that she might run into her neighbor again, she'd taken the time to put on jeans and a fluffy, oversized sweater instead of heading out in her house clothes.

Two minutes into listening to an opera aria—which, while incredibly beautiful, was starting to give her a headache—Haley searched her music app for another classical list that didn't have vocals. One playlist in particular caught her eye. When she pressed shuffle, a string quartet delicately bowed the melody of a familiar song.

Several species of birds seemed to be having a heated debate just beyond her balcony as Haley tucked her feet beneath her. Her hands slowly swept up and down the sleeves of her puffy sweater. The texture of this one always made her arms feel like they were suspended inside a cloud. It usually stirred joy in her belly, but now she wondered if relishing in the comfort of a piece of clothing was also childish.

Should all her garments be starched and rigid? Preferably black or gray? A barbed hand slammed at her chest as she looked down at the snow-white sweater.

She was *literally* dressed like a fluffy bunny.

"You're simply too hard to love." Jason's disappointed voice echoed in her ear.

To distract herself from the overwhelming wave that had been trying to submerge her for weeks, her shaky hands brought the tea to her trembling lips. The hot, dark liquid felt like it was slipping through a single-holed sieve; her throat was so tight. Her forearms tingled to the point of pain, like an electrical storm was building beneath the clouds of her sleeves. Teeth clenched tight, she used the last of her self-control to lower the plain white mug to the table before she broke.

As sweeping orchestral music floated around her, Haley completely failed at objective number four and cried harder than she had in weeks.

Harder than the time, in second grade, when PJ Domasksus told her that her mother had left because she hadn't wanted Haley. The cruel string of words had been confirmed by the dejected slump of her father's shoulders when she'd asked him if it was true.

Harder than when Mama Nena had died and the emptiness in the center of her chest felt like an endless void, a chasm that could never be filled. Even at ten, she'd understood that, though her father had been beside her at the funeral, the closest thing to family was lying in the flower-covered, oak casket.

"Hey." Yeti stood in the doorway to his sliding glass door, forehead pinched. "Are you okay?"

"No." She wiped her snotty and tear-streaked face with her sleeve as shame flooded her bloodstream. "But I'm sorry for bothering you." Haley lowered her bare feet to the cold concrete. "I'll go."

"Don't." His hand held firm pressure on her shoulder for two seconds before her eyes flitted to his. "Sorry." He pulled his fingers away as if she was on fire. "If you want to go inside, you should."

A staggered, halting breath drew into her desperate lungs as she buried her face in her hands.

"I shouldn't have touched you without asking permission. I'm sorry." His voice was a low rumble.

She couldn't bring herself to look up again and, instead, focused on the well-worn moccasins on his feet. His pinky toe nearly poked out of a hole in the side. "It's okay."

Haley expected the quiet stillness to be biting and icy, like all the moments that expanded between her and Jason, but the nearness of Yeti in his sweats was like sitting next to an oversized teddy bear.

And there was something else that kept pulling at her senses. "Why do you smell like Christmas?"

"What?"

She craned her neck to look at his shaggy face. "You smell like Christmas."

He pulled up the collar of his sweatshirt and sniffed inside. "I'm pretty sure I don't."

A laugh burst from her. Haley couldn't help it. The tension between her ribs was too tight. "I'm going crazy, then." She crumbled with a sigh. "Maybe I already am."

Some emotion that she couldn't place washed over his eyes before his lips downturned. "I've never had a good sense of smell, so maybe you're right."

Haley let her gaze flow to the bright, sun-soaked landscape beyond the balcony. It was unusually beautiful here. Having been born and raised near lush, rugged forests, she hadn't expected to be so taken by this dusty, arid land. Rocky sand was broken up by black-barked creosote plants dotted between brittlebush and patches of prickly pears, some of which were a playful purple. Deceptively cute, but not for touching. Every so often, a regal saguaro would pull from the otherwise low line of drought-resistant flora, its arms unabashedly reaching for the jeweled blue sky.

Yeti's pensive voice pulled her back to the balcony. "This is a violin cover of a Taylor Swift song."

"Yes," Haley said, tears immediately rewetting her eyes. "I can't even listen to classical music properly. I selected a playlist titled 'Running through a castle as my lover and I pine for each other,' like a *teenager*."

Yeti shifted his weight from one foot to the other and slipped his hands into the pocket of his sweatshirt. "Not every genre of music is for everyone, and 'Wildest Dreams' is one of the better songs on *1989*." He paused. "In fact, this is a really nice cover."

"You like Taylor Swift?"

He shrugged. "She's a popular musician, and it's a popular song."

Observing his obvious unease at her question, it was almost as if everything shifted. Some small transitional rotation clicked through her insides. She was still covered in mucus and tears, but this light felt like it was breaking through a pinhole in a three-foot-thick brick wall.

"But you know the name of the album."

Yeti's eyes flitted to the side. "When it ends up on a playlist, you get all that information. Once I see something, it's kind of always in here." He pointed to the side of his unbrushed head.

Haley almost choked on her own snot mid-sniff. "You have a photographic memory?"

"No . . . not exactly."

The pinhole expanded to the size of a nice, round marble. A wide smile pulled up her lips. "So, what you're *really* saying is that you're a Taylor Swift fan."

Yeti froze. There wasn't a better way to describe it. It was almost like a rigid wax version of her neighbor had replaced the one who'd been conversing with her seconds before.

Reanimation occurred with an audible exhale. "Looks like you're doing better, so I'm going to get back to work."

Before Haley could come up with an answer, he was through the glass door with the curtains in their secured location. The abrupt brush-off should have bothered her, but the odd conversation left her buoyed. The angry electrical storm within her had receded, popped like a shiny iridescent bubble hitting the cement floor.

Haley sat drinking her tepid tea and thinking for a long time before she scooped up her phone again. Perhaps it was okay to take a few hours to focus on her second reason for being thousands of miles from home.

A few clicks later, she shrieked with glee at the information on her screen. A brief whip of embarrassment zipped through her, but Yeti's curtains remained immobile. Haley exhaled with a creeping smile. If she left now, she could make it just in time.

Chapter 5

Hands firmly pressed on his kitchen counter, Yeti took another deep breath and willed his spiking heart rate to slow. The second he'd registered the noise coming from outside as his neighbor sobbing, he'd slipped onto the balcony to make sure she wasn't in a mood to hurl herself over the railing.

Everything had been cordial and neighborly until she'd hit him with that smile.

Now, futile thoughts and *impulses* bombarded him.

His body was still waging a major turf war against his mind when the sound of his neighbor's front door shutting brought his gaze up. His desk loomed in his eyeline, but there was no reality in which he could continue to work right now—not when this stupid emotion was swimming frenzied backstrokes in his veins. Yeti waited an additional ten minutes before grabbing his headphones and descending the stairs.

"Son of a bee sting! You good-for-nothing piece of junk!" A scratchy, irritated voice accompanied the breeze bending around the next building. Apparently, he wasn't the only one having a crap morning.

A tiny, older woman struggled with a personal, wheeled shopping basket. It teetered precariously off the sidewalk, its contents seconds from tumbling into a large barrel cactus. Yeti ran the last few steps, helping to save the woman's groceries from their needly fate.

"Thank you. Who says all young people are vermin?" The woman slapped his right shoulder, then grabbed a handful of muscle with an approving hum.

"Ah. You're welcome, ma'am." He was pretty sure he should have been offended at being blatantly objectified, but since she looked eighty years old, he'd let it slide. Yeti reached down for the cause of the problem—one wheel had popped off in a sidewalk crack. "Is it okay if I put this back on for you?"

Her dark-brown eyes seemed to be x-raying him. "Ma'am? I appreciate that someone raised you right, but there will be no ma'aming me."

"I apologize, Mrs. . . . ." He left the sentence open.

"Aster." The late-morning sunlight spring-boarded off her white shellacked ponytail.

"Mrs. Aster, would it—"

"No Mrs.," she interrupted. "Never got married. Just Aster."

"Aster," he began again, outstretching the offending object as his stomach growled. "Can I repair this for you?"

She put her hands on the waist of her purple paisley house dress and ruthlessly surveyed him from top to bottom. "When did you last eat?"

Yeti tried not to wince at her blatant examination. It was the second time it'd happened within a week. He'd gotten in the habit over the last five years of drifting along in the background, a specter not to be acknowledged.

"Eat?"

Aster lowered her barely visible eyebrows. "I didn't stutter."

He'd had a protein shake and a banana for breakfast, but his lips couldn't tell her that because his mind kept fixating on the fact that this had to be the weirdest day he'd had in a very long time. Maybe it hadn't been the worst idea to cut himself off from the rest of the human race if he was going to keep having impossible thoughts about his new neighbor and be scrutinized by the Asters of the world.

"If it takes you that long to figure it out, then it's been too long. Come on." The woman waved a crepe-skinned arm over the groceries. "You look strong. Pick this up and follow me." She turned on a Birkenstocked heel and strode down the sidewalk, muttering about people not feeding their bodies properly.

After a pause, Yeti picked up the cart and followed her into a ground-floor apartment.

"Be careful not to let Sebastian out," Aster called over her shoulder, flipping on a light switch that barely illuminated the room.

Thinking she meant a cat or small dog, Yeti quickly closed the door. Only when he turned around, a three-foot-long, green, scaly creature was sitting on top of an eye-level bookshelf. Its sharp claws gripped the wooden log beneath a heating lamp's amber glow.

Not expecting a face-to-face encounter with a large iguana, Yeti stepped back, almost knocking over a trio of potted plants. The entire apartment looked more like a jungle than a dwelling. Plants covered nearly every surface, including some walls.

"Oh, Bash, you big flirt." Aster affectionately rubbed a hooked knuckle under the lizard's chin, jostling his skin flap. "You can look, but he's not staying, so don't get attached." She ran that same finger down his spiny back before pointing it at Yeti. "Don't go telling the management I've got an iguana in here."

"No, ma—" He stopped himself just in time.

A *humph* sound left the woman's lips before she tromped into the kitchen. Below the microwave, a slow cooker steamed in front of a countertop-to-cabinet display of glass spice containers.

"Don't just stand there. Bring me my groceries," Aster snapped.

After helping her get boxes of dry goods into the upper cabinets—not quite sure how tiny Aster would get them down later—and handing her all the perishables for the fridge, the small shopping cart was empty.

Yeti stepped back. "Have a good—"

"Go sit at the table, and I'll bring you some soup. Then, you can leave," she said, busying herself in a cabinet with her back to him.

His impatient inhale brought a rich soil scent into his nostrils.

"I've got a great-nephew your age." She began ladling the soup into cerulean handcrafted bowls. "He doesn't come around as much as before."

Yeti's neck pinched, and he found himself sliding behind the same white MDF table that was in his apartment. Only, he didn't use the small round table for eating. He mostly did that at his desk while working. The kitchen table was perfect for his half-completed Ravensburger Krypt Black puzzle.

"Here." Aster set a steaming bowl of split pea soup and a homemade sprouted wheat roll under his nose. "Do you want water or lemonade?"

"Water is fine. Thank you."

Aster grunted before bringing back a glass and her own lunch. They ate in terse silence for a few moments before she pointed a finger at him. "You know what your problem is?"

Here it was. The criticism about his appearance. He was surprised it'd taken this long.

"You hide your scales instead of presenting them proudly like Sebastian does."

Yeti almost choked on the spoonful he'd placed in his mouth.

Aster took a large bite of bread with a smug expression. Another *humph* came from her, but this time, it was impossible to mistake that the sound indicated her satisfaction at his reaction.

Hot soup burned down his tight throat as he tried to understand *how* she knew. No one but his family and a handful of friends he'd intentionally lost over the years knew. He made sure of that. Yeti studied the pureed contents of his bowl as his mind worked overtime to justify her comment.

She's just making wild, random statements. Clearly, the woman is senile.

Aster's throaty laughter forced his eyes up. "If you want to think that, fine. I'm old, but I'm not that old. I'm only seventy-eight. You should see some of the ladies at water aerobics." She widened her eyes. "Real dinosaurs there."

Beneath his sweatshirt, his forearm hairs went on edge, and goosebumps rushed up his arms. He was easily twice the size of this woman and undeniably stronger, but every cell in his body screamed, *Get out!*

Aster sighed impatiently. "As much as you try to hide with all that hair"—she waved her roll around in an irritated fashion—"your eyes betray you."

The tension in his shoulders lessened a miniscule fraction, but his appetite had disappeared.

"You're like my great-nephew, broken and refusing to glue yourself back together. Don't you think it's time?" A solitary eyebrow lifted. "You have your whole life ahead of you."

When he didn't answer, Aster drooped with an exhale. As cantankerous and commanding as she'd been before, she looked every second of her seventy-eight years in that moment.

Even though acid was pooling in his stomach, he forced himself to pick up his spoon. He couldn't taste the savory soup anymore, only feel the consistency of it sliding down his throat, but he wasn't going to upset Aster further. He'd eat this meal, politely thank her, and never see her again.

Once they finished, Yeti cleared the table and moved toward the door, keeping an eye out for Sebastian. "Thanks again for lunch."

Aster waved a dismissive hand from her spot across the kitchen counter and turned her back to ladle soup into a large storage container.

His fingers made a jutting, hesitant journey toward the door handle, but eventually, he let himself out into the blaring sunshine. The skin over his nose pinched as his eyelids shielded his retinas from the contrasting light.

Yeti didn't remember getting into his car. Somehow, he was just there. His grip firmed on the steering wheel as his car hugged a curve, accelerating over a short hill.

His whole life ahead of him.

After he'd realized Aster wasn't some type of evil, telepathic psychic, it was that phrase that wouldn't leave his cerebrum. Some pessimistic naysayers with chips on their shoulders would point out that a bus could hit you at any moment. That you were never guaranteed tomorrow. But from a numbers standpoint, the odds of Yeti living into his elderly years were very good.

That hadn't always been the case.

All he could remember right after it happened was fighting against the overwhelming reality of his fragile mortality. That had been before drug-induced sleep dominated his days. The moments of brief consciousness had felt sticky and halting. Time had seemed to play tricks on his mind. It had taunted him, because in its barbed, laughing presence, he'd been overcome with soul-crushing pain.

And then, there were the non-hospital days at his parents' home, where he'd lain on their blanket-covered couch and stared at the village of pill bottles on the coffee table. The tall, white multivitamin bottle stood like an imposing church over the smaller orange bottles, the darkened—nearly brown—ones, and the skinny white one. His sister, Paige, had colored each lid with bright permanent markers to help him easily discern which was which. Despite Paige's sanguine colors, there were many days Yeti had wanted to destroy the village vignette. He wanted to be like Godzilla, not be a slave to the contents held within.

Finally, there had been the long, settling-in period when he hadn't been able to "get back to normal" like everyone expected him to. Three thousand things had triggered panic, danger had lurked around every corner, and it became nearly impossible to sleep. The little village had grown, more pill bottles joining the established homes. After that, it became easier to stay at his apartment, keeping things simple.

Predictable.

He was no longer trapped by his injuries, but mentally, he couldn't find a way to rejoin what was supposed to be his life.

Yeti was several miles down the I-10 before he realized he was heading to La Jolla again. His fingertips met his forehead with an exhale. He switched lanes, taking the next exit in Marana to turn around. Instead of taking the next entrance ramp to continue home, Yeti pulled into a shopping complex with broken asphalt. Hitting *Send,* the ring-back tone played only once through his car's Bluetooth system before Paige picked up his call.

An ocean breeze whipped through the speakers, its sound streaming around the interior of his car. "Ugh, not you again."

"Why aren't you in the lab?" he quipped, falling into their comfortable sibling squabbling pattern.

"Why aren't you at home?"

Yeti stared at the blinking neon signs of the run-down tienda in front of him. "How'd you know I'm not at home?"

Paige seemed to have sighed her breath directly into her phone, it came across so loudly. Yeti grimaced and used his thumb to decrease the call volume on his steering wheel. "If you were at home, you'd be too distracted by that glowing box of yours to call."

He thought about arguing that, technically, he had three glowing boxes, but instead, conceded with a considerably quieter exhale. "Bien vu."

"Aww, look at you trying French. Your pronunciation is off, though. It's *Bien vu*," she said slowly.

Yeti's hands scrubbed his face. "This is why I don't call you."

"Okay, big brother. I'll be serious. What's up?" Jazzy background music and chatting voices echoed over the line. "Thank you," Paige said to whoever was in front of her before murmuring in French about the essentiality of coffee and the time-saving awesomeness that was order-ahead.

Yeti was transported to the quaint cafe and coffee shop near her building at Scripps Research Institute, only a little over a mile from the beach. Salt air and the scent of kelp sprang from his memory. There was a certain peace that always encompassed him when he sat on the packed sand, running the damp granules through his fingertips. Because compared to the expansive Pacific Ocean, he—and all his tribulations—were quite small and fleeting.

"Hello?"

He blinked, zeroing back onto the black interior of his car. To reality.

His shoulders bunched. Perhaps he should have kept driving. At least then he wouldn't have to deal with these irritating emotions, just the sting of ocean winter wind lashing his skin.

"Hey." Paige's voice had transformed from its playful tone to a soft, cautious one. "I got you if you need me."

He cradled his head in his hands and nodded into them.

"Okay," Paige said with an uptick, always seeming to understand him before he did.

They rested in comfortable silence for a long while. Paige sipped her coffee, the background noise dropping away as she returned to her quiet office, while the torrent ripping through his mind slowly settled.

"I'm okay." He rolled his neck and straightened.

"All right." Paige let a pause rest before asking, "How close are you?"

His sister was used to this pattern, but it'd been a long time since he'd grabbed his keys and blindly drove for the beach. Years ago, he used to show up at odd times for odd reasons, but Paige always welcomed him with open arms before teasing him for some hollow offense—fetid feet, unkempt beard, that day's predictable clothing choice.

He rested tense hands on his thighs. "Not very. I only made it to Marana."

"Good." She paused again. "What are you going to do now?"

He shrugged. "Head back home to work."

"Or . . ."—that annoying quality crept back into the short, single-syllable word—"you could phone a friend and see what they're up to. Don't both Zane and Rowan work from home like you? I'm sure they could meet you for coffee . . . or dinner."

Yeti's thumb rubbed his throbbing temple. As much as he generally enjoyed their predictable patterns, this was one he could go without. "We've been over this—"

"Yeah, yeah. You made a mistake, *forever* ago. Don't you think it's time to stop beating yourself up over it?"

"What I did was inexcusable," he reminded her.

"So your ego inflated three times the size of your head, and you blew off one little wedding," Paige said with a following *psh*.

Those fevered months in Silicon Valley snapped to the front of his mind. Endless hours behind a screen with his two business partners on the precipice of the *next big thing*. Completely ignoring his family and those who'd always known him. Those who had doggedly stood by his side, even though his trips back to Tucson became more elusive.

Yeti had neglected calls and texts from his friends for months. Instead, he had listened to yes-men and his vapid, gold-digging girlfriend. He'd believed them when they said he was God's gift to software development. Then, it'd felt like a confirmation when his app had launched to unprecedented success.

On the night of his friend's wedding, Yeti had gone to some socialite's party. He couldn't remember whose, except for the fact that there was a viral video of him shared on, what else but, *his app*. The video still circled the internet, acting as proof of his attendance, of his complete and utter fall from decency.

"I'm here because I have absolutely nowhere better to be." A severely inebriated version of him had said that gem right before pawing at his girlfriend in a way that would have been predatorial had she not returned his sloppy kiss with the same gusto before the video cut out.

"You should reach out anyway." Paige's voice was softer.

"Those bridges are burned."

In another sadistic twist of fate, all four of his closest friends had reached out after the accident a few months later. Yeti hadn't been able to take the shame burning through his aching veins and screamed at them to leave. He'd *deserved* to be abandoned. He'd thrown whatever objects were in reach across the room until each of his friends had walked away, never to contact him again.

What hurt more than his injuries was that the snubbed groom had held out the longest.

Paige sighed over the phone, knowing they'd met their well-worn impasse.

"You should get back to work," he said, not wanting to argue further and hoping to close the subject. "I love you."

"I love you too," she said with an exasperated exhale. "I'll talk to you Thursday."

Every week, they had a planned call. Paige took off an hour early to catch up with him and walk the trails near the ocean, often describing what she was experiencing. It was a habit from when he'd been in the hospital, missing the world. She'd sat at his bedside with a notebook full of vivid descriptions, reading them as he weaved in and out of consciousness.

His spine relaxed for the first time since he'd left his apartment. "Thanks, Paige."

Yeti barely heard the catch in her voice before they hung up. "Anytime."

Chapter 6

A grating, incessant noise ripped Haley out of her Sunday morning slumber. Her lips twisted into a pout because she'd been happily consulting a talking hummingbird while crocodile shopping with Zach Abrams on a *breathtaking* tropical preserve. The instant Haley recognized the sound as the fire alarm, her legs clumsily stumbled out of bed. She was over the threshold of her apartment and spilling into the breezy morning air in seconds, grateful she was wearing an old men's sweatshirt and yoga pants instead of the thin sundress of her dream.

Muttering about how the winding, looping sidewalks of the complex were an evacuation hazard within themselves, she finally broke free of them. Yeti was hovering at the edge of the parking lot, several feet away from the large crush of people. A twisting mesquite tree stood behind him, its thin upmost branches bending in the wind that cooled her bed-warmed body.

Her forehead wrinkled as she strode directly toward her neighbor. Yeti's fidgety posture didn't match the calm, steady presence he usually exuded. He'd always emanated this soothing solidity. It was like standing next to a mountain ridge or a stately redwood tree. Grounding. Settling.

"Hey," she said.

His eyes darted between the tops of the buildings, swinging his keys from his index finger in a rhythmic, repetitive pattern. Thick black headphones hung around his neck as if he'd been away at the gym when the alarm sounded.

Haley waited, but when he didn't acknowledge her, she tried again, more forcefully. "Yeti. Hey."

When his gaze pulled down, the tension around his eyes lessened a fraction. "Oh. Good." The last word was said as a short, breathy exhale.

Before Haley could interpret what his slight moment of relief meant, Yeti's focus returned to its previous position. The vigilant quality of his attention made her stand beside him and follow his eyeline. Was she missing something? Each beige stucco building looked exactly the same as it had before—dusty and slightly washed out from hours of excessive sunlight.

"What are we looking for?"

She searched the rooftops for what was keeping Yeti so captivated—Santa with his reindeer, an alien spaceship, a Cirque du Soleil troop of roof jumpers. All Haley saw was the handful of palm trees that extended over the roofs of the two-story apartment buildings.

His hand fisted before he pushed it into the pocket of his sweatshirt. "Nothing."

Ripples of agitation radiated from him. She didn't know exactly why, but Yeti was freaking out.

Haley wasn't a stranger to witnessing others' anxiety. Very few people are comfortable with a needle being pushed into their arm. Her fingers tingled, knowing that, unlike at work when she'd use touch to soothe a nervous patient, it'd probably be weird to unexpectedly hold her neighbor's hand.

There was one thing left in her arsenal: words.

"I tried to crash my way into Zach Abrams's movie Tuesday."

"What?" His head snapped in her direction with his—almost as impressive as Zach Abrams's—brows pinched.

Even though Yeti was looking at her like she was a crazy person, he was looking *at her*, not staring at the apartment buildings. Victory sang a little ditty as it floated through her veins.

"Okay, I'm being hyperbolic." Haley let a small smile lace her lips. "I tried to be an extra in the movie, but while I was waiting in line at the casting call, a woman fainted and cut her head, and at the sight of all the blood, *another* woman fainted—"

"Is that hyperbole?"

"No, that part is true. After I helped the medics get the women situated, the casting director said they had enough people for the day." She shrugged.

A slight nod was all she got before Yeti's attention returned to the complex. His hand was out of his pocket, keys forgotten within, his fingertips playing an invisible piano on the seam of his sweatpants.

Her lips pinched, thinking.

"I guess since he's not answering my DMs on OnlyApp, I probably won't get to meet him while I'm here. Shame."

Yeti rotated his body to face her, fully focused now. "Wait. You're using OnlyApp to message Zach Abrams?"

A ribbon of unease slithered through her belly. Haley knew Jason would've responded with disgust upon learning that she'd been using Zach Abrams as a one-sided sounding board, but for some reason, she hadn't expected that reaction from her scruffy neighbor.

"Yeah." Her timid answer deepened his frown. "What's wrong with that?"

"Nothing, I guess." He rubbed his brow with a knuckle. "I just don't do social media."

His response made that burning, air-held-in-your-lungs sensation sweep through her chest. "I'm only asking him get-to-know-you questions, like *What's your favorite type of tamale? Have you always wanted to be an actor? Have you ever ridden a horse?*" That last question had come to her yesterday after trying to hike at the same time several equestrians were using the rocky trail. She'd ended up turning back after a quarter mile, not wanting to dodge digested hay any longer. "You know, things you'd ask a new friend." Haley left out the digital-diary aspect of her messages.

The weight of his scrutiny felt like it was compressing her vertebrae. "A new friend?"

"Um, yeah." Even though it was barely sixty degrees outside, a drop of sweat rolled from her armpit down her side. "Like you and me."

A pause settled between them before he said, "So, Coke or Pepsi?"

The tension in which she'd been imprisoned shattered, sending invisible miniscule pieces careening over the asphalt beneath them. "Beach or mountains?"

He nodded. "One hundred hours of absolute silence or forty-eight hours of mindless chatter?"

This bubbly sensation tickled up her esophagus as she fought the smile tugging at her lips. "That's oddly specific."

"Overcooked or undercooked popcorn?" he continued, undeterred.

She wrinkled her nose. "Who would want to eat overcooked popcorn?"

His gaze settled briefly between her brows before darting away. "Not anyone I'd want to associate with. I assume these questions were also used to suss out whether he was a sociopath."

A scoff flew from her mouth. "Zach Abrams is no sociopath."

Yeti's gaze ventured back over the buildings as a somberness washed over his face. "You never know. Some people's insides don't match their outside."

All the ground she'd gained felt like it was turning into fine-grain sand and slipping from beneath her feet. Haley didn't know why it was important to keep this man distracted, but the need to do so made her forearms itch.

Normally, she'd have seventeen different things to say to keep the conversation going. It was a good skill to have when you were trying to distract someone from their impending needle stick or needed extra time to find a viable vein. But right now, none of the words wanted to pass over her teeth. One moment pulled into two, which stretched into six.

Before time could further obey the rules of mathematics, she spurted out, "When's your birthday?"

"I'm sure a lot of his basic information is already on the internet," Yeti said as he continued to survey the complex.

"No, not a question for him. For you." That drew her neighbor's attention. "When's *your* birthday?"

Yeti bristled, straightening his hunched form as he leaned slightly away from her. "I don't see how that's relevant in your quest for Zach Abrams's attention."

She snorted. "Quest? You make it sound like I should be asking him, 'Good sir, doth preferth a broadsword or a mace?'"

A slight curve flirted with Yeti's mouth. "Hemlock or nightshade?"

Her jaw dropped. "Are you seriously suggesting that I ask Zach Abrams what kind of poison he would prefer I *kill him with*? Sure. That won't get me blocked or a restraining order filed against me. Not at all." She separated each word of her last sentence.

A chuckle came from Yeti's body a second before he ran a hand over his beard. It was almost as if, instead of trying to smooth out his facial hair, he was trying to cover the slight sound of mirth that'd escaped him. "That would be sufficiently dark and stormy, wouldn't it?"

Her mouth opened when a shouting voice interrupted.

"False alarm, everyone! You can return to your residences. Thanks for your patience," one of the day managers, an attractive, young-thirties woman with whom Haley had signed her lease, addressed the crowd.

"Great," Haley said, striding toward the complex. People began to dissipate, choosing different sidewalks back to their apartments.

Only when Yeti didn't move from his spot, she turned. "You coming?"

His eyes did another nervous scan of the buildings. "I just—" His hand ran through his hair. "I need a minute."

"Okay," she said, taking a step toward him.

"You don't have to wait for me. I'll be fine. I . . ." His exhale was as long as it was tense.

"You know. It's so nice here I should make being outside more of a priority. At home, right now, it's probably twenty-seven degrees. Look at me! I'm wearing flip-flops." She sat on a cement parking block and wiggled her midnight-blue toenails.

Yeti sighed. "Your friend was right." With his words, an infusion of iced saline coursed through her veins. She silently willed him to stop, not to say it, but he kept talking. "You—"

Before he could finish his sentence, Haley punched to her feet and marched back toward the complex. If he'd continued talking or tried to get her attention, she didn't notice it over the whooshing blood in her ears.

She didn't want to hear it, anyway. He was going to say she was too fluffy, too bright, too childish, *too naïve* to be taken seriously.

Haley wasn't naïve.

Even before her foolhardy attempt to be *dark and stormy*, she saw hardship every day at her job, often holding a crying patient's hand as they told her about their arduous health journey.

Her front door reverberated with a slam. Haley stalked around her living room, trying to dissipate the emotion coursing through her body. When a knock resonated on the other side of the wooden barrier, she didn't even check the peephole. She just swung it inward with a ferocity that widened Yeti's eyes.

"I was—"

"What's wrong with being positive? Do you want to tell me? Do you want to let me know the *harm* in trying to find the little things that bring you happiness? Seeing the bright side in different situations? Honestly, I don't see any. All I see is the good. Because you know what, Yeti? Life sucks. It does. And it's not like I don't know that. I *see it* just like everyone else."

After work this week, she'd tried to knock off every line item on her "Grow up" list. Even the perfectly cooked popcorn at the independent film theater couldn't keep her from the despair that followed watching *The Bridge*. Frida Kahlo's paintings were no doubt revolutionary, but they also made Haley's stomach twist. Those two tasks had nearly wrecked her emotionally. Friday night, she'd spent all evening numbly wrapped in a blanket she'd warmed in the tiny, stacked dryer, watching reruns of *The Big Bang Theory* to self soothe.

"I'm done with this. I'm not going to wallow in misery because life is hard. I'm choosing to find the good. I'm choosing to be like this because it's better than the alternative." Haley's hand cramped from her unrelenting grip on the door. "Screw Jason for not understanding that." Her chest heaved, but she refused to move her slanted eyes from Yeti's shocked ones. "And screw you too!"

"I—" He blinked. "I was going to say you shouldn't change."

Every facial muscle she had seemed confused as to how it should arrange itself. "What?"

"Your friend was right. You shouldn't change who you are." He paused, but a response was beyond her right now. After a few seconds, his gaze flitted over her shoulder. "The alarm stressed me out"—a swallow bobbed his Adam's apple—"so I wanted to say I appreciated you distracting me while we were waiting on the all-clear."

The air left her lungs in a loud rush. "Oh my goodness, Yeti. I'm sorry. I'm such a jerk."

The fierce way his eyes cut to hers stole her next breath.

"No, you're not." The sharp words hung for a breath before his expression softened. "I just didn't make myself clear."

A high-pitched objection squeaked from her. "I didn't even give you a chance to explain."

"I'm not the world's best communicator." Those broad, cotton-covered shoulders shrugged.

Haley barely trapped the frustrated groan in her mouth. "But I screamed at you before you could speak." Her hands flopped to her thighs. "I seriously need to bake you muffins and bring tea, and we need to start over."

"Don't. I don't deserve muffins."

That particular phrase sent an aching pulsing through her muscles, and she automatically doubled down, almost as if his words were an activation code. "I insist. This is happening. You will be the recipient of baked goods, and when you are, you'll be grateful I'm occasionally stubborn, because I'm a pretty good baker."

His chest expanded with a largely drawn breath as his lips pinched into a firm line. "Not blueberry."

"You don't like blueberries?"

"They have a weird mushiness to them."

"Mushiness? What are you, two?" The innocent jab was out before she could think about it.

When the corner of his mouth kicked up, the tautness in her chest lessened. "If two-year-olds don't have to eat blueberries, then yes. I'm two."

A smile broke over her lips. "Then you're the biggest two-year-old I've ever seen."

Fifteen minutes later, after discussing what fruit *was* acceptable baked into a muffin, Haley sat on her couch for breakfast. A grin curled her mouth as she crushed one of the blueberries topping her bran cereal between her molars.

Her mind was replaying the interaction with her neighbor when suddenly the activities she'd partaken in over the last week felt more foolish than Jason's claim that "idiocy defined her." Heavy stomping brought her to the kitchen to grab the list she'd penned after their breakup. Her hand crushed the paper into a miniscule ball before she threw it into the trash. It rested for half a millisecond before Haley picked it back up, ripped it to shreds, re-crumpled the slivers, and then tossed them back in with a flourish.

There.

She might not know why she was unworthy of love, but finding the bright side in situations wasn't it.

Even though a second prior she'd felt triumphant, cool hands wrapped around her ankles. They slithered up her calves, threatening to drag her to the abused linoleum floor.

Haley shook her head, fighting. There were things to do today. Muffins to bake. She grabbed her phone like she was frantically clenching at a frayed rope. Logging in and tabbing through OnlyApp strengthened her grip on the thin cotton fibers.

Technology was incredible. With a tap of the finger, the electronic impulses that constantly coursed through her skin would connect with the receiver built into her phone and make it possible for her to connect with an unattainable god. The whole thing was science fiction, particularly the part about Zach Abrams on the other end of the message.

Hey, Zach Abrams. Do you have any fruit aversions? . . .

Chapter 7

"I can't believe you got another job." Remmy's voice played in stereo from its position in Haley's dollar-store earbuds.

"It's just a shift here or there on the weekends like I do at the center in Maysville. The Red Cross always needs help. Plus, there's a blood shortage right now," she said, hoisting the six grocery bags dangling from her left elbow.

Jana, the Red Cross supervisor, had nearly cried in relief when Haley had called on her lunch break, asking if they needed additional phlebotomists. By the end of her hospital shift, she'd received an email stating that Jana had spoken to Haley's supervisor back home, expedited her official hiring, waved the new-employee training, and just needed her to come in tomorrow to sign paperwork.

"My sweet bleeding heart"—Haley could almost picture Remmy shaking her head—"isn't the point of this getaway to get a change of scenery and chase Zach Abrams? How can you do that if you're working non-stop? Knowing you, you're probably already staying after you've clocked out at the hospital to clean up the clinic or find other things that need doing."

Haley winced—she'd been caught.

"Well, my last attempt to get close to Zach Abrams imploded, as you know."

Last week, at the casting call, Haley hadn't even blinked when a thud sounded from behind her, and she found a young brunette sprawled on the sidewalk—neck fully extended, head cascading off the curb. Haley had crouched beside her, elevated her head, and shouted for someone to get help before quickly assessing the woman's airway, breathing, and circulation. The raised edge of the broken sidewalk had sliced into the side of the woman's skull, and unfortunately, head wounds tend to bleed. A lot.

"Don't make me think of it." Haley could hear Remmy's shudder in her words—she'd never been a fan of blood.

"Besides," Haley continued. "I promise I'm spending the rest of my time doing some sightseeing. Yesterday afternoon, I took a free Tai Chi class at this cool park. It was huge and had all these tranquil water features, like an oasis in the desert."

"Was that before or after delivering your neighbor the apple muffins?"

"After." Haley arrived at the base of her floating stairs and took a steadying breath. The open gaps between the rough-textured concrete steps always made her uneasy. She knew, logistically, that she couldn't fall between them, but it didn't stop her brain from envisioning gruesome ways her ankle would snap if it ever slipped between the gaps. "And tomorrow, after I sign the Red Cross paperwork, I'm going to the Tucson

Gem Show. It's supposed to be incredible. Gemstones the size of your head."

"Oooh, that does sound like fun." A pause settled over the phone. "I wish I was going with you."

Her heart pinched. "I wish you were too."

Now that she realized her disposition wasn't what drove men away from her, Haley felt slightly foolish for her wanderlust. With each day in Arizona, two things became glaringly obvious: one, unless she wanted to return to Maryland a lizard, she needed to up her moisturization game, and two, it might be better to use this time to take a break from men. It was past time for some healthier self-discovery. Inspired by her new plan, Haley had downloaded several emotional health audiobooks from the Maysville Public Library.

"Next time I decide to travel impulsively, I'll be sure to take you with me."

Remmy chuckled. "That's right, you will."

Haley's grin upon hearing her friend's laugh turned into a quizzical twist seeing the small cream envelope taped to her front door. *Dark and Stormy Cheerful Neighbor* was scrawled across the front in messy handwriting.

Haley snatched the envelope before pushing inside, suppressing the effervescent sensation trickling up from her stomach. "What are you up to this week?"

The bags met the counter with a varied chorus of clunks, followed by a *thonk* from the gallon of milk that had been freezing her fingers.

"The usual. Trying not to turn into a popsicle. Mediating divorce cases. Missing Margarita Mondays." The last part was said in a way that Haley knew her friend was deploying her tactical lip pout.

"I'm sorry, Remmy." She pulled open the fridge and piled broccoli, squash, and lettuce into the crisper. "Why don't you drink margaritas with Marcus?"

"Can't. He got sick off tequila in college and won't touch the stuff."

This tiny twitch pulsed between her shoulder blades as Haley tried to ignore the petulant, intrusive thought that fired off automatically. *At least you have someone to drink with when I'm gone. At least you're not completely alone.* The cheddar block bounced from its toss into the deli drawer before she made herself take a deep breath. *No. None of that. You're happy for Remmy's happiness.*

"Okay," Haley said. "How about he has a beer while you have a margarita?"

"Yeah, that could work." Remmy often fell into routines, and when she did, she didn't consider any alternatives unless someone else brought them up. It was ironic because Remmy solved problems for others all day long but never seemed to apply that same creative thinking to her own life. "But it won't be the same," she whined.

"Remmy Juniper Jones." Haley mock-hardened her tone.

"Okay. *Okay.* I'll go to El Guapo's with Marcus."

"Thank you." She closed the door to the refrigerator, the glass jars of condiments rattling from within. "Have some chips and guac for me."

Remmy drew in an exaggerated breath. "Wait! Why don't you go out and get some yourself? Aren't you in the birthplace of guac?"

"I'm not privy to the exact origin of guac, but it was probably nearby." Haley extended on the tips of her toes to put the bread and cereal on the top of the fridge.

"Do that for me."

"Do what for you?" she asked, folding the plastic bags into each other and shoving them under the sink.

"Go out tonight and have margaritas and guacamole. Then I'll know we're both having them. Under the same big sky. Like in that old movie from the eighties Memaw used to play on VHS for us. Oooh, why don't you ask Yeti to go with you? Surely a creature his size needs to eat occasionally. I'd expect rather frequently."

Before Haley could answer, the familiar beep of Remmy's phone getting another call resonated in the background. "It's Aunt Tara. I've got to answer this. Send me a picture from the restaurant. Love you. Bye!"

"Bye," she said, as Remmy ended the call.

Haley pulled her phone from her scrub pocket and earbuds from her ears, setting both on the kitchen counter. Groceries put away, she could no longer avoid the small cream envelope.

Inside, Yeti had written: *I'm sorry I don't remember your name. I'm sure you told me, and I forgot. I'm terrible about names if I don't see them printed. Anyway, thanks for the muffins. You were right about your baking ability.*

Haley felt something like the half-smile she'd seen on her neighbor's mouth lift her right cheek. Flipping the card over, she grabbed a pen from her scrub pocket and wrote *Haley* in her neatest print. Her purple sneakers were beyond the glass door and treading onto the concrete of her balcony before she'd even registered her motion. Over the weeks, she'd noticed that her neighbor often spent his evenings in his hammock, doing Sudoku with a pen.

Yeti looked up from his book, the cover image of *The New York Times* Sunday crossword collection peeking between his long fingers. Haley's mouth lifted at the sight of him snuggled into his hammock. The faded-green pillow beneath him made his long hair floof around his head, like he'd been adorably electrocuted. Her allergies to both cats and dogs—and bunnies, *ironically*—had kept her from ever having a pet of her own, but now part of her wondered if she could adopt a Yeti.

She laid the card over his closed and flipped book. "Read this."

Her neighbor lifted it to his nose. "Haley."

"Now you'll remember my name forever because of that photographic memory of yours."

Haley caught the precise moment he suppressed a smile.

"Have you eaten dinner?" The invitation popped out of her mouth. She hadn't planned on asking him, just showing him her name and then heading out to eat alone. Again.

His gaze fell to his bare feet. "Ah."

Heat swelled in her stomach as her mouth rushed to explain. "My best friend is demanding that I have margaritas and guacamole because it's Margarita Monday. We usually do that together every week, but . . ." Her brain finally caught up to the fact that his lips and shoulders had tensed as she spoke. "Just as neighbors," she hastened to add. "Obviously, I'm saving myself for Zach Abrams. Well, not *saving myself*. I'm not a virgin. I'm twenty-seven years old." She took a quick breath, lifting her palms. "Not that I'm hating on twenty-seven-year-old virgins or anything. To each her own, but Tony Barrasso took my V-card the summer before senior year, so all good on that front."

Yeti's gaze had ventured up the second she'd said *virgin*, and now his mouth was open—speechless.

There was no way her face wasn't magenta right now, probably her neck and ears too. Darn that Remmy for suggesting she invite him and noodling into her subconscious. This was a terrible idea. No. This had been an awkward, horrific, cringeworthy disaster.

"You know what?" She took a step back. "Just give me a suggestion, and I'll be out of your hair. I know there are, like, fifty Mexican restaurants within a square mile, but since you're from here, maybe you could tell me the best one." Her back hit the solid glass door before she noticed she'd followed that first retreating step with several others.

Her hand fumbled for the handle. "Never mind. I'll figure it out," she mumbled.

"Wait."

Even though she heard him and the creaking sound of his hammock, the muscles in her arms kept opening the door, as if acting in an independent reflex of self-preservation. One of her shoes was already resting on the rough, sand-colored carpet of her apartment.

"Haley, wait a damn minute."

It was the expletive that halted her movement, flinching. She'd often been the recipient of Jason's cutting curses peppered in with his insults. When Haley hazarded a glance in his direction, not an iota of Yeti's body mirrored the enraged exterior she'd expected.

Her neighbor had slipped back into his typical Yeti posture—standing with shoulders slumped, head slightly down, hands in his gray sweatshirt pocket. He blew out a remorseful breath and looked up.

"Guadalajara Grill." He paused, his amber eyes holding hers and forcing them into a momentary standstill. "They have table-side salsa and guacamole."

"Thank you." She was inside her apartment with the curtain closed before he could take another inhale.

Haley tried to ignore the burning sensation beneath her cheekbones as she moved into her small bedroom. Almost immediately, she caught her flustered reflection in the vanity over the sink. The far right side of the rectangular space had a doored-off shower and toilet area, leaving the sink and mirror open to the room. A small closet chunked off a little more space, completing the layout. The raw sunset pierced through the open window, highlighting the generic saguaro print photograph framed on the opposite wall above her queen mattress.

She wanted nothing more than to pull off her scrubs and put on her romper. The gauzy magenta fabric called to her like a soft and supple siren.

"Remmy will know," she said after a defeated exhale.

And Remmy would know because Haley had never been able to lie to her. She'd been successful in hiding her lack of happiness for the last year, but if questioned directly about whether or not she went to get margaritas, Haley would have to admit the truth.

She plucked loose the bow at the waistband of her scrub pants and began changing into pale-orange jeans and—yes, why the heck not—her fluffy bunny sweater. If she was going to have to eat guacamole and drink margaritas by herself in a foreign city, she was going to be as comfortable as possible. She even topped the outfit off with these cool, daisy-print flats she'd found at her new favorite thrift shop.

When Haley reluctantly opened her front door, a familiar shaggy face was on the other side, hand raised, as if to knock.

"Hey." His fingers returned to their home in his front pocket. "Do you still want company?"

Chapter 8

Yeti knew he was a madman for standing here, offering himself up to be rejected, but the broken way she'd run into her glass door . . . it had undone him. He couldn't be the one to abandon her, not tonight. Not when she'd bounded onto their balcony all luminosity and joy, and he'd pulverized that with his hesitation.

He hadn't meant to upset her, but he'd been hit again by how unfair life was. Because when Haley had asked him to dinner—even as neighbors—all he could think of was *before*. How *before*, he would have beaten her to it, and he sure as hell wouldn't have extended a platonic invitation. Though Yeti hadn't dated a lot in the past, there was something incredibly quirky and breathtaking about Haley. There was no way he wouldn't have asked her out.

Not when he could have stood a chance.

Haley pushed out onto the landing before locking her front door. "You're infuriating. You know that?"

The swing was instant. It took him a second to realize that it was *his* uninhibited laughter that filled the small space at the top of the stairs. She spun around, staring, like him parkour-jumping over the metal railing made more sense than him laughing.

Yeti quickly covered his mouth with his hand and subdued his merriment. "Sorry. That's the exact adjective my sister uses to describe me."

Haley blinked, suspended for a moment, before she moved to descend the stairs. "And here I was, thinking I was special and that you were saving your most irritating behavior for me." A dramatic sigh accompanied her hoisting the thin strap of her small purse higher on her sweater-covered shoulder. She was wearing that white one again. The soft one. "Life is full of disappointments."

It wasn't a choice to follow her down the death stairs. He simply did. "I told you I wasn't the best communicator."

There was barely room for both of them on the narrow sidewalk, so Yeti kept a pace behind her.

Her shoulders lifted, and he watched her intentionally lower them. "And why is that, exactly?"

The whole truth was an impossible thing, so he settled for a smaller one. "I don't really interact with anyone."

"What do you mean?"

He pulled his eyes away from her bouncing ponytail and sighed. "I work from home, and most of my professional interactions are done via email or text. I go to the gym every day, but I wear my headphones and use a barcode to check in. All my shopping is done with self-checkout, order-ahead, or delivery. Other than my weekly calls with my sister, or occasionally seeing my parents when they have time, I can go days without speaking to another person."

Haley plowed through the gravel section that separated the winding sidewalks from their covered parking spot without a word.

"Haley." He lightly touched her elbow, and her step hitched momentarily. "You didn't answer my question."

"What question?" she asked, head focused on the cars in front of them.

"Do you still want me to come with you?"

Haley flipped so quickly he almost crashed into her.

"What?" A flush streaked over her throat. "You're following me, but you're not coming?"

Pinpricks arched over his skin, toppling the pain squeezing behind his sternum. *This.* This is what Paige didn't understand when she kept encouraging him to reconnect with people. He did things like this—upset his friendly, kind, unattainable neighbor. His head dropped as his eyelashes rested on his cheeks with an exhale. For a breath, all he could hear was the crickets trying to compete with the hum of rush-hour traffic.

"Yeti." Her voice was soft, but it felt like a punch to the ribs because he knew what was coming next.

Why was he even out here? This was all so stupid.

"Get in the car."

His neck muscles whined at the speed his head snapped up. Haley disappeared into an ancient tan sedan and leaned over to manually unlock the passenger-side door.

It was another juncture where he should have walked home, but his body simply opened the door and lowered itself onto the scratchy fabric seat.

Haley didn't put the car in drive. She sat with her hands on the steering wheel, staring straight ahead.

"Okay, here's the deal," she said. "I'm lonely. I should have expected that I would've been, but I completely underestimated what it's like to move to a new city and not know anyone. In my small town, I can't go a day without running into someone I've known since I used to pee myself as a response to being startled." Her eyes darted over. "Kindergarten was rough. Anyway, I don't think I'm going to survive the next six weeks without occasional company. During the day, my patients fill my social coffers, and I'm always talking to Remmy, but . . ." Her sentence drifted off as her lips downturned.

"I could use a friend."

What had just come out of his mouth? He didn't *have* friends, especially ones he was undeniably attracted to. The catchy beat of Ace of Base's "The Sign" whispered from the car's stereo system, and Yeti briefly wondered if this was the worst decision he'd made since the one that had turned his entire life upside down.

But then, that stumbly smile lifted her cheeks. "Yeah?"

Since he didn't trust his voice, Yeti nodded.

Her grin stayed as she shifted the car into drive. "You didn't steer me wrong with the tamales. Let's see if you can go two for two."

◊◊◊

"Oh my goodness, I'm never going to be able to eat at El Guapo again," Haley mumbled over the large chip slathered in custom-made guacamole. "Is it possible to overdose on cilantro? Because if so, what a way to go."

He felt the corner of his mouth lift. "I'm glad I didn't lose my rank as Tucson's top food recommender. Perhaps I should moonlight as an influencer."

Something had loosened in him on the ride here. Haley had occupied every second of the drive with her words, often oversharing. There hadn't been that pressure for him to contribute, to say the right thing. She seemed completely content with his silent presence. As Haley told him entertaining stories of her day, his muscles had progressively slacked. Even though, initially, the car had stunk with a stale mix of takeout and cigarettes, when that spark returned to her eyes, the air seemed to sweeten.

"You totally could," she said from behind her lifted hand.

The warmth in her gaze caused the flicker of possibility to flit in his peripheral vision. Immediately, Yeti pulled his eyes down to the chip bowl and silently reprimanded himself for the foolish thought.

She needed company.

Nothing more.

"I'm going to have to learn how to make this." Haley went in for another round of salsa. "I won't be able to get anything like this back home. To be fair, we have incredible crab cakes. Maysville is an hour inland, but it's still close enough to the coast for great seafood. Nobody beats Maryland's crab cakes."

Their server returned with two fishbowl-sized margaritas. Tajín rimmed his jalapeno-flavored version while a halved pepper floated atop the ice cubes. The white salt of her rimmed glass stood in contrast to the deep cerulean of her margarita. Three lime wedges teetered precariously on the rim.

Haley took a deep suck from her oversized yellow straw. "Oh, wow. That's strong."

"The tequila's usually on the bottom." Yeti stirred his before taking a sip. Even with the small mouthful, the liquor shot straight to his calves. He pushed his drink subtly aside and made a mental note to ask for a water when the server returned.

Haley further integrated the ingredients in her margarita before startling as if she'd forgotten something. "Oh, will you take a picture of me? Remmy will want proof I actually went out. She's kind of relentless like that. It makes her a great attorney but, at times, an annoying friend." She gave a lopsided smile, using her thumbprint to open her phone's lock screen before handing it over.

Yeti couldn't help noticing the streak of blue nail polish dried on the back. "Say tequila."

"Tequila." She cheesed as she held up her glass.

Haley chuckled at the photo. "This margarita has some serious Smurfette vibes. Remmy'll love it." After a few clicks, she set her phone face-down on the cushioned booth bench. "So"—she leveled that steady gaze at him—"friends with a yeti. Do I get any storybook bonuses with that? Should I expect sparrows to dress me and pour my tea in the morning? Perhaps they could do something with my hair? They're obviously working wonders on yours."

It was a fight to keep the laugh trapped in his chest. "Unknown. Yetis are solitary creatures. I don't concern myself with the comings and goings of the fowl community." He tossed a guac-loaded chip into his mouth.

She puckered her lips while playfully scrunching her brow. "You're just sitting on all this dry wit and keeping it from the world? That's evil-genius-level hoarding of valuable resources."

"Why do you think I always wear dark clothing?" he deadpanned.

"Of course." Haley smacked her forehead. "You convene with all the other evil geniuses remotely from your apartment. You probably have a group text about savage things, like instructions on how to skin kittens, make hold music more mind numbing, and ways to increase the wait time at the DMV. Oh, and all the lost socks in the world. That's gotta be you guys."

"*Guys*," he huffed. "Over half of the council are women, Haley. We're not a sexist organization."

An uninhibited, barking laugh left her lips, and Yeti attempted to ignore the warmth flooding his muscles. He swallowed hard before focusing on the menu in front of him, studying images of entrees he'd eaten his entire life as if they were novel and fascinating. "Do you want to order anything else?"

"We don't usually, but this drink's so strong, maybe I should eat something with more substance."

"Probably." He flipped the plastic-covered page.

They ended up ordering burros—his a machaca to her bean-and-cheese.

Trumpets tangled with violins and the rhythmic strumming of a guitar while Haley admired the various paintings on the warm-yellow walls. They were positioned just above the dried peppers that hung beside each decorative wall sconce. The third one from the right caught her attention, and Haley tilted her face toward it as if it was the sun.

He should have been savoring her peaceful beauty, but Yeti couldn't help himself. The name had been racing back and forth in his mind since he'd heard it, zipping like an electron discharged from his atom. "So, Tony Barrasso . . ."

Haley groaned. "Didn't you say you're not good at remembering names you don't read?"

He lifted a shoulder. "Must have been a one-off."

"No." She waved her hand in front of her face, her cheeks pinking in direct correlation to the dwindling liquid in her margarita glass. "We're not doing this. We're not discussing Tony Barrasso. It's your turn to tell me something about yourself."

"My position on the council allows me—"

"*Other* than you're an evil genius."

He twisted his lips, thinking. The song ended, and another one began with a chorus of men's voices harmonizing in Spanish. "My sister's name is Paige."

She gasped. "Hold on. Let me flag down our server to refill your water. That must have been like running a marathon for you."

Yeti narrowed his eyes.

That playful scrunch was lining her forehead again. "Seriously, you need to tell me—"

Fortunately, he was saved by the delivery of a refill of chips. Yeti pushed the basket toward her. She needed to eat more to soak up all that alcohol. When Haley chowed down on another salsa-brimmed chip, his back settled further onto the booth's plastic seat.

"Do you really have a sister?" She lowered her voice to a whisper. "Or is she a figment of your imagination?"

Yeti rolled his eyes. "She's real. And she's a pain in my behind most of the time. Very similar to someone I've recently become acquainted with."

She ignored the gently laid barb. "Because my understanding is that evil geniuses don't have the best grip on reality."

Her careless comment about reality reminded him about his. That as much as this felt like a date, it wasn't. It could never be. He was careful to keep the disappointment from splashing across his face like an unwanted ink stain. Haley was in such a jovial mood he wanted nothing but to keep her there.

He was quickly learning her freely given expressions. When Haley was excited, her mouth slacked, her eyes widened, and she wiggled a little. An uneven smirk laced her lips when she was teasing him. But his favorite was how those two tiny lines at the bridge of her nose popped up once he'd annoyed her.

When Yeti leaned over conspiratorially, she mirrored his posture with such rampant glee it poked at his ribs. "That's where you're wrong. We have a better understanding of what the world is really like, and that's why we want to fix things by taking over."

Chapter 9

"Hey, Dad." Haley cradled her phone with one hand and gripped the back of her aching neck with the other. "Is Billy there with you?"

Thursdays were poker nights with the guys. Billy Eshom, the family friend she'd known since she was two—who was *also* her car insurance salesman—was a steady fixture at her father's nicked kitchen table.

"Yeah, why?"

She winced from her position on the curb, the lights of the police cruiser flashing beside her. "I was in an accident."

"You okay?" The emotion that crept into her father's words sounded odd reverberating over the line.

Her father rarely talked to her, rarely talked to anyone. He was often described as a "man of few words." Their conversations were usually repetitive and cyclical.

How's work?

The hospital's good, Dad. You?

Oh, can't complain.

The only time Haley recalled emotion crawling into his words had been the last time she'd asked him about her mother.

"Yeah." The rear bumper of her rental was detached, and her neck hurt in two places—along the back from jerking forward and hitting the headrest, and over her left clavicle where the seat belt had pinched her skin restraining her—but overall, she was fine. A little shaken, but fine.

"All right." A few seconds of silence was filled with the background noise of men's laughter. "Billy, Lee needs to talk to you."

". . . you know it!" Billy's boisterous voice barked in the distance. Memories of Billy's rotund belly perfectly filling the red Santa suit he wore as he handed out gifts at his yearly Christmas party swamped her brain. "Hey, kiddo. What can I do you for?"

Now that a warm voice was on the other end of the line, the words tumbled out of her. "I'm so sorry, but the rental I got coverage for was in an accident." Haley sucked in a quick breath. "I was driving home from a movie, and the other driver didn't stop at the red light and rear-ended me. But then they left. They hit reverse and drove through the parking lot next to me." On the last sentence, her voice cracked.

Haley patted the messy bun still intact at the crown of her head, trying to regain some composure. "I'm okay. I can move everything and don't need to go to the hospital, but . . . the bumper fell off."

Tonight, she'd decided to switch up her routine by enjoying the latest superhero action flick with a colossal tub of buttered popcorn. For the last week and a half, Haley had been filling a spiral notebook with crucial take-aways from her borrowed audiobooks. The *ah-ha* bulb had gone off several times, and once she'd finished what was available in the self-love section, she'd progressed to the books on relationships. Listening to those books had been much harder, churning her insides into knots as realization after realization hit her.

"Oh, Lee. I'm sorry." Honesty swept Billy's voice. "I'm assuming the rental's still operational."

She glanced up at the poor smashed vehicle. "I think so. I didn't move it. The driver in the lane beside me told me not to. She called the cops and stayed with me until they got here."

Thankful was a tiny, insignificant word with too few letters to describe how Haley felt about Delores, the middle-school math teacher who helped during the metal-crunched aftermath.

"No, that's good. That was the right thing to do. Did she give the police a witness statement?" The boisterous noises behind Billy settled to a concerned murmur.

"She did before she left." Already, Haley missed her warm presence. The cold of the curb was seeping through her corduroy skirtall and infiltrating her navy leggings.

"All right. Ask the police officer for the report number so we can get a copy later. You're not to blame, but without the other person's insurance to cover the damage, you'll have to pay for the repair."

A craggy boulder pushed on Haley's chest. Money was always tight, and she'd spent most of her savings on this whimsical desert adventure. She'd have to use a credit card to pay for the repair and pay it off as soon as she could.

"You'll need to inform the owner of the car and get it repaired for them," Billy continued. "Tomorrow, I'll look at your collision coverage and try to find you a good shop in the area. Is the bumper salvageable?"

Her gaze found the plastic protective cover laying on the asphalt, mangled. "I don't think so."

"Damn." He blew a breath into the phone. "That's okay, kiddo. It'll be okay. We'll get this sorted out. I'll call you in the morning."

The corners of her eyes flooded with warm tears, but Haley tried to keep her voice even. "Thanks, Billy."

If she'd been at home, this wouldn't have happened. She would have been driving her decade-old but sturdy crossover on the peaceful snow-covered streets, not on this six-lane divided roadway teeming with cars—many blasting music through open windows, even at ten o'clock at night.

"Miss?" The approaching police officer carrying a black citation holder kept her from adding tears to the splintered plastic scattered on the road.

◊◊◊

Haley sat in her covered parking spot for a long time after making the dreaded call to the car's owner, Livy. Since Livy had said she was going to be on a research ship funded by the University of Arizona's climate science program *nearish* the Bermuda Triangle, Haley wasn't sure when Livy would get her voicemail.

She was typing Livy's email address into the email app on her phone when two loud knocks on her driver's side window made her jump. A painful groan tore from her. Haley dropped her phone to grab her neck a second before realizing that she was about to be mugged on top of being the victim of a hit-and-run. Her left hand punched the door lock at the same time Yeti's glass-muffled voice said, "Haley, relax. It's me."

Her deep inhale did nothing to slow the already galloping pulse shooting blood to her extremities. The tingling, ready-to-fight sensation saturated her forearms and calves, but Haley forced her shaky fingers to remove her seatbelt and unlock the door. The instant the lock disengaged, cold night air infiltrated her car.

When turning her head made her grimace, Yeti's hand settled at the base of her neck. The touch was way too intimate, but Haley would have bitten anyone who tried to remove his skin from hers. The heat from his fingers and palm had already seeped into her strained muscles and tendons.

"I was going to ask what happened to your bumper, but it's pretty obvious with your neck pain." His voice lowered a few notes. "Are you okay? I mean, I know this hurts"—the tiniest pressure was applied by his hand—"but . . . are you okay?" Yeti's eyes were running over her V-neck, heart polka-dotted sweater and skirtall, searching for further injury.

Haley watched a drop of sweat roll from his hairline down the sharp slant of his nose and plummet onto the car's door jamb. "Why are you wet?"

"I just got back from the gym." His eyes were now fixed on the purpling bruise over her left clavicle.

Gratitude tiptoed across her forehead. Haley just needed a minute to think about *anything* besides the mess she'd found herself in. The mess she'd put her whole life in while trying to figure out something that she could've done at home. The only good thing about being in Tucson at the moment was the opportunity to ruffle her grumpy neighbor's feathers.

"Late-night gym sesh. Did you go this late to avoid other people?"

His brows dove together in irritation as his gaze snapped to hers. "We're not talking about me right no—"

"We never talk about you." Haley shifted to face him, careful to keep her head in line with her body. "Why are you always deflecting?"

Ever since Margarita Monday over a week and a half ago, they passed each other daily—often stopping to chat for several minutes. Afterward, she'd walk away from their conversations smiling. Then, the realization that her cryptic neighbor had yet again avoided answering any direct questions would hit her like an ice cube to the nose.

"I'm not—" He took a sharp inhale. "Answer the question, Haley. Are you okay?"

Two could play this don't-answer game. "You use my name a lot when you speak to me. Did you know that? Not a lot of people do that. It's kind of weird."

The tension seemed to increase in his shoulders. Yeti crouched in front of her, using his other hand to frame her face. Warm thumbs ran over her temples, felt for bumps under her hair, and settled again over the column of her neck as his eyes darted between hers. "What day is it?"

A slightly unhinged laugh exploded from her. "You're assessing my orientation?" He opened his mouth, but she cut him off. "Haley Kineman. Our apartment parking lot. Thursday, January 28th."

The relieved breath that blew over her face was cinnamon scented. Until this point, Haley couldn't remember a single moment in her life when she would've chosen cinnamon gum. Not when there were a myriad of choices on the bright, multi-colored displays in every grocery store. Not when *Juicy Fruit* had been an option. But as sweet cinnamon swirled and mixed with Yeti's clove scent, she craved the taste of that spice on her tongue more than she'd craved any flavor in her entirety.

Feeling unnerved by her sudden impulse, Haley tugged his sweatshirt-covered forearms away from her and moved to get out of the car. "I'm fine. Nothing to worry about. Just a little fender bender." He shifted backward as she stepped out and closed her door. "As soon as I can get some ibuprofen in me, I'll be right as rain."

Seemingly unconvinced, his gaze remained trained on her. The heat that she'd initially felt at her neck seemed to sweep through every one of her cells. Darting her eyes down, Haley strode toward the gravel path leading to the sidewalk.

Two large steps brought Yeti to her elbow. "Do you have Tylenol too? You should take both. And use a muscle cream. Do you have one of those?"

"You know, I would make some joke about you being a nervous mother hen, but I'm too tired." She tried not to flinch when moving her purse strap caused a searing sensation sprinting down her spine.

"I have both," he continued, undeterred. "I'll bring them over."

The rest of their winding walk through the complex was silent, and Haley was halfway up the concrete stairs, too exhausted to care about shattered ankles, when she realized she'd left Yeti at the base.

"What is it?"

His nose wrinkled before he took a deep breath and ascended the stairs. When they both reached the top, she couldn't stop the unexpected shimmering trying to explode from her chest.

"Did you just hold your breath going up the stairs?"

His eyes darted to the side as he took a small step toward his front door. "No."

"Oh my goodness, you did!" Effervescence was bubbling over, spilling on every surface around them, obliterating her neck pain. "I'm afraid of them too."

His mouth curved slightly. "Really?"

"I envision splintered bones almost every time I climb them."

Yeti nodded. "They're a death trap. So far, holding my breath has kept me from being sacrificed to the stair trolls. At least going down them isn't as bad, since you can't anticipate your fall into the abyss."

A wide smile pulled up her lips. "I feel exactly the same way."

His gaze stalled on her mouth, and Haley was certain she could feel every cold air molecule entering her lungs.

Yeti's eyes ripped away, causing his hair to flop over his shoulder. "Take some ibuprofen. I'll get the Tylenol and IcyHot." His keys were out of his sweats pocket and his front door was shutting before she could respond.

Disorientation swept like a hot, tempestuous wind through her body. Surely, Yeti hadn't just *stared at her mouth*.

Her neighbor was this safe entity, gruff on the surface but actually kind, not . . .

No, she mentally shook her head since her neck wouldn't allow a proper shake. She must have unknowingly bitten her lip in the accident. It was probably all puffy, and bloody, and gross.

It was after she'd dropped her purse on her bed and swallowed the burnt-orange pills that Haley noted her unremarkable face in the bathroom mirror. Nothing to see here, folks, just her normal, on-the-thin-side lips.

The loud knock at her front door caused her to jump and then wince.

Yeti was frowning at his ringing and buzzing phone when she opened her door. He quickly ignored the call with one hand while holding out the medicines in the other, barely raising his eyes from the screen. "Let me know if—" He couldn't get the rest of that sentence out because his phone rang again, drawing his attention.

Quickly taking the medicines, Haley said, "Thanks for these. I'll get you replacements when I can."

His eyes bounced up. "You don't need—" An irritated growl cut off that one as he silenced yet another call. This time, his thumbs flew over the screen in a furious attempt to out-speed whomever was calling him.

The train of thought Haley had tried to stop earlier crashed through, kicking up dirt while splintering iron blockades as if they were made of spider silk. It presented itself like a heaving, imposing thing, each loud puff of the engine impossible to ignore.

It was Yeti's hands that snagged her attention first. She'd already noticed the spongy criss-cross of veins on the backs of his hands—occupational hazard. Anytime she saw a nice vein, her mind hummed in appreciation, the way one might after smelling cake fresh out of the oven.

But now Haley noticed the firm grip of his fingers on the phone, the way the device seemed diminutive in his palm. Next was the tight bunch of his shoulders and their rhythmic movement. Breathing was another one of those predictable, mundane things, but watching Yeti's shoulder's seesaw, Haley felt a rebellious kitten unravel yarn inside her chest, altering something that couldn't be undone.

Then her gaze shifted up, almost methodically. Shampoo-commercial hair. Pinched lips peeking out from wild facial hair. That sharp nose. Enviable lashes. Amber-brown eyes circled by a darker outline she hadn't noticed before. The thin ring almost seemed to serve as a hedge, preventing the warmth from seeping out and dissipating.

"Haley?" His brows twinged with concern, his focus now steady and unrelenting. "Are you okay?"

Somewhere in her belly, the flicker of embarrassment at being caught staring was efficiently dismissed. His phone continued to chime, but the melodic arrangement of notes was a strange, far-off sound. It took a second to notice that the ring tone had been overshadowed by the rhythmic rushing of blood in her ears.

"Yes." Haley barely had the wherewithal not to nod and cause herself further pain.

When the phone simultaneously rang with a text and a call, Yeti reluctantly tore his gaze away.

"I, um—I'm going to—" She swallowed, trying to clear her dry mouth while ignoring the tiny little needles that had carelessly traversed down her legs. Thankfully, her arms seemed to regain some semblance of function, and their motion kick-started her brain. "I'll let you get your call. Thanks again. Goodnight."

By the time Yeti looked up again, she was already closing the door.

"Okay, okay. You have me," he barked from the other side of the wooden barrier. "Are you happy? You know if I don't pick up the phone right away, it's because of something important." Several heavy steps preceded the slam of his door.

The second the lifting, floating feeling from overhearing her scruffy neighbor's words traipsed through her body, it was almost like a shinier version of herself swept it out with a metal-bristled broom. *Nope. No space for this anymore. We're not letting men define our self-worth.*

Haley took the Tylenol bottle to the bathroom sink, swallowing two tablets with a fistful of water and mentally agreeing with her newly polished and educated self.

But her smiling reflection didn't seem to get the memo—it was nice to be important.

Chapter 10

It felt like three days had passed by the time Yeti convinced Paige to hang up. She'd pestered him about what had kept him from instantly answering, but he refused to tell her. There wasn't a reason to tell Paige about Haley—about how the short moments conversing with Haley felt four thousand times more colorful than the rest of his predictable routine, about how he'd become concerningly addicted to their daily interactions, or about the fact that witnessing her in pain had shredded his intestines.

An anxious buzzing had ping-ponged in his chest seeing Haley injured, and Yeti hadn't thought, hadn't used a micron of common sense. Instead, he'd been a stupid, reckless man. The quick hugs he gave his parents and the occasional rough-housing he did with Paige were diminutive compared to the feeling of Haley's warmth beneath his palm. Wisps of blonde from her askew bun had teased the back of his hand as his heart had scrambled to memorize the texture of her skin.

The need to know she was okay had been suffocating. His nerves had skyrocketed with each evasive answer, tightening an invisible vise over his tense ribs. Muscle groups had throbbed with an incapacitating intensity while his mind spun frantic circles. Yeti despised the hospital to a magnitude many couldn't fathom, but he'd been prepared to drive her there himself, to stay with her if need be.

By the time he noticed she'd only been bumped and bruised, it'd been too late. The balance he'd barely been harboring during their brief encounters had been decimated. Now he had to live with the memory of her pulse strumming beneath his thumbs, the vibration of her laugh permeating the bones of his hands, and the impossible way her eyes dilated as they met his—like she'd wanted him to lean in and kiss her.

Yeti's shoe caught on the slight lip between the scratchy carpet and the linoleum entryway, halting his pacing. He hadn't been able to stop moving since he'd gotten home. A restless hand tore through his hair as he paused by his desk to toss his phone on the solid rubberwood.

His fingers tapped an irregular rhythm on the surface as his computer chair called to him like a seductive enchantress. Even his keyboard glowed in anticipation, somehow knowing he'd cave to his basest desire. Time patiently waited as Yeti fought himself, almost languid in its demarcation of seconds.

The springs of his chair sighed when he sank into it. His fingertips flew over the keys before a derisive snort left his nose. The avatars he'd abandoned years ago were still functional—the ones he'd used to test the app during development. His old partners should have disabled them.

A thick swallow halted him only a second before "Haley Kineman" appeared in the search bar next to the OnlyApp logo.

The shuddering breath Yeti stole as the page loaded sounded like a gale blasting in his ears. Her account was listed under @LeeKineman, but it was undeniably her. Haley's sunny smile beamed at him. Her bio only contained one phrase that somehow encapsulated her: *Life is in the details*.

An itchy feeling of intrusion slithered up his spine as Yeti clicked through each of her content tabs. OnlyApp had differed from its social media predecessors because it seamlessly separated its photo streams from its video streams into tethered categories. A user could choose which medium to scroll through depending on whether they wanted to observe silent frames or watch up to three-minute-long videos.

Haley only had one seventeen-second video of a summer rain coursing through thick green leaves, but she had over two thousand photo posts. The smiling one he'd taken of her holding a comically large glass of tequila over a week and a half ago stared back at him. Several others corroborated the stories she'd told him about her Tucson sightseeing adventures. The last two posts were a landscape shot Yeti recognized as the view from their balcony and a simple snap of the front of a Red Cross Donation center, urging her modest one hundred and forty-nine followers to donate blood.

Prior to her arrival in Tucson, she was most often photographed with a woman he assumed was Remmy. She was taller than Haley, with darker skin, her curly black hair uniquely arranged in each of their photos. Everything else seemed almost random—a field overwrought with purple dead nettle, soap bubbles in a scrubbed saucepan, a closeup of who was probably Remmy's great-grandfather laughing at a family picnic—but Yeti understood that each photo was a sliver of Haley, of what she loved enough to share with the world.

Dirtiness washed over his skin, but he kept clicking, reading each short caption. He was a disgusting stalker now. After confirming that she followed Zach Abrams, Yeti clicked on the celebrity's last post, trying not to scowl at the face Haley was enamored with.

Reluctantly, Yeti had to admit the man looked good on a horse.

A few clicks further brought him to an *Arizona Daily Star* article about the movie. It was a cinematic tribute to Tucson-local-turned-one-of-America's-most-influential-musicians, Bobby Carter. The movie was set in the former-rancher-turned-singer-songwriter's heyday of the mid-sixties. Critics were already predicting, based on the director and cast, that the film could sweep independent film festivals and maybe even the Oscars.

Yeti clicked through three more articles about the actor, reading about his multiple charitable works. A sinking sensation pulled at his calves because Zach Abrams appeared to be a decent human being, not the Hollywood dirtbag Yeti hoped he'd be. Bitterness washed his tongue because when he had been met with *much smaller* fame, he'd acted like he was better than Bill Gates and Steve Jobs combined.

When Yeti had been headhunted by Google right out of college, he hadn't been surprised. By that point, he was an established polyglot, intimately knowing over ten programming languages, and had barely needed to study for his interview. He had, however, maintained the humility his parents had instilled in him, even though one of the head developers had watched his interview, gawking in astonishment.

Three years later, when he and his former business partners had decided to branch out from their day jobs and upend the social media game, things changed. Success abounded, and Yeti became careless with the relationships he should have cherished. He'd listened to his girlfriend, Amber, encouraging him to strip those who'd known him the longest from his life. He'd let fame within the Silicon Valley world and money change him.

Until fate did some rearranging of its own.

When the memory blindsided him, his exhausted body couldn't fight it.

Pinging. Beeping. Buzzing.

Strange.

The last thing he could remember hearing was the surprisingly loud roar of the roof collapsing. Yeti tried to move, but his limbs ignored his commands. It was as if he was suspended in some strange precipice, like right before waking from a dream.

Another sound crept into his cranium.

Paige.

The relief flooding him had its own thick pulse. His sister's words sounded garbled, like she was gargling salt water.

"What do you mean you're not coming back?"

A computerized version of Amber's voice broke into the room. "Look, I'm sorry, but I can't. Do you want me to tell him it's okay when it's not? I can barely look at him." An unmistakable retching sound echoed over everything.

"But you told me you'd come back. That you'd support him through this."

"I lied."

Iced scalpels sliced through his raw nerve endings.

Paige stammered for a moment before she hissed, "Go to hell, you heartless monster."

His brain was momentarily distracted by his sister's harsh response—Paige didn't swear. The phone bounced on the bed, tapping his shin.

Then, everything became too sharp, too bright, too contrasted. It felt like a demon was twisting bony, barbed hands over his chest, his arm—pinching and clenching his skin. The sensation was relentless, slivering him with its unimaginable brutality. It shouldn't be possible to feel this amount of pain. There should be some safety switch in the human brain that shuts the body off at this magnitude.

He remained motionless, paralyzed in his flaying torture, until the sound of Paige sobbing snagged his attention.

A second before he gained control of his body, an impenetrable wall of sound capsized him. It was only when he felt Paige's frantic hand on his wrist and heard his name drop from her lips that Yeti noticed the blood-curdling scream had come from him. His eyes blinked open, taking in a blurry hospital room and the three running staff members before a drug-induced sleep mercifully took him away again.

Paige had convinced him to undergo laser treatments once he'd fully healed, but his main motivation in agreeing had been for the functionality he'd gain, not aesthetics. Even though his scar had softened and smoothed with each treatment, Yeti understood that no woman would ever want to look at, let alone touch him again.

His shoulders caved forward, his forehead falling into his palm. Agonizing seconds passed as his back heaved with uneven breaths. It took several minutes to realize that the faint sound of rain was coming from the tab he'd left open, playing Haley's video.

Rainfall was a sparse, coveted occurrence in the desert. Tucsonans spoke about water like starving people about food because the arid landscape never had enough of it. When it did rain, often during the summer monsoon season, every living thing soaked it up. Like how he'd been absorbing Haley's light whenever he was lucky enough to be in her presence.

Yeti pushed away from his desk with a curse, his chair toppling when it couldn't glide seamlessly over the carpet beyond his floor mat. He needed to knock this off. This stupid fantasy he'd built up in his head wasn't real. Even if she seemed to brighten whenever she saw him, there was no world where someone like Haley would ever want to be between his arms.

They were neighbors. *Temporary* neighbors. Nothing more.

Rationality did nothing to blur the anger simmering beneath his breastbone. If he hadn't just come from the gym, he would have already headed out. Lifting weights allowed him a sense of control that even coding didn't. Sometimes, code went awry. If he picked up a weight and put it down, he always got the same result—soreness and a feeling of accomplishment.

There was nothing to do to fix this. This just *was*.

Yeti closed all the OnlyApp tabs and opened his work files. After fifteen minutes of typing a jumbled mess, it was obvious that working would not serve as an adequate distraction. His shoulders sagged as he dragged his fatigued feet toward the bathroom. It'd been years since he'd used his prescribed sleeping medication to rest his racing mind, but Yeti didn't see another way out of this turmoil. He swallowed the pill dry, went through his evening routine, and lay, staring at the ceiling, waiting for the chemicals to obliterate the world.

Chapter 11

The only good thing about waking up early the next day was that Zach Abrams had posted a couple of short videos of him herding cattle. That answered her question about riding a horse! The videos were *magnificent*. The way his toned, jean-covered thighs clung to the heaving sides of his chestnut Quarter Horse as one leather-gloved hand gripped the reins . . .

Ooof.

He'd been attractive in his other movies, but those short clips were enough to momentarily distract her from the throbbing soreness radiating down her neck and back. Zach Abrams was so handsome he literally blocked out pain—impressive.

Not wanting to move from her semi-comfortable side-lying position, watching the two sixty-second videos on repeat, Haley lingered in bed even though she knew she should fill her empty stomach with pain killers.

"What do you think about staying in bed all day?" she asked of Zach Abrams's galloping form.

The video auto-restarted. "Ugh, you're right. Always so pragmatic."

Pressing her eyes closed, Haley rose in halting degrees. She eventually made it into the shower, where she stayed much too long, allowing the hot water to soothe her aching muscles. Any minute now, Billy would call her with the information about repairing her rental car. After that, she'd have to go to work.

A cursory web search told her the replacement bumper could cost anywhere from five-hundred to two-thousand dollars. Haley hoped because the sedan was older, the price would be on the lower end of the spectrum.

Towel-wrapped and brushing out her wet hair, her phone rang with a digitized version of "Walking On Sunshine."

"Hey, kiddo," Billy said as a response to her hello. "I've got good news . . . but there's a catch."

◊◊◊

Haley hated calling out of a shift, but Billy had coordinated with a repair shop in south Tucson that could do the replacement for an incredible $675.50. The only caveat was that she had to deliver it ASAP. This bill was going to nearly deplete her savings, but at least she wouldn't go into debt over it.

The entire time she drove, spoke with the repairman at the shop, and attempted to arrange for a rideshare to take her back to her apartment, Haley's phone exploded with messages. News about her fender bender was clearly cycling through Maysville's rumor mill, leaked by one of the seven men at her father's poker game.

Before she could type out a response message to Melinda, her boss back home, Haley's phone rang. She stared at the screen for two rings before answering.

"Hello?" It was impossible to hide her dubious tone. Haley couldn't remember a single time her father had called her.

Her dad cleared his throat. "Uh. Morning, Lee. How are you doing?"

The scent of automotive oil arm-wrestled with rubber tires as Haley took a deep breath.

Good, almost made it out of her mouth.

She almost followed the script.

As Haley paused, it was like some impatient director was waiting in the wings, a tattered and highlighted tome in his hands, gesturing wildly at her. But she'd been listening to relationship gurus almost every night. Literally. One author had even narrated her own audiobook, so her voice, ideas, and research had been pushed directly into Haley's brain, giving her the courage to tell the truth instead. Even though Haley generally overshared with anyone who would listen, she'd never had an honest conversation with her father.

"Not great, Dad. I'm homesick, my neck hurts, and I'm worried that this repair will cost more than they estimated. The only thing keeping me going at this point is that my job here is awesome, the food's phenomenal, and I don't need a jacket to stand outside."

"Oh." Haley could picture her father fidgeting, probably picking at the divot in the kitchen counter by the sink. He always did that when he was uncomfortable with something.

She shielded her eyes against the rising sun. "Yeah."

"I'm glad work's been good."

Haley should have been expecting it, but *'I'm glad work's been good'* was a splintering blow that made her suck an agonizing breath through her teeth.

It was a struggle to keep the strain out of her voice. "My ride's here. I've got to go."

"Oh, sure." He paused. "Take care."

"You too." She hung up and stared into the empty street before her, liquid pricking at the edges of her vision.

Morning traffic hummed in the background while Haley waited for the tension in her chest to pass.

"Did you need a ride, mija?" The mid-fifties shop manager was leaning out of a repair stall, smudged tool in hand.

Though he'd obviously meant the endearment in a passing way—the way the middle-aged server at Dave's always called her "hun"—that particular epithet in the wake of her father being emotionally inaccessible made her throat squeeze.

"No. Thank you. My ride should be here any minute," she lied, holding up her phone.

He nodded and headed back to work.

Haley organized for a rideshare before she answered the messages still pinging her phone. As much as Jason had espoused that no one but Remmy cared for her, Haley must have tenaciously crawled into the hearts of her friends, neighbors, and coworkers. The rideshare driver picked up and delivered two other people to their destinations on her way across town. Meanwhile, Haley's fingers flew over her screen, returning well-wishes with words of gratitude.

"You're a popular lady," the driver said when Haley finally set her phone down with a sigh.

Before she could even answer, Remmy's caller ID lit up her screen. "Uh. Is there any way you can let me out over there?" They were crossing the bridge over the wide, dry Rillito River, nearing a small shopping complex on the north side.

"Sure, just change your destination."

A few swipes later, Haley was standing beside a local coffee shop nestled beneath a few cottonwood trees. The riverbed stretched beyond, and small shrubs and grasses grew where water had once flowed.

She picked up Remmy's fourth call.

"How dare you get in an accident, not tell me first, and then ignore my calls? I had to find out from my mother, who heard it from Dad, since he'd been at poker last night. Third, Lee. I was third in line to find out that my best friend was hurt!"

Haley had to progressively move the phone away from her ear as Remmy's volume increased. She found a spot away from the patrons sitting at the outdoor tables and leaned over the metal railing separating her from the bike and running path several feet below. A handful of exercise enthusiasts passed by, taking advantage of the mild Arizona morning.

"I'm sorry. It was late last night. And you're two hours ahead of me, remember? I didn't want to wake you up in the middle of the night for a fender bender and a little neck pain." All her hollow excuses felt like ash in her mouth.

"Third." Remmy's word was harder than the steel railing pressing against Haley's belly.

"I know. I'm sorry. I should have told you first." Her lungs burned as her voice wavered. "There's so much I should have told you."

It was time to come clean—to explain why she'd felt she'd needed to escape all she'd ever known to sort out her life, why Haley couldn't tell her closest friend the truth.

"Oh, honey. No. I take it back. I'm not really mad. Well, I'm mad, but I'll get over it. Please don't cry. What can I do?"

"Just—Just listen, okay?" Haley took a fortifying breath. "Remember that bad fight in third grade, and Mama Nena would only let us play again if we promised to always tell each other the truth?"

"The one where she declared us sisters afterward?"

Haley pushed away an escaped tear. "Yeah. So, when I told you Jason was a little . . . emphatic in our breakup—"

"With his laundry list of complaints—which, by the way, are completely unfounded—yes, I remember."

Haley had only shared a few details of Jason's breakup speech with her best friend, omitting the verbal bashings she'd been receiving daily.

"I—" She swallowed, her sandpaper tongue brushing against the roof of her mouth. "Well. Um."

After a quick pause, Remmy asked, "Can you put the call on video?"

A click brought her friend's worried face into view, her navy suit almost blending into her black office chair, eyes bouncing around the screen in assessment. "Lee, what's wrong? Are you okay?"

"No." Haley watched her own jaw clench on the screen as she fought back tears. "I haven't been for a while, but . . . I think I'm working my way back."

It's funny how a moment can knock you sideways, rearrange your atoms, and then reassemble you stronger. Haley figured that would have been the accident and the unexpected outpouring of love in its aftermath, but no. It was a few blurted sentences beside an auto shop. Even if her father hadn't reciprocated, even if she felt battered and broken afterward, she'd finally been honest with him.

That was *huge*.

Now it was time to follow that vulnerability with another one.

She let her exhale wisp along the air currents following the path of the river. "I think my relationship with Jason might have been toxic." Remmy's eye twitched, but she kept quiet. "The thing is, it didn't start out like that. Jason was charismatic and complimentary in the beginning, but over time . . ."

Her eyes flicked down, remembering that, with Remmy at law school, it made sense when Jason argued that Haley should spend all her time with her boyfriend. That it made sense he didn't like her spending time with her coworkers after work when she could be with him. That he was right in saying Remmy's relatives weren't really hers, so Haley should say no when they invited her to family gatherings while Remmy was out of town. Before she knew it, Haley had lost touch with the community that had always supported her, and her world revolved around Jason.

"It was like how they describe boiling frogs. You don't realize the pot is hot until it's too late."

It had been when Remmy and Marcus had moved home over the summer that the first inklings of wrongness had tapped on her temple.

"I wish I'd known." The sorrow and regret steeping Remmy's words drew Haley's gaze.

"He was good at hiding it. The more I think about it, he never said or acted unkind when we were around others, and . . . I was ashamed because I believed the things he told me."

In her research, Haley had written words like *gaslighting* and *love bombing* and come to grips with the fact that she'd been at the receiving end of two long years of manipulation.

"Oh, Lee," she sighed.

"I thought I had to leave town to figure out what made me so unlovable." Her shrug brought the video screen up and down. "He'd said over and over that you were the only person who cared about me. That everyone else was just tolerating or pitying me. He kept reminding me that my mom left, and that my dad could barely stand to be in the same room as me—"

"Stop!" Remmy took a deep, steadying inhale, regaining her composure. "Your mom never knew what she was missing. She left when you were a baby. She probably had her own issues that had nothing to do with you. I know for a fact that if she'd gotten to know you, she wouldn't have been able to leave you."

An unhinged sob broke from Haley's chest, tears warming her cool cheeks.

Remmy steamrolled along. "And your dad loves you too. He's just a quiet, solemn man. On some level, I think he's probably still a little broken that your mom left you both. He's never dated, even though I know my parents have tried to fix him up several times over the years."

A memory pushed forward—being eleven and asking her dad why everyone called her *Lee*. Her father had been cleaning gutters and threw down a pile of soggy leaves, barely missing her. He gruffly stated that Lee was her name. That evening's dinner had been quieter and colder than usual, and Haley had never brought up the subject again. Maybe her mother had named her, and hearing *Haley* was still an icy spike to the ribs.

"Obviously, my family and our community loves you too. I'm sure your phone has been buzzing all morning." Her slight smile twisted into a vengeful frown. "If I'd known about all the crap Jason had pulled, I'd have whooped his skinny behind. I still might." Remmy let out a loud exhale. "You hid it too well. I didn't know you were so unhappy."

"I'm sorry," Haley whispered.

"Don't be sorry. You were taken advantage of by a manipulative jerk. Ugh. I want to hug you so bad. Why do you have to be so far away?"

She shrugged weakly. This whole wanderlust idea seemed really overrated at the moment, even though the bright sun was illuminating a landscape that was often featured in nature magazines.

"I hope Zach Abrams is worth it," Remmy huffed.

Haley's sob turned into a watery laugh.

"You believe me, right?" Remmy's lopsided smile was tender. "You see now how much you are loved? Not just by me, by everyone?"

"Yeah," Haley managed.

Remmy beamed. "Good. Because you know I'm always right."

"Not always." Haley twisted her lips to the side, brushing the tears from her face. "Remember the mascot incident sophomore year?"

Her friend's eyes rolled so hard Haley was sure she'd strained her eye muscles. "Jaguar. Tiger. What's the difference?"

"Spots. Stripes. And I'm pretty sure, some genetic distinctions."

"That's it." Remmy's gaze went off screen as keystrokes accompanied her words. "I'm flying out to knock some sense into you. Believing that good-for-nothing, low-life buttnut over your best friend of twenty-one years."

"Language!"

"You're not the boss of me." Remmy continued to type, muttering expletives.

Haley groaned. They'd obviously reverted to their seven-year-old selves. "*Remmy Juniper Jones.*"

Remmy's scrunched up nose brought her eyes with it.

"I love you," Haley said. "And I'm sorry. I should have listened to you. It was just hard after hearing his voice in my head for so long." Remmy's gaze softened. "As much as I'd love to see you, I'll be home in four weeks. I still need you to pick me up from the airport. You can kick my behind then."

Satisfied, Remmy leaned back in her chair and folded her arms. "Deal. And I love you too."

A few minutes later, after cleaning her face with the inside of her overall bib, Haley moved toward the coffee shop. It was about time she flooded her empty stomach with caffeine. Thumping, groovy jazz spilled out the doorway as a mom with two kids in matching dresses held it open for her. Saying thanks and moving inside the purple-walled store, the ubiquitous burnt-coffee scent enveloped her.

"Oh, we got another one," the bearded, beanie-wearing barista with glasses called from the register. "Cloud caramel macchiato."

"Not another cloud caramel macchiato." The barista behind the espresso machine smiled. He was a near spitting image of the man at the register, except for four additional inches in height and a different colored beanie atop his head. "I've been making those all morning."

"*Cloud caramel macchiato*," the one at the register sang, winking and handing the receipt to the college-age brunette on the other side of the counter.

"*Cloud caramel macchiato*," the barista harmonized, pressing pulverized espresso beans into the silver portafilter.

Their energy was like Pop Rocks doused in soda, and Haley *loved* it. It was moments like this when she felt something bigger than herself was rewarding her, knowing she'd cherish it more than others.

After the accident and the cathartic call with Remmy, *this* was just what she needed.

"*Cloud caramel macchiato*," she let her mezzo-soprano voice float above the men's.

A delighted laugh exploded from the man behind the register. "Yes! That was awesome!" He slapped the counter, turning to his partner in crime. "Kyle, did you hear that?"

"Oh, I heard it." He grinned, topping the cold foam with caramel sauce.

"Nicely done, stranger. What can I get you?" His badge read *Kevin*.

Bright, shimmery rosé bubbled in her chest. Kevin and Kyle in matching beards, glasses, and beanies, singing about coffee. Haley almost whispered *thank you* under her breath.

Her smile stretched so high her cheeks hurt before remembering her looming repair bill. "Oh, just a cup of water."

"No, no." Kevin waved away her answer. "What do you really want?"

Her eyes flicked to the board behind him. She could simply walk the rest of the way home to even out the cost. "I'll take a sweet iced tea—large, please—and a fruit tart."

Haley began digging through her small purse for cash when Kevin interrupted. "This one's on me."

"No, that's not necessary."

"I insist." He grinned, picking up a plastic cup and writing on the side. "Just come back and sing with us again sometime."

After she finished her scrumptious fruit tart, Haley floated through the three-mile uphill trek to her apartment. Before she knew it, she was inside her doorway, toeing off her sneakers, and typing *Hey, Zach Abrams. Are you a coffee or tea person?*

Chapter 12

Haley's heart pistoned to an alarming rate when slam over repetitive slam jolted her out of sleep. It only took a second to notice that she'd fallen asleep, fully clothed, on top of her covers. Her jostled phone's lock screen read 3:27 a.m. The blinds to her window were still open, the sliver of a waning crescent moon providing the room's only illumination.

"Come on! We have to get out!" a voice shouted.

Bolting from her bed, Haley ran, sock-footed, into her main room. She intended to shoot out of her front door when she noticed Yeti's frantic form behind the glass door to her balcony. Her neck muscles complained as she pivoted and changed directions.

Yeti's eyes were wide as he continued to pound his flat palms against the glass. "Hurry! It's not safe!"

Her fingers fumbled with the sliding door's locking mechanism, and when she finally got it open, he grabbed her wrist. "Come on, Paige. We have to get away from the house."

Then he pulled her arm *hard*, dragging her behind him as he began sprinting back to his apartment.

The wrenching action tore at the already aching muscles of her neck and back and nearly lifted her off her feet. Haley used her free hand to pull back on her captured arm as an excruciating scream streaked from her belly. Yeti spun, blinked hard, and then the unyielding grip on her wrist dropped as his fingers flew through his hair.

"Haley?" His head whipped around, trying to get his bearings. "What—What happened?"

Her breaths heaved in and out of her open mouth as she continued to hold her injured limb, too stunned to speak.

"What's wrong with your arm?" His face contorted in agony. "Did I—Did I hurt you? *Oh no.* I did, didn't I?"

"You called me Paige." That was the single detail her brain fixated on.

A slow, deliberate inhale raised the shoulders of his dark-gray, long-sleeve shirt as his eyes widened. "I'm sorry. Are you okay? Let's—Here." He gestured toward her open balcony door. "Let's go inside and get you taken care of."

Haley hesitated. As much as Yeti's behavior, until the moment he'd anxiously grabbed her, had been gentle and caring, an ingrained part of her whispered warnings. She now knew with blinding certainty how much he could hurt her if he wanted to—how much stronger he was than her.

Frustrated fingers ran through his long hair again. "At least sit down." He pointed to her patio chair.

She didn't take her eyes off him as she slowly lowered herself onto the cushioned seat, trying hard to mask the wince that wanted to run across her face. An instinctive part of her didn't want to show weakness.

His next movement sent an unexpected emotion sprinting through her bloodstream. Gray-and-black flannel pajama pants hit the concrete as Yeti knelt beside the chair, his open, outfacing palms hovering in front of his chest in a cautious manner, like he wanted to run them over her in assessment but didn't want to touch her again without her permission.

The hollowed expression on his face allowed her to run her fingers up her arm, feeling the joint of her tender shoulder before squeezing up to the back of her neck.

"I made everything worse, didn't I?" he murmured.

"What happened?" she asked, lowering her voice to match his. "Were you dreaming?"

A hard swallow accompanied his nod. "I haven't sleepwalked in years, but. . . ." He let that sentence drop off. "I'm sorry for hurting you."

"What was happening? In your dream," she clarified.

The slight moonlight illuminated his puff of breath. Haley's feet were slowly turning to ice on the chilly concrete, but she willed herself not to shiver as she waited for his answer.

"I was trying to save Paige—you—from a house fire."

Several beats of silence fell between them as her stomach tried to test the limits of concavity.

"Did you—" Haley paused, letting her hand slowly drop from her throbbing neck. "Did you actually save Paige from a house fire?"

When his head bent in a yes, her fingertips flew to her lips. "Oh."

Suddenly, his behavior at the false fire alarm two weeks ago made a lot more sense. Questions flooded her mind. She wanted to ask how bad the fire was, was anyone injured, when it happened, but she kept her lips pressed to the pads of her fingers.

"It's been on my mind more than normal." His words were said to the balcony floor before he raised his gaze. "I'm sorry for hurting you." Sincerity etched into the subtle creases of his eyes. "I wasn't trying to."

Her mouth opened, but nothing came out.

When Yeti's head bowed again, breathing became more difficult. Haley ran her shaky hand over her ribs before the answer arrived in her groggy mind—almost like a sleepy toddler rubbing its cherubic eyes. Her neighbor wasn't some cruel, vindictive person intentionally attempting to harm her like Jason had. He was just a flawed human.

Like her.

"I know you weren't. It was an accident. Accidents happen." Stilted silence pulsed with a heavy throb at her temple. "One might say what you were trying to accomplish was heroic." When Yeti looked up, she framed her mouth as her eyes cut to the side. "Don't worry. I won't tell the council. I wouldn't want you to lose your evil-genius street cred."

The breathy, "You're incredible," that left his lips as he shook his head shouldn't have warmed her as much as it did. Haley was in the middle of mentally doing her new we-don't-care-what-men-think song and dance, missing some of the choreography, when his voice distracted her.

"Do you always sleep in overalls?"

When she glanced at herself, pain smacked her aside the head as if to say, *Slow movements, dummy!* Her nose wrinkled as a grunt left her.

"Haley." Yeti looked like he was witnessing thirteen puppies being skinned. "I'm so sorry."

She rose to standing, all the muscles of her neck and right deltoid screaming at her as she moved. "Come on. Let's have a glass of warm milk so we can get back to bed."

There was no way she'd be able to sleep if she left her neighbor this devastated. Time for an old-fashioned remedy and some simple hospitality.

"I've got chocolate chip cookies too," she said, padding through her open balcony door.

Haley was using her good hand to reach for two mugs in the kitchen cabinet when the soft whooshing of the glass door whispered closed behind her.

"Let me do that."

The inundation was immediate. His heady clove scent engulfed her, the heat of his chest hovered just beyond her back, and when his arm reached past hers, his ridiculously silky hair brushed her cheek. Her eyes fluttered closed, and then he was gone, rummaging in her fridge and microwaving milk.

"I like what you've done with the place."

"Thrift-store buys for the win," Haley said, pressing her fingers onto the cheap Formica countertop to ground herself. "I had to do something to make the place a little more personal. That living-in-a-hotel feeling was bothering me. Most of these were less than two dollars, so I'll just donate them when I leave."

She'd purchased a variety of colorful and decorative tablecloths to cover the unadorned beige walls in the living room. A quilted table runner now topped the coffee table, and a particularly lovely blue throw that felt like faux mink was now her standard snuggle item while watching TV or scrolling on her phone. Her fingers often brushed the soft fabric, imagining she was petting a fluffy monster.

"I have a feeling you'd like this one better. Though, the sentiment seems more applicable to me." Yeti handed her a smiling cartoon prickly pear "Don't be a Prick" mug—another thrift-store purchase, but one Haley was *definitely* taking home with her.

Her lips tried to smile, but masking how much pain she was in was taking all of her mental focus.

When she turned to reach for the cookies, Yeti stepped forward quickly. "Haley, I—"

She startled, twitching her stinging muscles and spilling warm milk over the side of her mug. "*Ouch.*"

An expletive tore from his mouth as he set his mug down. "When's the last time you took something?" His eyes were serious as they hovered a mere twelve inches from hers. "If you took it before bed, you're probably due. Don't move. I'll get it for you. Do you keep it in the bathroom?"

Haley refused to let her breath hitch. "On the vanity."

As Yeti strode away, she set down her mug, wiped her milked hand on a Hawaiian-print kitchen towel, and allowed her ceramic-warmed fingers to massage the base of her head.

Yeti was back with white and burnt-orange pills in less than thirty seconds. "Do you have a heating pad?"

"No," she said after choking down the medications with milk.

"If you've got rice, you can make one with one of your socks you're wearing." He was already looking through her cabinets.

Haley's brows twinged as she picked up the plastic container of cookies. He was displaying that same odd, worrisome energy he had last night.

"I know how to make a rice sock, but I'm not using these. I'm sure they stink since I walked three miles in them yesterday."

The cabinet door banged closed. "Why?"

Slowly, Haley turned her body to face him—no more head turning for a while. "What do you mean, why? Because I wanted to."

"You wanted to walk three miles?" Yeti asked, stepping into her personal space again. His fingers collected the storage container and set it on the counter beside them.

Haley jutted her chin up—gently. "Yes. I did."

She might have been a compulsive oversharer, but he didn't know everything about her. For all he knew, her favorite pastime could be walking. She could be a *champion* walker.

His arms folded over his chest. "This has nothing to do with the car accident?"

Haley started mirroring his stance but got halfway before the natural shoulder raise required to neatly fold her arms in themselves caused her to wince. She pushed her hands into her green overall pockets instead. "Aren't you supposed to be apologizing instead of interrogating me?"

When his face fell, Haley felt the sensation through every muscle fiber in her feet. The ground was slipping again. "I didn't mean—"

"No, you're right." His words were almost whispered to his crossed arms before they dropped. Yeti attempted to find a home for his hands, first trying his sweatshirt pocket before realizing that he wasn't wearing one, and then he couldn't find refuge in the missing pajama pant pockets either. In the end, he ran one hand over his scraggly beard. "I should g—"

"Make it up to me."

His eyes flicked up with confusion, and the same emotion spiraled in her stomach. She *should* let him go home. She *should* go back to sleep and forget this ever happened. Her recently formulated no-men plan was sinking in quicksand, imagining what it'd be like to be pressed against a yeti.

Perhaps yetis didn't even count as men. They were mythical creatures, after all.

Haley ventured a step closer, lint pushing under her nails from their jammed position in her pockets. "Tell me something. Big, small, anything."

His shoulders raised, and then something slicked over his face, quick and fleeting, like oil rolling off polished metal.

"Blueberries are mushy."

There was a brief, suspended moment when everything froze before the corner of his mouth ticked up.

Her exhale sounded more like a growl, but bottle rockets were exploding in her chest. "Here I am, trying to be hospitable, and—"

"A cardinal mistake when dealing with someone like me." Haley heard the upward lilt in his voice.

Shaking her head would have been excruciating, so her pointer finger came out in full force. "You are—"

"Infuriating?" Yeti offered. "At least I'm not pretending to be—"

"If 'dark and stormy' comes out of your mouth right now . . ." She widened her eyes, threatening.

"I wouldn't dream of it." Though he shook his head, that slight curve was flirting with his lips again.

Was it her, or did he just float a few centimeters closer?

"You better not." Haley moved to playfully jab her index finger to his chest to close the rest of the distance between them, but her finger never made contact.

Yeti retreated with two exaggerated steps, like she'd intended on punching him instead of poking him. Though he tried to regulate his next breath, it came out shaky and halting. "It's late. I should go."

Her cheeks stung as if she'd been slapped. "Sure."

After three thudding heartbeats, he was at the balcony door, pausing and turning halfway to face her. "I'm sorry about hurting you. Let me know if you need anything. I'm just on the other side of the wall."

Then he was gone. Haley stared out the glass door to the blackness beyond as Remmy's Great Aunt Lola's favorite phrase repetitively ran through her mind.

Eventually, it spilled from Haley's mouth. "What in Sam Hill just happened?"

Chapter 13

Each of Yeti's keyboard's near-silent clicks felt like gongs sounding in his exhausted brain. Unlike Thursday night, when he'd obliterated his consciousness with a sleeping pill, he wanted to be functional if Haley needed any help. So, after he'd returned home early this morning, he'd sat at his desk, doing the only thing that made sense to him.

Because the way Haley had looked at him last night did not make sense.

Haley *leaning in* and then reaching out to touch him, even in a small joking manner, did not make sense.

For the first time since he'd moved to this sturdy, cinderblocked complex, Yeti cursed its excellent sound quality. It was something he'd been grateful for when he lived across the complex in a downstairs, internally facing unit before he relocated to this one in mid-December.

But now it was tearing him apart, not knowing if Haley was awake, if she was okay, if she'd been able to go back to sleep, because his buzzing body hadn't allowed him to.

A little after ten, the closing of her front door fractured the silence. Twitchy apprehension bunched his shoulders. As much as he should have probably pretended he hadn't heard the sound, Haley had her own gravitational pull.

"Hey." When he leaned out of his door, she was locking hers.

Heat sprinted down his forearms at her obvious displeasure upon seeing him. As much as Yeti hated witnessing her pinched expression, that was the best thing about Haley. She displayed everything so easily. He never had to guess how she was feeling or what she was thinking, which made last night even more puzzling.

"Uh. Hey." Haley tucked her fingers inside the cuff of her oversized yellow cardigan.

"I wanted to apologize again for last night." He leaned on the doorjamb, attempting to appear calm.

"No. It's okay." She waved a hand. "It was an accident."

The silence between them could have been used as a torture device to crack even the most seasoned spy.

"Okay, well. See you around." Her brown, combat-style boots took a step toward the death stairs.

"Do you need a ride somewhere?" It was getting really annoying how his mouth kept spurting out sentences against his will.

Haley thought for entirely too long before answering. "I'm just heading to the grocery store across the street. I can walk."

He'd already been too forward and awkward, acting as some sort of gatekeeper, but he didn't want her in any more pain than he'd already caused. "And carry home groceries when your muscles are already strained? No. Just—" Yeti leaned back inside to swipe his wallet and keys off the kitchen table. "Tell me what you want, and I'll get it for you. I could use a break, anyway."

When she paused again, the tendons in his neck tensed to the point he feared they'd snap.

"Working on a Saturday, huh?" Haley peered in his open door, her tone softer. "What are you doing on all those screens? Hacking nuclear codes for your evil takeover?"

Yeti wasn't one to look a gift horse in the mouth.

"No. I could hack into most things, but nuclear codes are highly frowned upon unless you're comfortable with jail time, which I am not." He'd spent enough time chained to beds by thin plastic tubes to compromise the freedom he had now, even if he didn't always use it fully.

"So, you're an evil *computer* genius," she said, a ghost of a smile on her lips.

The emotion clicking through his chest shouldn't have felt as breathtaking as it did. "Sadly, I'm just a normal software developer," Yeti said, keeping his tone even. "Nothing too exciting. Truly boring, really."

Her eyebrows twinged as she took her assessing gaze from his workspace to his face. "You don't like what you do?"

He placed his hands in his pockets, as if hiding the small amount of exposed skin would rectify the naked feeling that accompanied Haley looking at him like that. "No. I love it. It's just boring to most people."

"Why would you assume *I* would think that? Maybe I find computer stuff riveting." She mirrored his posture, tucking her hands into the pockets of her white culottes.

The corner of his mouth quirked. "The fact that you just said 'computer stuff' leads me to believe otherwise."

She huffed. "Fine. I don't know much about computers. I don't even own one. But that doesn't mean I couldn't listen to you talk about it like a good friend." Haley quavered over that last word, the beginning stretched out longer than the end.

Yeti barely stopped himself from pressing his eyelids closed. In addition to nearly ripping her arm out of its socket, he'd given his impulses too much leash last night. It had been harder to control them within her intimate kitchen and with how incredible Haley had looked, freshly woken from bed, pillow lines still creasing her cheek.

Before he had a chance to answer, Haley said, "I'm on this new honesty kick since my accident." His head tilted, confused. She'd been so forthcoming in their interactions already. "Well, not since the accident. Since I did a bunch of research and realized I'd been in a toxic relationship for the last two years." Yeti was grateful his hands were in his pockets, because they fisted at the idea of anyone mistreating her. "My ex was a real buttnut—excuse my language—so I don't think—"

"Haley, relax." He held up his palms, seeing the line she was trying to draw in the sand. "We're just friends. Neighbors. I don't want anything more," he lied. "I don't really do relationships, anyway." At least that last sentence was true.

Before Yeti could chide himself again for not just letting her reject him and walk from his life, she grinned.

"Oh . . . okay, then." The relief on her face was a tangible thing, like if he'd brushed her cheek with his fingertips, they'd come back sticky with it. "In that case"—Haley gestured to the stairs—"after you."

He kept his expression even. "You just want to sacrifice me so the trolls will be too busy feasting to notice you slipping by."

Haley hit him with that full, wide smile, and he had to tighten his abs to prevent himself from reacting.

"I would never." She pressed a hand to the chest of her snug butterfly-print tank, and Yeti used the excuse of dutifully descending the stairs to avert his eyes.

A moment later, they crossed the rocky path as he pulled keys from his pocket to unlock his black Audi R8 sitting a few slots down from her vacant parking spot. The immaculately buffed sports car stood at visual odds with the standard coups, sedans, and minivans littering the apartment lot, but Yeti liked that. It was the one part of his life he didn't mind people staring at.

"Holy crap. Is this your car? Apparently, being an evil computer genius pays *very well*." The appraising gaze, that usually centered on him, ran the length of the car. Her hand lifted to slide over the glossy exterior before she froze.

"You can touch it."

Haley glanced up with such mischievous delight it pulsed like a beat in his chest. "You're sure? I'm going to smudge the wax job with my grimy fingers." She wiggled her hand.

A smile tugged at his lips. "I'm sure."

The appreciative hum that accompanied her hand smoothing along the metal finish made it impossible to not imagine what it would feel like to have those fingers sliding up his back and into his hair.

Calm down. You just declared yourselves friends.

Yeti cleared his throat. "I wouldn't have taken you for a car person."

"I'm not. I mean, I've never been one before." She pulled her fingers back, even though they looked like they wanted to explore further. "But this car is . . . is it weird if I say hot?" Her eyes darted up to his amused ones. "Is that offensive?"

"My car doesn't have any feelings, Haley. It's an inanimate object." He opened her door. "When was the last time you took your pain meds?"

"Right before I left, why?"

He should drive her to the store and take her home, but an alternate idea was like a floodlight in his brain. "If you're feeling okay, I have something to show you. Something I think you'd like, but it's a bit farther than the grocery store. Do you have the time?"

She fiddled with the clasp on her purse. "I don't think—"

"Please, Haley." It felt as if all his blood was slamming against his temples as his mouth betrayed him again.

Her eyes flicked up, locking on his before a subtle nod dipped her chin. "Okay."

◊◊◊

The parking lot of a family-owned restaurant had been roped off to display various lowriders, trucks, and classic cars, all sporting colorful, custom paint jobs. Yeti parked in the nearby neighborhood, and they followed a family of four to the busy lot. The slight desert wind was stronger here in the valley than at their apartment complex. Fluttering yellow pennant flags hanging from eight-foot-tall steel poles twisted around the periphery.

"They're so colorful." Haley clapped her hands in front of her chest like a kid on Christmas and raced toward an old VW Bug covered in decorative, front-to-back rainbow stripes.

The way her eyes light up.

Her reaction was precisely the one he'd hoped for, and damn if it didn't make him feel like he'd single-handedly vanquished an army of stair trolls.

"There are some true artists here," Yeti agreed, walking over.

The chrome of the bumper and side mirrors had been shined to the point of optimal reflection.

"I love it," she said to the patterned stripes over the hood, folding her hands behind her back to prevent touching the roped-off exterior.

After fully appreciating the Bug, Haley moved to the next vehicle. The lowrider had swirling, intertwining lines in magenta, turquoise, and dark blue along its side. White-wall tires matched the white anchoring outlines within the design.

"Gorgeous," she whispered to herself.

"Thank you," said a man in his early forties, wearing a Muñoz Custom Body and Paint T-shirt. "This is one of my favorites."

"I can see why." Haley beamed at him before rapid-firing questions. "How long did it take to paint? Does it require a team? How do you get those lines so sharp?"

The man laughed before explaining the process to Haley, but Yeti didn't hear a word. He stood just outside the conversation and watched the way she absorbed his words, as if the man was relaying the secret to immortality.

"Alan! I haven't seen you in forever."

The man paused in his explanation to rotate and hug the approaching woman, and Haley dismissed herself with a cordial, "I'll let you catch up. Thanks for chatting with me."

Haley was halfway toward the green-and-brown truck with a smiling woman's face on the passenger door when Yeti asked, "Do you always do that?"

"Do what?" She bent at the waist to analyze the brunette's perfectly painted teeth.

"Make it seem like whoever you're listening to is important."

She straightened quickly, turning to look at him with a furrowed brow. "They *are* important."

Yeti nodded, his eyes flicking to the truck's tires. Haley had always made him feel seen in a way that was often unnerving. He'd thought it'd been something unique to him, but now he understood that was how Haley was with everyone. Serrated hooks jabbed into the muscles of his shoulders and brought them forward.

"Everyone matters, Yeti." When annoyance laced its way into his nickname, he glanced up. "Every person I meet has their own story, their own life. We can't all be gold medalists or Nobel Prize winners. Some people just stay in one little corner of the world and live a small life. But they're important too. They have to be. Because if they don't matter, then . . ."

Something turbulent rolled over her features, but Haley pivoted before he could identify it.

"I need something to eat," she spurted, striding toward the two food trucks lining the other side of the parking lot.

One was a taco truck, but it seemed that the sweet scents coming from the fair-themed one lured her feet. A sandwich board next to the truck boasted corn dogs, funnel cakes, fries, fresh-squeezed lemonade, and cotton candy. Haley stopped fourth back in line behind two college-age men in backward University of Arizona ball caps.

Yeti hovered just beyond her shoulder. "Did you miss breakfast? Is that why you were going to the grocery store?" His intestines twisted, thinking he'd kept her from food because of his selfish desire to show her handcrafted beauty in an attempt to make her happy.

Happy was nice, but satiating hunger was a primal need.

Haley didn't turn her body to him, just kept staring straight ahead. "I ate breakfast. Cotton candy's my favorite, though."

The proprietor of the food truck handed two pink ethereal swirls to a mother with jumping kids at her knees.

His spine settled. "My treat, then."

"I've got it." She stepped forward in line, her jaw still tight.

"Please. I'd prefer if—"

He wanted to finish that sentence, to fix whatever he'd obviously blundered, but the two men in front of Haley wouldn't stop talking. They passed glances backward as they traded tawdry remarks and barely attempted to hide their inappropriate hand gestures. Yeti had never been in a fistfight, but every muscle in his body tightened. Even his toes were ready to inflict whatever damage was required. Haley glanced back at him, seeming to notice the agitation wafting off him in concentric pulses.

"You don't have to wait with me if—"

"It's not that," Yeti interrupted. "But can we get the cotton candy later? I'll buy you two. Let's just step out of line for a second."

His hand found her elbow, but she tugged it away. "No. I want a cotton candy, and I'm getting it. You don't control me. No one controls me anymore."

Even though Haley's last sentence felt like the first punch to his jaw, Yeti had to deal with the jerks in front of her first. When the two men moved forward, Yeti stepped in between Haley and them.

"Sorry, Haley," he said through tight teeth. "But I can't let this go."

Chapter 14

Several things happened in quick succession. Haley's jaw popped open at the sight of Yeti ripping the two men in front of her a new one with a blur of angry Spanish. The men puffed up, almost challenging him, returning his furious Spanish with their own. As much as Yeti towered over the two men, Haley didn't want to bear witness to a car-show brawl. She was about to lay a hand on his tense back when a familiar-sounding word dropped from his mouth, and the tone of the conversation instantly flipped. The men took slight, retreating steps with raised palms. Then, the woman through the food truck window shouted, "Next!"

"Sorry, man," one said. He sent a chastened nod in Haley's direction before turning to order.

Her hair was hurting from how her pinched forehead pulled at her ponytail. The men left with two corn dogs and sheepish looks a second before Yeti ordered her a cotton candy.

"What the heck was that?" When her voice returned to her, it was nearly shouting.

"What was what?" Yeti took the outstretched fluff of sugar and held it out to her.

Snapping the paper stick from him and taking a large bite out of the side, Haley stalked away from the droning hum of the truck's generator. Her tongue worked over the ball of compressed sugar. Only when she'd reached a silver 1930s Ford coupe sprayed with painted bullet holes did she stop. She didn't look for Yeti, knowing he'd followed her. He'd been following her all morning, just a step out of reach.

With glucose slowly slithering down her throat, Haley could phrase the second sentence with less aggression. "Please explain to me what just happened."

Yeti ran his hand over his forehead and through his hair. "They were saying inappropriate things about you. It was hard to listen to, and I had to do something."

Even though her brows tensed reflexively, some traitorous part of her softened at the idea of him defending her. Ignoring how her dumb heart accelerated in her chest and clearing the corseted-gown-wearing "my hero" responses from her mind, Haley managed to say, "But it seemed like you were telling them off, and they didn't back down."

She could see his jaw muscles clench even with his beard. "If they'd been decent human beings, they would've apologized from the start, but they didn't. I didn't want it escalating and you getting hurt." His voice lowered. "I've already hurt you too much."

As much as that sentence felt like a flood moving through her, something pricked at the side of her throat. "What were they saying, exactly?"

Yeti's shoulders tightened again. "Nothing appropriate to repeat."

She nodded. "Why didn't they stop when you confronted them?"

"They said I should be happy about their 'compliments.'" He swallowed, pressing his hands into his pocket. "When it was obvious they were jerks, I switched tactics."

The entire scene played before her vision again, and understanding struck.

"The word you used. Everything changed after that. I've heard it before—mana-something?"

"Hermana." Haley wasn't prepared for the way his mouth changed when it wove itself around non-venom-spewed Spanish. "I told them you were my sister."

There was this one time in third—maybe fourth—grade when she'd been trying to do a cherry bomb off the monkey bars and horribly miscalculated. She'd landed flat on her back, and it'd felt like the air had been suctioned from her lungs. Even though Haley had been the one to request that their tenuous relationship remain platonic, hearing all those hard s's and t's falling from Yeti's lips hurt the same as that fall.

"Right, no. That makes sense. It'd be super gross to say untoward things about someone's sister." Haley stuck out her tongue in an attempt to make her words believable. "Well, bro." She plastered a smile on her face and pointed with her cotton candy. "I see a psychedelic station wagon calling my name. Let's not let those two *pendejos* ruin our morning."

◊◊◊

"You're seriously not going to question this blonde-haired, blue-eyed, Maryland-born girl's perfect use of the word pendejo?" Haley asked in the car on the way home, thirty-five minutes later, when she'd finished her cotton candy and they'd exhausted all the cars on the lot.

His lips rose slightly as he shook his head. "Now who's the enigma?"

"Oh. It was always me." She winked.

It's amazing what an entire ball of sugar and some mental straightening can do to your mood. She'd figured it out. Yeti equals hairy, grumpy, male-sized Remmy.

Easy peasy.

"This innocent, small-town-girl thing is an act. I'm actually here to take down the council by infiltrating its computer science sector. Your number's up."

When Yeti's laugh floated out the open windows, tumbling onto the dusty xeriscaped lawn of the passing adobe house, victory shimmied through Haley's veins.

This was her new goal: Yeti's merriment. If he was going to insist on driving her around town and showing her beautiful things, she was going to at least provide entertainment. He clearly didn't laugh enough, and though she wasn't comedian-level funny, she'd always been tenacious once she set her mind to something.

Haley glanced at the digital representation of an analog clock on his dashboard—almost lunch time. *Friends* had lunch together. Brothers and sisters *certainly* did, especially if they had no one else to eat with. As much as Yeti seemed to prefer his solitude, Haley got the impression he was more lonesome than he let on.

"What do you say we eat something before returning the Batmobile to the cave?"

His eyebrows arched. "Didn't you just inhale an entire cotton candy?"

"I offered you some," she countered. "And that's mostly air, anyway. Once, when I was a kid, I smushed the whole thing right after I got it. It was smaller than a baseball—and a lot less fun to eat."

His warm, rumbly laugh felt like it was tickling her spine. Haley shifted her shoulders to dissipate the emotion she wasn't supposed to be feeling, and an involuntary groan left her lips.

Yeti's gaze cut to her. "I didn't want to offer initially because you work in the medical field and doctors tell you not to, but I have some old morphine tablets you can have if the other medicines aren't working for you." His somber tone was a sharp contrast to his bright laughter, and she ached to flip it back.

"So, you're also a drug dealer. Well, I guess even bad guys need a hobby. You probably meet some interesting characters with that side hustle."

The car rolled to a stop at a red light, and Yeti fully turned his body to her. "I'm serious, Haley. I don't like seeing you in pain."

As his eyes locked on hers, breathing ceased. Just completely stopped, like it wasn't a necessary life function. Gratefully, the car behind them alerted Yeti to the missed green light, and he turned his attention to the road, so she didn't asphyxiate.

For the umpteenth time that day, Haley had to override the sensations inundating her body.

No one wants to see a family member in pain. You wouldn't want Remmy to be hurting. Same thing.

"I'll think about it," she murmured.

Yeti nodded to the windshield, focusing on the road. She expected the silence between them to be strained, but instead, Haley felt wrapped in a cloud. Of course, that could be attributed to the surprisingly powerful seat warmer she was nestled into.

Several minutes later, he asked, "What do you want to eat?"

"How's your Japanese?"

"Rusty."

Fizzy green bubbles were sprinting through her. "That's a shame. I really wanted to see you order sushi fluently. Or even better, get behind the counter and show the itamae who's boss."

"The who?"

"The sushi chef."

"Ah." He paused. The music from his sound system was a barely audible undertone. "No, my evil mastery is in *other* subjects."

Haley's stomach clenched as her legs fidgeted reflexively.

You did not hear innuendo in that sentence.

You. Did. Not.

She kept her tone light, definitely not watching his strong hands as they turned the steering wheel. "Okay, Mr. Tucson, where's a good place to get sushi?"

The car slowed to roll over the high entryway to a shopping complex before he whipped it into a parking spot.

"Will this do?" He pointed to a red-roofed building set aside from the main strip mall. *Oshiki Sushi* was printed above the door.

Haley couldn't help the laugh that burst from her. "Yeah. That'll do."

Twenty minutes later, several platters of colorful, tasty morsels laid in front of them. Though they'd been chatting nonstop since they'd been seated, Haley brought up the subject that had been poking at her temple. "So, you're bilingual."

"Yeah." He took a sip of steaming green tea, and Haley thought that was going to be the end of it. "Mom's half Mexican American, and she wanted us to have a connection with her father since we never got to meet him. There are pictures of me with him when I was a baby, but he died before Paige was born."

"Oh." The somber word escaped her throat.

"Yeah." His lips twisted to the side. "I never knew any of my grandparents. They all died before I was four. Outside of my dad's brother, who I've never met, we don't have any extended family."

She paused in chewing a roe-topped salmon slice and held her hand over her mouth. "I don't have an extended family either. It's just Dad and me. Remmy has six cousins, two aunts, an uncle, all four of her grandparents, and one great-grandpappy."

They ate in a comfortable quiet for a few beats before Yeti said, "Paige is also fluent in French, but I can only understand it."

Confusion must have shown on her face because he clarified, "Dad's French Canadian."

Haley nodded, then turned her focus back to her plate to keep the look of victory—over learning something about the elusive Yeti—from showing. With the amount of information he'd just divulged, she was seriously resisting the urge to shout, *"Stop the presses!"* over the din of the restaurant.

"There's a joke about multilingual geniuses in there, but I think I'll leave it alone," she said instead.

He looked up from his clenched chopsticks with a satisfied gleam. "I didn't even list all the programming languages I know."

"Ah, finally." She rubbed her hands together. "We're getting to the *computer stuff.*"

Yeti rolled his eyes and shoved half of his slivered ginger pile into his mouth. "How's Zach Abrams hunting?"

Haley straightened her lips and attempted to do her best David Attenborough impression. "The North American movie star seems to be quite resistant to the hopeless pleas of the female. It appears his rigorous filming schedule might be to blame. If only she'd made it into a role as an extra, then this unimportant commoner might have stood a chance."

"You're important." The force behind his words pulled her gaze. "Didn't you just get pissed at me over that?"

Haley paused, the sting of wasabi stunning her tongue.

"Touché," she said with a heavy wink.

Yeti shook his head, muttering something to his plate.

"What's that?"

His eyes bounced up, playfully glaring. "Nothing."

"Anyway"—she picked up another piece of sushi, deciding to bulldoze through—"I think it's pretty obvious that all I need is an introduction. Once that happens, it'll only be a matter of time before he falls madly in love with me. I'm talking sweeping-orchestral-music love, become-his-whole-world love, can't-function-without-me-in-his-arms kind of love."

"Growing-old-together love," Yeti said, popping another piece of ginger in his mouth.

A wide smile tugged on her cheeks. She loved when they went back and forth like this. "Fight-but-still-want-to-kiss-the-lips-off-the-other-person love."

"Matching-cardigans-on-checkers-night-at-the-retirement-home love."

"Matching-*tattoos* love," she countered.

"Packing-up-your-entire-life-to-be-with-the-other-person love."

"That's a good one." Haley tapped her lip with her index finger. "Hating-their-weird-hobby-but-still-doing-it-with-them kind of love."

"What are we talking about here—fly-fishing or taxidermy?" His forehead was adorably scrunched.

She flipped her palm. "It doesn't matter, right?"

Yeti paused to swallow a large bite with a hum. "Okay. Sharing-a-box-of-dye-when-you-go-gray kind of love."

"Aww. That's adorable, but I'm never dying this." She pulled at her ponytail, tickling her cheek with the ends of her hair. "When I go from almost-white to white, I'm not turning back."

"Yeah. I guess you'd have to have the same hair color as your soulmate to share the box dye." He tilted his head, thinking. "Bocce-partners-for-life love."

Her brows pinched. "You're kind of fixated on elderly love, and as much as I'm sure Zach Abrams would age like a *fine wine*, I want years of youthful love first."

"Fair." Yeti nodded, his expression sobering. "But I feel like old-people love is the goal. Anyone can love for a few years. Loving someone for a lifetime is something else entirely."

Her sip of ice water burned down her throat. Haley pointed to the lone sashimi piece left on the center platter to break the tension. "Do you want the last piece?"

"All yours." He laid his chopsticks neatly together on his plate.

While she was stuffing her face, Yeti handed his credit card to the server before she'd dropped the check.

"Hey." Haley nearly spit yellowtail all over the table. Covering her mouth, she said, "We should at least go half."

"This is muscle-injury payback." He leaned back in his chair, pointing to his shoulder. "Arm, almost out of socket. Remember?"

She huffed. "And when is that going to end?"

"When you no longer hurt."

In actuality, she should have taken ibuprofen an hour ago, but bantering back and forth with Yeti over sushi had been so enjoyable her neck didn't ache at the moment.

"It doesn't hurt."

"Don't lie to me, Haley." There was a warning to his tone that made her stop her automatic counter-argument.

The server returned his card and the check, and Haley finished her water while Yeti scrawled an indecipherable signature.

"Were those even letters or just evil-genius symbols?" she asked as they rose from the table, determined to steer the conversation toward lighter territory. "You know you're not supposed to let the general public see those."

Yeti's slight smile stayed on his lips all the way to the exit. Then he held the door open for her, and Haley had to intentionally hold her breath as she passed his body. It was only with the bright sunshine piercing her retinas that her brain tried to make sense of the barely audible words he'd muttered after she'd stepped outside.

Mentally, Haley shook herself. There was no way he'd said, "Running-joke love."

Chapter 15

"I think I might know someone who could help you get into that movie," Yeti said once they were settled into the warmth of his car, headed north again. "If you don't need to get back right away."

"Really?" Roman candles were bursting behind Haley's irises.

"It's not a sure thing, but I have some"—his mind auto-corrected to *had some*—"friends that own a local theater. Maybe they have a connection or a colleague who might know those working on the movie."

He was certain his friends didn't want to see him, but Yeti was already in too deep. A steady thrumming pulsed in his forearms as he turned the wheel. There was a high likelihood that showing up unannounced would completely backfire, but he didn't care. The only thing that mattered was keeping that smile on Haley's face. The need to do so scratched at his throat like thirst.

Haley slapped her palms on the dash in a giddy-up motion. "What are we waiting for? Let's go."

A chuckle escaped his mouth before he flicked on his turn signal. The longer he spent with Haley, the harder it was to trap the errant laughs that wanted to be free. Every smile came easier, sprung forth with a life of its own.

The small community theater was only a few blocks east of the restaurant. If you didn't know it was there, you'd drive right by it. All World Theater was sandwiched between a popular Jamaican restaurant and a laundromat with green awnings topping the brick exterior.

Once inside, the sound of hammers reverberated around the little theater space as sawdust and latex paint filled Yeti's nostrils. Two women in splotched overalls were constructing what looked like a dystopian, industrial backdrop for a play. To the left of the stage, a 1940s propaganda-style UGC ad had been marked with graffiti.

Watching Haley absorb the scene almost distracted him from the persistent taste of bile at the back of his throat. This reunion was going to be tense, but hopefully they'd look past his bad behavior to assist Haley. Yeti's shoulders pinched as they walked down the short aisle separating the low-lying stage from the audience.

When his friends strode from backstage into the flooding lights, it was Haley's reaction that scrunched his forehead.

"Kevin and Kyle!" She barreled toward the edge of the stage.

"Haley!" Kevin's face lit up as he rushed toward her, hopping down the last step, double-footed, like a jubilant child.

A smile lifted Kyle's lips until he saw Yeti. He lumbered over with crossed arms, attempting to burn a hole into Yeti's skull through his tortoise-shell glasses.

Time was a slippery thing. Though it had been years since he'd seen the friends that were crucial in his life for so long, Kevin and Kyle looked like an idyllically preserved memory. Their attire reflected their artsy, hipster personas. Kevin had a scarf over his juniper-print button-up and black skinny jeans; and Kyle wore an oversized, southwestern-print cardigan over tan joggers. The only difference was a round bald spot apexing Kyle's dark curls and that both of them had slight creases at the corners of their eyes and mouths.

Kevin gave Haley a quick one-armed hug. "How's the neck pain?"

"Better today." Her fingers touched behind her ear as a grin rose on her lips. "Thanks for asking."

As much as Yeti had been aiming to bring Haley joy, a thick knot tugged at the side of his neck. "You already know each other?"

"We met at the coffee shop. She's got quite a set of pipes," Kevin said.

"You sing?" Two emotions bombarded him: the desire to hear her voice expand in melody, and the flushing jealousy that his friends got to hear that sound first.

"Oh, no," she hedged, a sheepish look on her face. "Not really. Just in the shower and the car. You know, like everyone."

Bitterness flooded his mouth, overtaking the lingering ginger flavor from lunch. Had he known he could have Haley's singing in addition to her comforting chatter, Yeti would have turned the music up.

"You work at the coffee shop too?" Haley asked his friends.

Kevin shook his head. "Not officially, though we did throughout college. Ground Street Coffee is my wife's business, so Kyle and I will help out every once in a while. All the baristas called out the other day because the flu is sweeping the UofA campus."

Yeti's stomach soured at the casual mention of Becca, of the wedding an arrogant version of himself had chosen not to attend.

"I don't believe this." Kyle's words were spat like venom, eyes unrelenting.

"I *know*, right?" Kevin said, scratching his neatly trimmed beard. "If I knew the bass player from the popular *ZZ Top* cover band, *AA Bottom*, was going to be here, I would have brought something for him to sign." He patted his clothes, looking for a fictitious pen.

Haley's fingertips barely caught her snicker.

"I hate to tell you this, but auditions for *Jesus Christ Superstar* were last season. Though, we could have used you as the understudy with that hair." Kevin's lips contorted in a regretful twist as he ran his fingers through his own short strands.

Haley was having a hard time keeping her shoulders from shaking. She looked like a baking soda volcano that some mischievous kid had just loaded with vinegar, seconds from erupting.

Kevin adjusted his black, half-framed glasses, scrutinizing. "I know I should make a Chewbacca reference, but I've always been more of a Trekkie."

Yeti had been silently enduring Kevin's half-hearted jabs, awaiting the real explosion—the one that would send shrapnel tunneling through his skin. Kyle opened his mouth, but Haley spoke first.

"I call him Yeti." The squeaky quality of Haley's high-pitched words yanked a shocked laugh from Kyle. The sound ricocheted off the first few rows of seats before he straightened his lips, pulling his shoulders back.

"That's perfect!" Kevin's eyes glinted. "But shouldn't he be wearing all white?"

"I think he's a rare breed," Haley said, a smile wobbling on her lips. "I've never seen him in anything that wasn't dark. Usually black, but occasionally gray or dark blue."

"Simply riveting!" Kevin's voice dissolved into an English accent. "We must telegraph the Royal Society of Biology and inform them. Such a specimen—and in the flesh. Astonishing."

Yeti tilted his head back with an exhale, focusing on the black ductwork above.

"You're seriously not going to say anything?" The force of Kyle's words snapped his vision back in place. "Tell us where you'd rather be, perhaps?"

Yeti opened his mouth, but sound vibrations refused to slither through his vocal cords. The force of his past mistakes hit him like a thousand-pound sandbag to the forehead. He shouldn't even have been here. He shouldn't have been traipsing around Tucson, chasing some life that wasn't his anymore. He'd finally gotten to a point where things were under control, balanced, and then his new neighbor careened through that like a cannonball on steroids.

"I'm the one that dragged him here today." It felt like one of the stagehands had hit him with a wooden beam when Haley's fingers gave his right bicep a brief, supportive squeeze. "I've got this massive crush on Zach Abrams, and I've got it in my mind that if I can make it into his movie, he'll have no choice but to fall in love with me." Kyle softened, watching her self-deprecating shrug. "I know it's a long shot, but do you think you can help me out? I've heard you two are the ones with connections."

Kyle paused before answering. "No, unfortunately. A lot of people were trying to get into that one, but the production company has it sealed tight. As far as I know, they've got everyone they need."

"You win some, you lose some." An uneven smile was striving to maintain a presence on her face. "So, um, do you want to sing something? That was fun yesterday." She tapped her lip. "Okay, here's an old one. Let's see if you two know it."

"Oooh. I love a challenge." Kevin rubbed his hands together, joining Haley on the distraction express.

Kyle only took his flinty glare from Yeti's face when Haley's voice lifted above the noise of set construction. Yeti recognized the song instantly. It was from one of Paige's favorite movies. A short, painful breath left his parted lips. Haley had completely underplayed her abilities. He'd sat through enough of Kevin and Kyle's productions over the years to recognize raw vocal talent.

"'Singin' in the Rain.' Classic," Kevin said before taking over the rest of Gene Kelly's line from her.

Kyle never joined in. He subtly shook his head as Haley continued with Debbie Reynolds' parts from "You Are My Lucky Star."

Everything in him wanted to interrupt, wanted to shout, *"Haley, stop!"* but this whole endeavor was already shot to hell. The least he could do was let her finish her beautiful attempt to smooth over something that was irreparable.

Haley and Kevin harmonized the last line of the song, crescendoing toward the last word. None of the set designers or other staff acknowledged the impromptu singing. After a beat, Yeti finally spoke.

"I never reached out because I knew there was no fixing things." Several seconds of stillness froze the four of them in place as he ran a hand over his face. "Some things can't heal, will never go back to the way they were . . . I'm sorry for coming here today. I just—" How could he explain that he was only here because of Haley? Because, with her, everything seemed different. Possible. Life with her was too bright, too noisy, and impeccably flawless at the same time. "I should've known better. We'll leave."

"Hey," Kevin said, the softness of his voice twisting Yeti's stomach. "I'm okay with you."

It was Kevin who had kept texting the longest, kept asking how Yeti was doing, wondering if he could help with anything. At times, Kevin's kindness had been more excruciating than his daily pain.

Because Yeti hadn't deserved it.

Just like he didn't deserve his forgiveness now.

"Would I have preferred one of my closest friends not to blow off my wedding? Absolutely. But you were young and stupid, and that was years ago. We can put it past us." A small smile tweaked the corner of his mouth. "Dorm bros for life."

"'Dorm bros' sounds like it's got a story behind it," Haley said, her voice artificially saccharine.

Kevin eyed him for a breath before explaining. "When we started college, the UofA underestimated housing needs for our freshman class. They took a dorm study room, smushed five beds into the space, and called it ours. Since we all got along so well, the next year, we moved off campus and rented a house with more leg room. We lived there until graduation, when we went our separate ways."

"Except, the rest of us never stopped getting together. Never stopped supporting each other." Kyle pushed at his temples, his jaw tightening. "You haven't even asked about Zane and the hell he's been through. You're expecting me to believe that Mr. Social Media doesn't know what's been going on?" Kyle's voice peaked, drawing the attention of several stagehands.

"I deleted all my accounts—" Pinpricks arched over his skin. "What happened?"

"He and Tessa got divorced."

Yeti staggered back a step. "What?"

Zane and Tessa had gone from friends to dating during college, and then, with her pregnancy senior year, husband and wife. Outside of his parents, they had the most stable and loving relationship Yeti had ever seen.

"*After* she fought Non-Hodgkin's lymphoma for two years," Kyle snapped.

"She—What? Is she okay?" Partially digested sushi was creeping up his esophagus.

"Yeah." Kevin's tone was gentler than Kyle's had been. "She's been in remission for a year."

"Oh," he breathed, his shoulders sagging forward.

"If you're going to randomly drop in on someone, it should be him. That is, if you actually want to catch up and not just ask for a favor." Kyle's words were like forty-five hundred papercuts doused with lemon juice. "I've got work to do." He disappeared behind a thick velvet curtain.

The awkwardness that hovered in Kyle's wake was ugly and heaving, and it sucked all the energy from him.

"I should get back too." Kevin's lips flickered in a wavering grin. "It really *was* good to see you again."

Chapter 16

They were silent again on the drive home, but this time, itchiness was marching back and forth between Haley's shoulder blades. It dragged muscle soreness behind it like an irritable toddler schlepping an oversized blanket. The desire to rub the back of her neck was oppressive.

Yeti hadn't spoken since they'd left the theater, and by his overly hunched stature, it was clear he'd taken Kyle's words to heart. In trying to help her, he'd obviously torn open some very old, very messy wounds.

"You could call Zane," her voice whispered over the Imagine Dragons song murmuring in the background. "Do you still have his number?"

Remmy's mother's voice popped up in her head, telling her not to meddle, but Haley ignored it.

Of all the versions of him she'd seen today—protective-and-angry Yeti, playful-and-bantering Yeti—Haley hated seeing him reduced to melancholic Yeti. The impulse to console him was a gargantuan monster tugging all of her limbs.

She needed to fix this before they got home. Otherwise, the minute they got back to their apartments, he'd lock himself up again. Haley didn't know him that well, but somehow, certainty over this sang in her bones. The road increasing in elevation for the final stretch toward the complex felt like an audible ticking of a doomsday clock.

"Walking on Sunshine" screamed from her purse before Haley fished her phone out and silenced it.

"It's just Remmy. On Saturdays, we usually do something together, so she's probably missing me," she said.

A subtle bob dipped Yeti's chin.

When the phone rang again with her best friend's smiling face, he said, "You can answer it. I don't mind." Yeti rolled up the windows, decreasing the background noise.

"Hey, can I call you back in a few minutes?" resonated at the same time Remmy's tear-stricken voice sobbed, "I think Marcus is cheating on me."

As much as she'd been completely engrossed in a plan to help Yeti a second ago, Haley immediately flipped gears. Heat bloomed through her body, rousing her satiated, wasabi-coated nerve endings. Her shoulders rushed forward, and her free hand clenched into a fist on her thigh.

"*What?!* He better not be if he doesn't want to lose a finger."

Yeti's face snapped in her direction.

Remmy's humorless laugh filled her ear. "I know I can always count on you to inflict bodily harm on my behalf."

"Always," she said darkly. "Now, explain so I don't go to jail for dismemberment without due cause."

A long and shaky exhale resonated over the line. "At first, it was little things I didn't notice until you left. Once a week, he'd stay at the office and then come home an hour later than normal. One time, he smelled like flowers, but he'd also come home with a few groceries and claimed that a woman in the checkout ran into his suit with her bouquet."

So far, all of that was purely circumstantial. No burning red flags. Marcus could have been working late, and his story could have been legitimate.

"But today . . ." her voice squeaked.

"What happened today?" Haley asked, coals smoldering beneath her breastbone.

"Today, he was supposed to have lunch with David. He left and came back after being gone for three hours. Only twenty minutes before he came home, David posted a picture of himself wrapped up in a blanket with the caption 'I officially hate the flu.'"

Haley's stomach bottomed out.

"Naturally, I panicked. I was pacing back and forth in the living room when Marcus came home, and I couldn't help myself. I asked him how lunch was, and he told me all about how it was nice to catch up and even detailed what they ate. I just stood there, listening to lie after lie, struggling to keep a calm face."

"Oh, Remmy."

Her best friend sniffled. "Luckily, I was dressed for the gym, so I told him I was glad he had fun and I'd see him later. Then, he leaned in to kiss me goodbye." Her voice broke. "Lee, it was so hard letting him kiss me after he lied to me like that." A loud sob shook from Remmy. "What do I do now?"

"I think you get definite proof, right?" Haley hadn't noticed that they were sitting in Yeti's covered spot, the engine idling in park. How long had they been back?

She unbuckled her seatbelt and moved to get out of the car. As much as Remmy most definitely needed to discuss this with her, Haley didn't want anyone else to hear how Remmy's life was falling apart. Once outside, her eyes met Yeti's for a fraction of a second before he locked his doors and started up the path to their apartments.

Trapped air was hostage in her lungs, but Haley held back, pacing along the narrow line of dirt separating the parking lot from the desert beyond. She'd fix the Yeti problem after this. Remmy came first.

"If I was in town, I would tail him for you. Find out where he was really going. I'm sorry I'm not." A spiky ball twisted and rolled in her belly.

"It's not your fault that Marcus is a cheating buttnut."

"Still, I wish I was there holding you right now."

"Me too," Remmy said weakly.

Silence hovered between them for a few heartbeats as surging helplessness made Haley feel like she'd been thrown into the cactus beside her.

"Any response from Zach Abrams?"

Haley's initial response was to balk over talking about her celebrity crush at a time like this until a thought occurred to her. "Remmy, do you need a distraction?"

"Yes, please," was a watery plea.

Dry desert air filled Haley's lungs to the brim. "How about I send him a message right now? Want to help me draft it?"

Remmy sniffled. "Uh-huh."

"Okay." She put the phone on speaker and toggled to her one-sided conversation with Zach Abrams. "This morning I went to a classic car show with Yeti and got cotton candy. A lot of my questions seem to be food related," Haley mused, thumbing through her DMs. "I guess I could ask about his favorite fair food."

"You went out with Yeti again?"

"Don't make it sound like we *went out,* went out. It was just as neighbors. Friends," she said firmly, as if to remind herself. "He's honestly a male version of you every time you get hangry."

When Remmy's pearlescent laugh came over the phone, Haley's blood shimmered. "You've got to take a picture of this guy for me. I keep imagining a literal yeti."

"That's pretty much him."

Even as the sentence fired off, her body automatically refuted it. There was a lot about Yeti that was desirable—his warm, amber eyes; his *unfairly* soft hair; his distractingly large hands; and the fact that, under his baggy clothes, he was probably hiding a wall of muscle. He was also considerate, always worried about her feelings or if she was in pain. He had the same protective instincts that were still flowing through her veins on Remmy's behalf. He took jokes at his expense in stride . . .

"*Lee.*"

"Huh?"

"I asked if you were going to ask Zach about cars this time to break up all the food talk."

"Right." Haley pulled her vacant gaze from the multiple-armed saguaro—which looked like it gave great hugs—to her phone. "Hey, Zach Abrams," she read as she typed. "What's your favorite type of car?" She hit *send*. "Can I do anything—I mean *anything*—for you?"

"You typed that to Zach Abrams?" Remmy gasped. "That's pretty forward."

"No, not for him, for *you*."

"Oh," she sighed. "*Besides* kick the crap out of Marcus?"

The idea circled her brain. "I could."

She could put the plane tickets on a credit card and pay them off little by little.

"No. You're not coming home. We went over this yesterday. You've got to finish this adventure of yours, and I'm going to make sure this is really happening first. After all, maybe I'm wrong. Maybe Marcus was doing something he thought was embarrassing and didn't want to tell me."

Haley jumped on that idea. "Like, every month he gets his back waxed while you're out with me."

Remmy's soft chuckle lifted Haley's lips. "Yeah. Or he's got a standing appointment with Madame Toma." The town's tarot-reading fortune teller had a little shop out of her garage.

"We could be completely wrong. He could have a legitimate reason for lying to you." Even as the words came out of her mouth, they tasted like ash.

"Maybe." Remmy's voice was small.

"I love you." Too much force was put behind the sentence, but impotence flowed through Haley because she couldn't tuck Remmy into a tight hug.

"I love you too." Another sigh echoed. "I'll figure this out. I'll call again if I need you."

"Call *anytime*. And that offer still stands for me to come home. I can pack up and be there in a day."

"Thank you." Haley could almost see Remmy straightening, putting her natural strength forward. "I've got this for now."

"I know you do."

After they hung up, Haley continued to pace over the dusty ground for a long while. Then she traversed the winding pathways of the complex, thinking about Remmy and Marcus. Her and Yeti's apartments were on the edge of the property facing the desert, but several others were tucked into each other with only a slim barrier of palo verde trees and creosote bushes between buildings. She walked past the wrought-iron fenced-in pool, imagining that it probably got a lot of use in the warmer months.

A determined flush crept over her collarbones. There was nothing she could do to help Remmy today, but maybe she could save a Yeti.

Her knuckles rapped the wood of his front door in a playful two-bits rhythm. Haley was prepared to go another round when her somber neighbor appeared.

"Your friend okay?"

"No. Remmy's had a tough time with love over the years, and until now, Marcus has always been so incredible . . ." She let out a long, noisy breath. "It's not fair. She deserves better."

Yeti nodded, his shoulders tensing. "No one deserves to be lied to."

"Yeah. This whole thing stinks."

Four kids skipped past the base of their stairs as they stood in thoughtful silence.

"Did you call Zane?" she asked gently.

Yeti's gaze dropped to the floor. "I did, but it went to voicemail." He backed into his apartment. "I should—"

"We forgot my groceries." Her hand flew to the back of her neck. With everything going on, she'd almost forgotten about its dull throb. "Do you mind? My neck is bothering me again."

There was a brief pause while he warred with himself. To seal her victory, Haley fished ibuprofen pills out of her purse and swallowed them dry, clearing her throat for good measure. Deep down, she knew the dramatics were unnecessary. Yeti was too much of a gentleman to refuse her. A rough exhale flowed her way, but he was already reaching back into his apartment for his keys.

Chapter 17

Haley haphazardly tossed items into the grocery cart. Organic tofu joined Flamin' Hot Cheetos next to Brussels sprouts and a jar of tahini. Since Yeti generally subsisted on takeout, he wasn't the person to judge her food choices. The whole time she shopped, Haley kept up a verbal litany that he couldn't have disrupted even if he'd wanted to. Instead, Yeti let the sound of her voice wash over his tired skin.

The interaction at the theater kept cycling through his mind. Somehow, he'd carelessly assumed that his friends were doing well. Paige was always getting on him to reconnect with them, but he thought she just didn't like how much time he spent alone. Had she known about Zane and Tessa? Was that why she was always pushing?

Zane suffering without him being able to help felt like swallowing a chunky, chalky antacid without chewing it. He'd left a message on his friend's voicemail, but Yeti doubted Zane would call him back.

"There's got to be a reasonable explanation," Haley continued. "Marcus *loves* Remmy. Like, in a make-you-want-to-gag-but-also-clench-your-hands-in front-of-your-chest-and-melt kind of way. This has to be a mistake. Something else is going on."

Haley tossed soy sauce in before tugging on the front of the cart to whip it into the next aisle. Three cans of black bean soup nearly smashed the chips as they bounced in. Her phone pinged, and she paused to pull it from her purse.

The repetitive pattern of the waxed floor tiles kept fading to Kyle's glaring face. Shame flooded Yeti's muscles, ripping apart the fibers. He should have at least checked in, but why check in on someone you'd ostracized? It took a second to realize that the background music of Haley's voice had ceased.

Haley stood frozen—mouth open, eyes wide and fixed on her phone. Even from his spot behind the handlebars of the cart, Yeti could see she'd pulled open the app he'd built. His creation that led to the destruction of everything else.

Yeti drifted over her shoulder, close but not touching. Large, gray, stacked bubbles of text settled on the right—a written version of Haley's tumbly speech—but one on the left caught his gaze.

"These messages are intriguing. I dig them."

"Holy crap," Haley whispered.

As Yeti stared at the white text bubble on the screen, another one followed it.

"To answer your most recent question—Aston Martins."

Haley rotated her neck, those blue eyes finding his. The initial shock of reading the screen was now obliterated by the idea of wrapping his arms around her waist and pulling her into him. He'd never been the possessive type, but everything in him wanted to draw her close, to bury his nose in that sweet dip beneath her ear and breathe her in.

Why hadn't he done that before?

Ah, yes. Because she'd clearly laid out that they were only friends. Haley didn't want him. She wanted the celebrity that, unbelievably, was reaching out to her.

As much as this had been his goal when he'd taken her to Kevin and Kyle's theater—to deliver her to the man who *was* worthy of her—now Yeti wanted to keep Haley to himself, like a selfish scumbag.

"Zach Abrams is messaging me." Her sentence elevated in volume as it neared its competition.

When her gaze fell to the screen, so did his. An orange circle orbited the edge of Zach Abrams's profile photo, indicating that he was currently using the app.

Haley spun so violently her hip checked the cart, bumping it a few inches away. "I have to say something. What should I say? He's *waiting*. Oh my goodness, Zach Abrams messaged me back. But that makes no sense because why would someone who literally could talk to anyone in the world decide to talk to me? He called me intriguing. Intriguing! I'm probably the least intriguing person alive. I'm plain vanilla. Insipid white bread. I literally have blonde hair and blue eyes. So predictable."

"You're talking like he's better than you again." He barely kept the growl out of that sentence.

She zeroed in on him, her lips slightly parted like he'd stunned the words out of them. Imagine him being able to bring bubbling Haley to breathless silence—*laughable*. Even so, as her eyes bounced between his, it was a monumental struggle not to frame her face with his palm and gently brush her lower lip with his thumb.

She sucked in a quick breath. "But it's *Zach Abrams*."

Somewhere in the distance "Daydream Believer" hushed through a crackling speaker, other patrons ambled by, and the scents of rotisserie chicken, ammonia, and cardboard fought for his attention, but all Yeti could notice was the way Haley's collarbones rose and fell as she stared at him.

"He's just a man, Haley. Just like me and millions of other men on this planet."

Yeti didn't realize how, but his words released her. She took a step back, peeking again at the phone clutched in her hands. "Zach Abrams is *not* just a man." When Haley brought her face up, it radiated in jest, her smirking lips pulled to the side.

He fought the tug at his mouth, quickly sliding into his new favorite game. "He's a regular, disgusting male."

Haley's exaggerated gasp drew the eyes of a few onlookers in the aisle. "You take that back."

Yeti crossed his arms over his sweatshirt. "He gets diarrhea with the stomach flu, just like the rest of us."

Her phone dropped onto the child seat of the grocery cart as both hands covered the sides of her head. "No!"

Yeti couldn't help that everything in him rose. This was what he wanted. This back and forth with her. Not the hollowing knowledge that Haley would have this much—or more—fun with Zach Abrams.

He ticked off his fingers. "He's got morning breath, dead skin on his feet, stinks when he sweats—"

"Stop!" Her palms flattened over his chest as she firmly pushed him back a few inches.

The puff of air leaving his mouth would have led one to believe she'd sucker punched him in the stomach instead of playfully shoved him. Already he was trying to override it, like a segment of wry code that needed to be extricated and replaced. It was only a good-natured shove between friends. It didn't matter that he wanted to feel the warmth of her palms over his heart more than he wanted anything in his life.

"Ah, mmh." Incoherent sounds came from his sawdust-coated tongue. "You're right. He's probably a great guy with very clean feet."

Haley stared at him, her shoulders seesawing as her squirmy fingers gradually lowered to her sides. She blinked a few times before responding.

"It could be fake. Or a joke."

His brows pinched together. "Why would it be a joke?"

"If it's not a joke, then the world doesn't make any sense. Pretty soon, moisture is going to be pulled from the ground and rain into the clouds. Then, animals will start talking to me, and—"

"What did he say? Let's come up with a response." Yeti couldn't stand to listen to her degrade herself further.

And helping Haley converse with her celebrity crush was what a good *friend* would do.

"Okay." That wobbly smile danced across her face as she picked up her phone and handed it to him.

Yeti reread the short sentences he'd already memorized.

"I dig it," he scoffed. "Who talks like that?"

"Stop critiquing the movie star who deems me worthy of conversation." Her finger poked his bicep.

Yeti had to intentionally count to three before lifting his gaze. "I'm not sure this warrants a response at all. He never asked you anything, just commented on your prior message."

A strangled sound left her throat as her fingers gimmied for the phone. "There's no way I'm not going to say *something*. Preferably something enigmatic and sexy and filled with enough wit to make him instantly smitten with me," she said to the screen.

His hands fisted in his pockets as Yeti studied the boxes of ready-made dinners behind Haley. Who knew Rice-A-Roni had so many flavors?

The side of his head pounded as Haley murmured to herself over possible responses. Even though *You're just friends* ran repetitively through his brain, this deep, sinking feeling poured through him. It fell like a saturating rainfall through his intestines until it settled, heavy, on the tops of his toes.

This was an unsolvable problem, but his brain was a six-lane highway, and he was standing in the middle of it. Options presented themselves and were dismissed faster than the electrical impulses prompting his jaw to clench. If the next message from Zach Abrams held any indication of the star wanting to meet Haley, he would back down. That would be the right thing to do. Undeniably, Haley would be better off with the philanthropic celebrity.

But . . .

Yeti's next series of thoughts would certainly earn him his alleged namesake with the morally gray choice he was about to make. Because if this was one of the last chances to spend time with Haley, he was going to make the most of it. He just had to keep up the charade that he was helping her move toward her goal.

"I'm attending a public lecture on black holes hosted by the College of Science this evening. Why don't you come with me, and you can recap it for Zach?"

"Black holes?" Haley looked at him like he was psychotic before a barking, uninhibited laugh escaped her. "Black—" She wheezed, shaking with laughter and doubling over.

Yeti glanced at the entertained passersby, but Haley didn't seem to care. When her heaving breaths finally evened out and she wiped moisture from her eyes, Haley hit him with that smile. "You evil geniuses really know how to stay on brand."

Stupid. Stupid. Stupid. The words sang through his mind, but his chest was exploding.

He made a show of grumbling and scowling, but his fake discontent didn't dim Haley's light.

"I'll go on one condition," she said. "*I* get to feed you beforehand. What sounds good? Greek?"

Greek happened to be his favorite, but Yeti stalled because he didn't like the idea of her paying.

"Oh, come on." She bounced a tiny bit.

This time, he didn't fight the smile tugging at the corner of his mouth. "Let's make it a fair trade, then. Once we get these groceries unpacked, you take me to that thrift shop you're always talking about."

Haley didn't need convincing. "Deal. I'd never cover those gorgeous locks with a flat cap or a fedora, but maybe you can find some new kicks. Oooh or a bolo tie to match your sweatshirt?"

A chuckle escaped him. "Sure."

She spun, holding her phone to her chest and almost skipping down the aisle toward the bank of dairy fridges.

"Lucky man." An older gentleman passing by nodded in Haley's direction.

"Yes, sir. I am." Yeti gave an agreeable smile before following Haley with the cart.

At least for the next few hours.

Chapter 18

While others might wrinkle their nose at the overwhelming mothball scent of the thrift store, Haley took a deep, satisfied inhale. She'd been shopping at thrift shops all her life, mostly out of necessity. But her choice became intentional in middle school after Patrick Aldrich made fun of a well-loved sweater. The next day, she'd doubled down by wearing a more eclectic outfit. She'd felt uncomfortable, trying to stand out all that day, but Patrick never mentioned her clothing choice again, and her personal style evolved from there.

Most of her stuff came from Goodwill, and generally, her wardrobe resembled what one might purchase in a big-box store, but Haley had always enjoyed the chance to shop at a place like this—where buying vintage clothes was celebrated. The store was a visual cacophony of color. Even the exterior had been painted an eye-piercing yellow and aqua. Fully loaded, circular racks stood with barely enough walking space between them. There was an entire wall of hats and an overflowing costume section in the back.

Her gaze drifted over to Yeti, silently evaluating his impression of one of her beloved places.

"What are you looking for?" His fingers carelessly skimmed the rack of clothes in front of him.

He didn't look up, but something in her knew that he'd noticed her watching him.

Haley couldn't help it. Ever since she'd touched his chest in the grocery store, it was like a transition had happened. They were both playing their roles of friendly neighbors perfectly, but this invisible tension clicked and spiked just out of view.

At the grocery store, her body had recklessly made decisions without mental consideration. When her brain had finally played catchup, all it could focus on was how strong he'd felt—even through a fluffy barrier of cotton. Images of her sliding her hands underneath his sweatshirt and up his stomach had played like a movie on the backs of her eyelids.

When they'd split ways for her to put away her groceries, unease had cramped her forearms. He'd said to knock when she was ready, and Haley had taken more care than she should have changing for a casual lecture with a friend. She'd knocked on his door, wearing black jeans and a snug indigo crewneck sweater covered by her black lightweight coat. Then, she'd given him a cheesy smile and asked, "How's my dark and *starry* outfit?" Yeti's shoulders had sighed in a way that ribboned in between each of her ribs, further compressing the air out of them.

"Nothing in particular," Haley answered, pulling her gaze away. "That's half the fun of thrift shopping. Sometimes you come in for something you need, but other times, things you didn't know you needed speak to you." When she hazarded a glance at Yeti, that half-smile was on his lips.

Haley took a leisurely perusal of the various bobbles in the jewelry case beside her. There were several versions of the Claddagh ring and other decorative silver bands next to the rings set with polished stones—quartz, turquoise, agate.

"There's something about owning an item with a story that's comforting, even if you never know that story. Like jewelry. I like thinking about who owned it before and how they received it. Was it a Mother's Day gift? An impulse buy? Their favorite thing to wear on a date?"

That last word burned her esophagus. She shouldn't have used it.

This isn't a date.

Her shaky index finger touched the transparent barrier between her and a black-centered ring with silver petals surrounding it. Something about it was a perfect hybrid. The shape of the ring was undeniably that of a cheerful flower, but the dark center somehow balanced it, making it stronger.

"Somethin' catch your eye?" an older man with an impressive salt-and-pepper mustache asked from the far end of the counter.

"Oh." Haley glanced up. *No* was forming on her lips, but an unrelenting pressure pulled at her collarbones. "The flower ring. This one, please."

"The hematite one?" He pulled a ring of keys from his belt and opened the case.

"Umm."

The man pointed a freckled finger to the same ring she'd been admiring.

"Yeah, that one. Thank you."

On closer inspection, a detailed silver braid encircled the stone, and tiny silver balls were artfully placed between each petal. She turned the ring over, glancing at the price written on the white paper tag—$32.71.

"You should get it."

Haley should have noticed Yeti's warmth behind her, his clove scent surrounding her. It was all she could focus on now as her breath hitched.

The man chuckled. "She might want to try it on first."

"Right." Haley laughed along, although heat flushed her skin. "I probably should."

The band was too big for her ring finger but settled nicely over her index finger.

"Looks good," the man said, nodding. The compliment was a genuine expression, not the false words of a salesperson trying to make a sale. Haley got the distinct impression that this proprietor didn't care whether you bought something or simply window-shopped. "Why don't you hold onto it while you look around?" A knowing smile laced his lips before he made himself busy at the far side of the store, rearranging hanging Halloween masks, using a long, teal-painted pole.

"Do you like it?"

Haley couldn't stop her eyes from fluttering closed as Yeti's deeply voiced question blew over her shoulder. Her head dipped in a sedate nod.

"Let me get it for you."

She was about to argue. This was far too intimate. Friends—*no*, neighbors—didn't buy each other jewelry. They didn't stand too close. They didn't touch each other, even innocently. They didn't talk endlessly with each other until even the silences between them felt warm and comfortable.

Her inhale was met with, "Please, Haley," and she couldn't say no.

Why could she never say no when he asked like that?

◊◊◊

While they had been filling their bellies with lamb and tzatziki, they both seemed to settle back into a more friendly, neutral state. For Haley, the tension from before still lingered, sparking and snapping below the surface, but Yeti seemed completely comfortable. He'd openly answered her questions about the UofA—his past major and what it had been like being a student here. She'd nearly choked on the kalamata olive from her Greek side salad when he'd casually mentioned that the *student* population of the University of Arizona was four thousand larger than the entire population of Maysville.

Shuffling into the large auditorium that was to hold the lecture, they found open seats near the aisle a third of the way back. Yeti gestured for her to sit first. It was another one of those unconscious gentlemanly things he'd been doing all night, along with making sure she never walked on the street-side of the sidewalk.

"Thank you." Haley plopped down and primly intertwined her fingers over her folded knees—her foot facing *away* from him, just to be safe. They people-watched for a while before the dean of the College of Science began speaking onstage. The dean thanked their sponsors, welcomed the high school science educators in attendance, and introduced the speakers.

Two scientists stood slightly offstage. One was a tall man with a mop of blond curls and honest-to-goodness brown elbow patches on his tweed blazer. Under his jacket was a simple white collared shirt, followed by jeans and Teva sandals. He wiggled his toes as the dean spoke. The female speaker wore a perfectly tailored burgundy skirt suit with sensible black heels. Her long brunette hair flowed in effortless waves around her stylish glasses. Her presence emanated warmth and competence.

As soon as they were introduced, the two speakers raised their hands in a wave and then moved to opposite sides of the stage. A large screen displayed digitally mastered slides. Each speaker was mic'd, and Dr. Pérez held a small device to switch the slides in her hand.

Even though the lecture had been prepared for the general public, Haley had a hard time following it. As some of the grittier nuances of astrophysics flew right over her head, she could at least enjoy the obvious camaraderie between the two speakers. That, and Dr. Tremblay kept making physicist dad jokes.

The whole thing was reminiscent of a well-executed TED Talk. And Haley should know, she'd watched over a thousand in an effort to educate herself since she couldn't afford a formal education like the one Yeti had received. It was amazing what you could learn from podcasts, free video lectures, and audiobooks from the library.

The hour seemed to sail by, and Dr. Pérez clicked a final time with a broad smile. "Thank you all for coming."

The dean came back onstage with information about the next lecture the following weekend before the house lights came up, and the crowded auditorium began to empty.

"What did you think?" Yeti asked with unanticipated eagerness in his voice.

"Honestly, some of it was a little beyond me, but the speakers did a great job. Their energy bounced off each other so well."

When Yeti's smile broke wide and earnest across his mouth, it caught her by surprise. "Yeah, they're always like that."

People standing beside them prompted them to move along, but Yeti hesitated for a breath before heading toward the stage instead of up the aisle.

"Where are you—"

"I just want to say hi real quick."

"Oh, okay." Maybe he'd taken a class from one of the speakers.

A few people were standing in a haphazard line, asking questions of the two scientists. Yeti stood back until everyone had had a turn. Eventually, it was just the four of them.

"So?" Dr. Tremblay looked at Yeti, as if seeking his critique.

Haley's brows pinched as her neighbor laughed. Who was this jubilant body-snatcher who palled around with astrophysicists, and what had he done with serious Yeti? It usually took her an hour to coax this version from him, and these two scientists received it in seconds. Haley worked double-time to prevent the flush of jealousy from staining her cheeks.

"Great as always," Yeti said. "I liked the new joke about 'understanding the gravity of this matter.'"

Dr. Tremblay let out a warm, rumbly laugh and gripped Dr. Pérez's elbow. "I told you that one was good."

Dr. Pérez only half-smiled at Yeti with a slight head tilt—the motion jumping him into action.

"Ah. Right. This is my friend, Haley. Haley"—he paused—"these are my parents, Teresa and Oliver."

If the word *parents* hadn't been enough to detonate three sticks of dynamite in her throat, his warm hand sliding under her cropped jacket at the small of her back did.

Haley was pretty sure Dr. Pérez—Mom!—caught how her eyes shot open before she controlled her facial features enough to extend her hand with a semi-shaky, "Hello." Yeti's fingers lingered for one, two seconds before her lower back almost shivered in their absence.

After her shock was locked back between her rib bones, Haley's customer service skills rushed to the forefront to save her. "Nice to meet you both. That was a very educational and entertaining lecture."

"So glad you enjoyed it." Oliver smiled.

As they kept talking, Haley tried to keep her brain from melting as Drs. Mom and Dad continued to bounce commentary off each other, just as playfully as they'd done during the lecture. Yeti even volleyed a remark here and there, and Haley struggled to keep her face pleasantly placid.

"Are you heading to the brewery?" Oliver asked.

The dean had mentioned an informal discussion open to the public at a nearby microbrew following the lecture.

"Oh, no!" Haley coughed, bringing her hand to her mouth in a fake yawn to cover her outburst. "I've got work really early tomorrow, but the three of you should go." Yeti was staring at the side of her face, but she didn't acknowledge him. "It was, um, nice to meet you both." She let her friendliest smile lace her lips, knowing it didn't reach her panicked eyes, before she turned to leave, snagging Yeti's gaze. "See you later."

Yeti seemed to catch the hint and stayed behind as she tried not to run like a cheetah from the stage. The aisle seemed to elongate as she climbed, but finally, Haley broke from the auditorium into the crisp night air. Blessedly alone.

Chapter 19

It only took a few moments to find Haley muttering to herself, going the opposite direction of the garage where his car was parked.

"Haley!"

Her head snapped toward the sound of his voice, but she continued striding away from him, her fingers rising to curl around the back of her neck.

Yeti fell in step with her fevered pace. "Where are you going?"

"Um . . ." She hesitated. "For a walk."

An aggravated growl escaped him. "But it's dark, and you never know who could be out here."

"Are you saying your alma mater isn't a safe place for women?" she clipped, continuing to rub her neck.

The agitation that had begun brewing the second her retreating form strode away from him mounded. It was a rising, uncontainable thing—maroon and multiplying by the second.

"How were you planning on getting home?"

The path forked, and she jerkily shot left. "Uber. Lyft. Yellow Cab. Take your pick."

"*Haley.*"

"*Yeti.*" She stopped her in her tracks, meeting his gaze. The low-wattage lights of the walking path cast half of her face in an amber shadow. "I know you're rusty at the whole normal-parts-of-society thing, since you mostly live in solitude, but one does not simply take a person to meet their parents without notice."

His chest puffed as irritation sprinted to each exterior surface—finger pads, kneecaps, even the tips of his damn ears. "Why not? Lots of my *friends* have met my parents over the years."

Her mouth popped open, and even as anger ravished his intestines, the impulse to slide his fingers through her hair and bring those lips to his pulsed through him.

A forceful exhale blew over the sidewalk. "It's not the same."

"Why, Haley?" He pressed into her space. "What makes it different?"

He was being such a jerk. Surprising her with a parental introduction was a chump move. When they'd arrived at the lecture, he'd planned on leaving afterward, never notifying her of the relationship between him and the speakers. Yeti could have told his parents later that he'd needed to leave right after the lecture. Centennial Hall held twenty-five hundred people. He and Haley could have easily slipped back into the night undetected.

But part of him had wanted this reaction—expected it, even. Haley was right in that he wasn't the best at navigating social interactions anymore, but he didn't think he was misinterpreting *this*. He'd noticed how she'd leaned back slightly in the thrift shop. He'd caught how her eyes had fluttered closed through the tiny mosaic glass pieces of a decorative mirror hanging behind the counter.

For the first time in years, Yeti wanted something other than his quiet, predictable existence. He wanted noise, and light, and Haley constantly babbling in his ear.

"Because—I—Because—" An unsteady inhale separated each word.

"Ethan!" The sound of his dad's shout snapped his head over his shoulder.

Oliver jogged in their direction. "Glad I caught you. About tomorr—" When his gaze swept between the two of them, he took a quick, receding step. "You know what? Never mind. I'll text you." He nodded to Haley. "Nice to meet you again."

Oliver's eyes flicked cautiously to his before striding away.

"Ethan." When Haley's shocked mouth tried out his name, the T sound tumbled over her teeth like a sigh instead of the sharp pop Yeti had always formed.

The sound was a blow he wasn't prepared to take. Pinpricks radiated over his chest and shot down his arms as his lashes pressed firmly closed.

"Your name is Ethan?"

A ragged exhale shuddered from him, hearing it again.

His father had unknowingly armed Haley.

Ethan dropped his head, staring at the dark sidewalk and running a hand over his beard. Hearing his name from her lips was a reminder of who he *really* was, of what even the golden-hearted Haley wouldn't want.

What nobody wanted.

He'd spent too much of today playing pretend.

"We should go. It's time I took you home." Ethan took a step in the direction they'd come from, not waiting for her response.

Haley whispered his name again, as if in disbelief, hesitating only a heartbeat before following him.

◊◊◊

For as much as Ethan had previously wanted Haley to fill the space surrounding them with her stories, he'd been grateful that the car ride home had been silent. They'd even managed to numbly get upstairs and mutter goodnights without incident.

Except . . .

Except, he'd noticed how her eyes kept darting to him as she'd clumsily reached for her door handle, missing the first time.

Except, he'd heard the tremble in his name, felt how it sent a heated wire searing through him when it husked from her lips.

Ethan stood beside his kitchen table, his keys digging impressions into his palm.

What if . . .

Sure strides brought him to his closet. Most of it was filled with comfortable hoodies and sweats, but a small corner was relegated to more traditional attire. All of it was new, tags still attached. Each time Paige visited, she snuck a new item in like a crow. The fabrics she'd researched and selected were supposed to be incredibly comfortable. His sister using her hard-earned money to buy him expensive fabrics annoyed him, but Paige often reminded him that since he'd used part of his OnlyApp earnings to wipe out her student debt and buy her a brand-new, safer bungalow in La Jolla, she possessed disposable income.

His fingertips explored a flannel shirt that was debatably softer than the hoodie he was wearing. Ethan's pulse hammered the underside of his chin as a staggering breath drew into his lungs. If he was going to do this, he wasn't going to scruff Haley's beautiful face with unkept beard hair. The fabric of his hoodie momentarily blinded him before he tossed it into the hamper.

He'd seen the electric razor that his sister had snuck under his sink. It was next to the package of no-tug hair bands, scissors, shaving cream, a razor, and a not-so-subtle note that stated *USE THESE* in all caps.

His chest stretched as he clumsily wrapped a hair band around his hair, securing it into some semblance of a low ponytail. A beat-up, rusted-out car felt like it was sitting on his throat as he stared at the black paper that had been over every mirror in every apartment since the accident. His hand ran over his beard with a loud exhale.

The necessity of daily massage had made the ridges of his scar something his fingers knew well, but Ethan avoided seeing himself whenever possible, often working through each crater and whirl without looking down.

Ethan knew what would be seen in his reflection—dragon skin on the chest of a man. The remains of where heat and snarling fire had attempted to swallow him whole. Irregular breaths jostled his shoulders as he tugged at the black corner.

He caught the panic in his eyes before the rest of the paper fell away.

His scar started where his neck met his shoulder, engulfing the front of his left arm just past his elbow before cutting sharply across his chest and tucking beneath his right armpit. It continued down his torso until just above his waistband, dipping slightly below on the left side.

The unique pattern of geometric shapes, remnants from his skin grafts, momentarily caught his eyes. Ethan focused on his scissor-laden hands, trimming his beard. Clumps of coarse hair fell onto the Formica countertop. The buzz of the electric razor clicking on sounded like a freight train as he brought it to the corner of his jaw.

As shaky fingers systematically destroyed the small barrier of hair he'd developed over the years, his brain buzzed. The cooling sensation of shaving cream filling his palms allowed him to catch his breath, but even strokes were challenging with his heart stumbling around in his chest like an uncoordinated toddler.

There was a very real possibility that Haley would react to him like Amber had. Though, her *no* would likely be the tenderest he'd ever receive. That knowledge made it possible to step outside of the world he'd built and try for something more, especially if there was a chance Haley wanted him back.

Once the sink was cleaned up, Ethan pushed most of the black paper back in place—except for where his face reflected back at him. He'd need that space now. Trading his sweats for jeans, he pulled the flannel over his chest. When he moved into his main room on the way to the front door, a familiar computerized voice stopped him mid-stride.

Remmy.

Unease slithered through him at the idea of eavesdropping, but his feet didn't seem to have any qualms about padding toward the balcony door.

"You're kidding me. *Zach Abrams?*" Remmy's digitized voice shrieked. "The man you've been crushing on for years? He messaged you back. This is *fiction*. There's no way this is real life."

"I thought you'd like the distraction." Haley's voice sounded . . . uneven, uncertain.

His face pinched. She should have been over the moon, like she'd been at the grocery store.

"This is the best thing to ever happen to you. I forgive you a million times over for skipping town on me if this is the result." Remmy's gasp was comically loud. "Your wedding is going to be *gorgeous*."

The jubilant sound of Haley's barking laugh pierced him through the chest.

"Slow down there, tiger. There's no saying we'll ever meet, let alone get married."

"But you've got to try. I mean, this is a once-in-a-lifetime thing. It'd be idiotic not to try."

The long pause that hung in the air seemed to be set there just to torture him.

"Lee!"

"No, you're right."

Ethan's vision grayed at the corners. Of course, Remmy was right. The best thing for Haley was Zach Abrams.

Before Ethan understood what was happening, his keys were in hand, and he was breaking into the cool evening air. His progress came to a halting stop, finding Aster seated at the top of the death stairs.

This time, her muumuu was covered in an old-fashioned, gray flannel jacket. Tiny, tumbling waves patterned the azure fabric escaping beneath. Beside her tight, stubby ponytail, Sebastian's eyes stared directly at Ethan. His long, striped tail wove around her waist and disappeared behind a gap in the railing.

Aster mindlessly patted his spines, like one would do with a newborn baby, turning to glance at Ethan. "*Humph.*" She rotated back toward the complex. "Lorraine always did have a strange sense of humor."

"Excuse me?" He blinked.

Aster heaved with an exaggerated sigh and rose to standing, walking down the stairs without even holding the railing. Ethan's heart jumped to a techno beat. Even though Aster seemed like a very capable seventy-eight-year-old, her spit-fire personality couldn't protect her from the inevitability of age-induced osteoporosis. Ethan rushed behind her, but Aster batted his outstretched hand away like a mosquito.

"I don't need help this time. You do." Her critical gaze swept him once she landed on the sidewalk. Sebastian followed suit, turning his spiked head. "Oh, you like him, don't you?" she said to her scaly companion before giving Ethan another ruthless once-over. "I suppose he's got his merits."

"I— Ah . . ."

"Not very eloquent, though," she stage-whispered to Sebastian.

Ethan was getting a headache from the pinched position of his brows.

"Okay," Aster huffed. "Come on. You're lucky that I used to cut Joel's hair all the time. We can finish that makeover of yours."

His hand pushed over his forehead, realizing that the chance he'd been about to take had evaporated. Soon, Haley could potentially be in the arms of Zach Abrams, or returning to Maryland, and he'd be back to where he'd been four weeks ago before her energy had perforated his peaceful existence. Suddenly, shaving his beard felt impetuous.

"That won't be necessary."

"Nonsense. You've—" The sound of his ringtone interrupted her. "Go ahead." Aster leaned back with an *I'll wait* expression.

Since Paige would only continue calling until he picked up, Ethan dragged his phone out of his pocket. Only Zane's contact information lit up his screen.

"Zane. Hey." He failed at keeping the surprise from his voice. Though Ethan had hoped his friend would call him back, a part of him had thought he'd screened and ignored him.

"Ethan, wow. It's great to hear your voice. How are you? I've missed you."

When Ethan had first met Zane, it took some time getting used to his emotive ways. It's not that Ethan's family was particularly closed off, but Zane always said exactly "what was on his heart." It was a phrase he'd used often. Ethan knew that losing his dad at fifteen had a lot to do with Zane's sincerity.

"Ah, I'm all right." Aster glared at him, clearing her throat. "Hey, um, I know I called, trying to catch up, but I'm with my neighbor right now. Is there any way we could get dinner this week or coffee?"

"I gotcha. How about Friday? Bluey's? Seven-thirty?" The uptick in Zane's voice made Ethan's chest wrench.

"That sounds great. Thanks, Zane."

"The pleasure's all mine. Seriously. I'll see you soon."

Aster spun and flicked a beckoning wrist the second he lowered the phone from his ear. "Let's get this over with."

"Aster, I—"

"Don't *Aster* me." She was already striding away, the slap of her sandals an impatient ticking.

His neck popped as his gaze and exhale floated toward the stars.

"Come on. I made lemon poppyseed cake, and if Sebastian eats it all, he'll get sick." When Ethan brought his chin down, Aster's expression softened.

He'd already come this far. Though Haley had been the initial reason for the change in his appearance, his parents would probably be pleased if he showed up to breakfast tomorrow with a new haircut.

Aster's firm hand met his back with a hearty *thwump* when he fell into step beside her. "This'll be fine. You just can't see it yet."

Chapter 20

Though the delicious scent of bergamot filled Haley's nose as her lips cradled the ceramic edge of her mug, it didn't matter. She might as well have been drinking hot dirt. The few hours of sleep she'd managed last night had been broken and filled with manic dreams. The ones where you miss something, or are late for something, or are always somehow left in the dark even when you're standing barely dressed on a light-flooded stage, addressing your high school graduation class.

This morning, she'd risen and said her daily mantra: *Make today better than the last*. But even as that sentence fired off automatically, Haley couldn't help pulling out all the incredible parts of yesterday. It'd been like one long, complicated, breathtaking, infuriating, amazing day.

The weirdest part about the whole thing—and there had been a fair amount of weird sprinkled in there—was that she hadn't sent Zach Abrams a message back. Though Haley officially stood by the line that she was trying to think of the most captivating thing to say, last night, lying in bed while spinning her new ring on her index finger, Haley had to admit the truth.

She'd been waiting for the need to text Zach Abrams to be obsolete.

She'd been waiting for Yeti—no, *Ethan*—to frame her face with his hands and finally release her from this tension prison.

Haley ran a wobbly hand over her scrub top and poured her full cup of tea down the drain. At least she had a shift at the Red Cross today and wouldn't be obsessively replaying yesterday in her mind. Oh, who was she kidding? She'd be doing that while putting needles in people's arms and collecting blood for those in need.

Her mind was stuck in a thrift-shop loop as Haley pushed outside. The biting, cold air rushed to prick at her eyes and nose when she heard Ethan locking his front door.

Anticipation spiraled and curled through her veins, trying to guess what version of him she'd receive this morning.

Only . . .

There was no way her wild imagination could have predicted what her eyes were telling her. Ethan wasn't standing there, keys in lock . . . Some gorgeous, well-coiffed man was.

Three things kept Haley from looking over her shoulder and confirming that she'd just left her apartment: Ethan's undeniable clove scent, the sharp slant of his nose, and the evenness of his brows.

Everything else was changed.

For one, he wasn't wearing his trademarked uniform of hoodie and sweats. His shiny black shoes reflected the Arizona sunlight, their tops covered by fitted black slacks. A crisp white Oxford was tightly fastened at the neck with an efficiently knotted, light-gray tie. Somehow, her body sagged with relief at seeing a storm-gray cashmere sweater layered over both. The soft, almost hoodie-like fabric gave her something to ground herself.

Because when she looked into the familiar eyes of the person she'd been spending a lot of her time with, Haley felt lost.

Ethan's thick, wavy hair had been cropped. It still held several inches over the top, but the sides and back were neatly trimmed. The most startling thing was the change to his face. The sharpness of his nose should have prepared her for the cutting edge of his jaw, but since it had been hidden by a rather bushy beard, Haley hadn't the slightest idea. Now, however, everything about his face seemed too angular, too masculine.

"What—I mean—You—" she stammered.

The corner of his mouth tugged up, and though she'd seen that half-smile a hundred times, without the beard as a cloak, it sent heat loosening the tendons behind her knees.

Almost immediately, Ethan stiffened, straightening his lips, jamming his hands into his pockets, and moving down the stairs.

His sudden absence smacked her in the belly. Haley quickly closed and locked her door. "Wait. Where are you going?"

He paused, half-turning his face. "Brunch."

"With Zane?" She couldn't hide the hopefulness in her words.

Last night, Haley had counted the days. Twenty-eight. Shortest month of the year. Normally, the first day of a month brought a joyous, "Rabbit! Rabbit!" from her mouth, a superstition to ensure good luck. But even if Ethan wouldn't allow her to get closer to him, it was important to Haley that he had *someone* when she left. The idea of him alone in his apartment made her bones want to disintegrate.

"No. With my parents."

Thoughts of last night flooded her, flushing her earlobes. Haley wanted to reply, but her twitchy muscles couldn't seem to remember how breathing worked.

Ethan's eyes ticked to the pulse point in her neck before catching on hers. They were laced with something unreadable. When his thick, dark lashes pressed firmly closed, the word shouted inside her skull.

Regret.

The same emotion bounding through every cell in her body.

"I've got to go."

He twisted back around, pounding down the remaining steps and stalking around the corner. He'd never moved that rapidly before. Not running, really, but definitely moving purposefully.

Away from her.

Something inside Haley snapped.

The plastic bag containing her lunch and water bottle hit her welcome mat with a slap. Haley could barely hear the sound of her sneakers racing down the stairs over the buzzing in her chest. She wove through their complex and caught up to Ethan just before he got to the parking lot.

"You don't get to walk away from me," she nearly shouted at his back.

Her muscles quivered to a halt when he spun in the gravel, sending tiny rocks flying away from his shoes. A layer of dust coated his shiny toes, and she thought, *Good!* Haley wanted to pick up a handful of desert sand and toss it over his head.

"What's going on here?" she demanded.

His body transformed with the same emotion rapidly cascading through her bloodstream.

"What's happening is that I'm trying to do the right thing." His hand raced through his cropped hair. "Damn it, Haley, *Zach Abrams* messaged you yesterday, and you're chasing me through our complex. Have you texted him back?"

"No." The word came out with the defiance of a surly teenager.

Ethan shook his head. "Why? Why not? You should be texting him right now, telling him something witty and enigmatic that will make him fall in love with you." He spat out the last few words like they tasted like rotting meat.

Haley pulled her shoulders back, trying to hide the fact it felt like she'd been struck. "Is that so unthinkable?"

"No. That's just it." He ran a frustrated hand over his beautifully smooth face. "You're incredible. He's perfect, and—" Ethan stuttered over incoherent syllables for a few seconds before finishing with, "And I've absolutely had diarrhea before."

Her hands flung into the air. "What does that have to do with anything?"

An exasperated growl slipped through his clenched teeth. "This was a bad idea. This whole thing was stupid. I'm stupid for thinking . . . Look"—he jutted out a hand—"just let me leave, okay?"

"No!"

Ethan blinked at her forceful answer, and honestly, she'd surprised herself. But Haley wasn't going to let him walk out on her, not when there had to be another reason he kept pulling away when they got too close. Her brain had already recolored their past encounters, like an artist putting a final varnish on a painting, alighting the truth with perfect clarity.

She'd doubted her experiences last night. She'd told herself she was making something out of nothing, but now Haley understood.

Ethan wanted this as much as she did.

His chest heaved as his anger transformed into something else. Silence filled the space between them for a few stumbling heartbeats before he went to smooth a hand over a beard that was no longer there. "You need to let me leave, Haley. I'm messed up."

Though he'd let go of his irritation, hers continued to bounce between her ribs. "That's established. You're evasive, you'd rather suffer than allow yourself to let go and smile, and you're terrible at letting people in."

A deep breath lifted his shoulders. "No. You don't understand."

Her body seemed to advance on its own, only stopping when she was inches from him. Standing slightly higher on the path, it brought his lips, and the lingering scent of cinnamon gum, closer to hers. "So, explain it to me."

Ethan tensed at her proximity. "Just let me do this for you. You're better off with him. That's obvious. We shouldn't even be standing here having this conversation." A muscle in his jaw twitched. "Why are you being so difficult?"

"It's not like Zach Abrams asked me out or anything. And even if he did—"

"Stop." His gruff word cut her off. "You're good enough for him."

"Am I good enough for you?"

They stood at an aggressive standstill for a couple of seconds until something shifted. The invisible cords of pressure between their bodies snapped and broke. She could feel it. She could feel the way his collarbones loosened as he subtly shook his head, his gaze never leaving its locked position on hers.

"Haley, don't."

She sucked in a halting breath. "You keep saying my name."

His lips parted, and it was almost as if the coarse, sandpaper words fell out against his will. "I like the taste of it in my mouth."

The distance between them grew diminutive in a fraction of a second. Haley couldn't tell if she was leaning in, or if he was, or if some cosmic hand was pushing them both, but it didn't matter. All that mattered was she needed sweet cinnamon on her tongue, so she pressed her lips to his.

Ethan's body went eerily still for a split second before his jaw slacked, and a ragged exhale washed over her skin. Fire ignited behind her breastbone when his lips softly brushed hers—once, twice—before his tongue almost hesitantly touched her lips. A broken sigh left her mouth open, and Ethan explored slowly, gripping her ribs and pulling her to him.

Her fingers rushed through the short hair on the sides of his face before twisting into the longer parts over the top. It was still *so soft*. A relieved sound escaped him, and Haley chased the vibrations with her tongue, needing to hear it again. Something in the way he held her, how he kissed her, was needling its way through her essential organs, fundamentally changing them.

It didn't make sense. This was a first kiss. It should have been clumsy, or messy, or at the very least good but exploratory as they learned each other, but kissing Ethan felt like they'd done it thousands of times.

When he pulled away a fraction, she'd never experienced a stronger internal objection.

"Haley, you shouldn't—" He kissed her again like he had no control over it, like his lips belonged on hers. "You won't want—"

She silenced him with her mouth.

Haley wasn't sure how her back became pressed against the stucco wall beside the path. She knew she hadn't walked there, so Ethan's firm hands, hot against her waist, must have carried her. Her focus was distracted by how his hungry lips fit over hers, how his spicy tongue made her blood shimmer, and the weight of him pushing her against the slightly spiky wall was absolutely heavenly.

"Yeeaaaahhh. Get it!" A trio of older teenagers skated through the parking lot, hooting and laughing.

An automatic chuckle bubbled up her esophagus, but Ethan rubbed his swollen lips with his fist and looked like he was going to be sick.

"I should let you get to work." He stepped back, focusing on the dry brittlebush beside them.

A hot tingling swept up the back of her neck and across her face because she should've seen this coming. After all, it'd always been this way with him. A little sweetness before sour washed over everything. The chipper morning desert mocked her as the rapid, repetitive call of a cactus wren dug into her temple. Even the ever-present click of crickets—a generally pleasing sound—seemed to be flippantly asking, *What'd you expect?*

But . . . he'd kissed her like she was elemental to his existence.

"Ethan?"

When he looked up, his gaze bounced around as his lips downturned, like seeing her kiss-flushed face was torture. Whatever battle he was waging below the surface, his fingers drifted up and slid over her jaw, palming the back of her head below her ponytail.

His eyelashes closed as he sighed. "Why are you making this so hard?"

"It doesn't have to be," Haley whispered, knowing that she'd be leaving in four weeks, but not wanting whatever *this* was to end.

When he brushed his lips against her forehead, she felt it. It was as obvious as the large capital letters at the end of a black-and-white movie. Every single cell in her body yelled at her to fight, to reason with him, to jump on his back if needed, but her mind reminded her that you can't force a person to be with you when they don't want to be.

So, when Ethan murmured, "I can't," into her hair and walked away, Haley let him.

Chapter 21

All Ethan wanted to do was drive to La Jolla and curl up on Paige's uncomfortable houndstooth couch—the one she manically cleaned but perpetually smelled like stale coffee cake. As much as he'd been allowed to blow off social events before, missing his mother's sixtieth birthday brunch would be inexcusable. It didn't matter that, in this moment, he felt more broken than he did after the fire, after each hospitalization, after each lost relationship.

Kissing Haley had confirmed what he'd been trying to push out of his mind since her snot-covered, flushed face looked up at him and smiled. The feeling that, with each subsequent interaction, had etched further into his marred skin.

There was no way to assign intellect to the way he felt about Haley.

There was no rational explanation.

You weren't supposed to love someone you'd only known a handful of weeks. You weren't supposed to feel like you'd found the person who was made for you. You weren't supposed to be shattered by having their lips on yours because it confirmed that you were right.

Dry air filled his lungs for one final breath before Ethan stepped into the historic hotel's main entrance. His dad had rented out one of the dining rooms to celebrate his beloved wife and invited twenty or so of their closest friends. A runaway toddler streaked past him down the main hallway, followed shortly thereafter by a harried father, before Ethan found the right room.

Two gorgeous heirloom chandeliers hung from the wood-beamed roof of the immaculately decorated room. The round tables set for eight held exploding snapdragon centerpieces—his mom's favorite flower—among the copious silver and glassware. Everyone was standing and chatting, their voices layering over the classical guitarist who played from her stool in the corner. Out of habit, Ethan clung to the edges of the room, finding refuge beside a brimming recessed bookcase.

When he turned to examine the antique spines, a high-pitched squeal preceded a pair of thin-but-strong arms hugging him from behind. The tenacious squid only let him go enough to spin him around, nearly knocking him into a nearby gilded frame.

"I can't even—I mean—Whoa!" His sister's matching brown eyes took him in, hands bracing his shoulders. "I *love* the haircut, and thank goodness you got rid of that beard. I was always worried you'd get some sort of infestation." She shivered before picking an invisible piece of lint off his sweater. "I'm so glad everything fits. I honestly thought I was buying moth food this whole time. But look! You actually wore it." Paige's gaze couldn't seem to focus. It kept bouncing over his attire.

Normally, he'd find some way to push back or joke, but it already felt as if he'd been in battle for twenty-three hours just standing there. "Dad said you couldn't make it."

"I didn't think I was going to, but everything finished out last night around ten, so I drove straight here afterward." Paige was practically bouncing. "You look so good, Ethan. Like, it's scary."

He tilted his head, some semblance of his former self arriving from whatever torpor state it'd been in. "Good or scary? I don't know if you remember English class, but those are antonyms."

Paige didn't bite. "Scary good. Has Mom seen you yet? You didn't even need to get her a present. This is it."

"*Ethan*." Mom's warm, firm arms were around his shoulders before her hands fussed over his jaw and ears, murmuring in Spanish. "You didn't need to do this. We love you the way you are. You could have worn your sweatshirt. Are you comfortable?" She ran a gentle hand over his chest. "The shirt's not too scratchy?"

Ethan blinked against the dampness sheening his eyes. "No, Mom. Paige bought me all these. They're very comfortable."

His mom framed Paige's face with her palm as a server came by, offering mimosas. He and Mom took one, but Paige declined and asked for an espresso instead.

"I put you at the table near the exit," Mom said once they were alone again, motioning toward the French doors. "Feel free to slip into the courtyard if you need a break. I'm sure Paige wouldn't mind some sunlight after being trapped in her lab, finishing out her experiment."

Ethan was used to them making accommodations for him, even though he hadn't needed them over the last year. They'd never made him feel like it was a burden. A knot formed in his throat. "I'll be fine, Mom. Enjoy your party. Happy birthday."

She kissed both of her kids' cheeks before heading back to the center of the room to be among her friends.

Trying to dissipate some of the emotion swelling in his chest, Ethan elbowed his sister. "The last thing you need is more coffee. How are you this awake after getting to bed at 4 a.m.?"

"Four-thirty," she corrected. "And I got about five and a half hours before they woke me to get ready." Paige ran a hand over her sleek green sheath dress, rotating side to side as if to show off how lovely she looked. "Nice, right? Since I've been doing so much research finding clothes for you, I got myself a little something." She pulled at the fabric at her waist, and it easily stretched six inches. "This dress looks fancy, but it's made of butter-soft, flexible material. I could do cartwheels in this thing."

"Even with the heels?" He motioned his glass to her feet, knowing his sister hated heels but was trying to make an effort on their mother's behalf.

Paige punched him in his right arm. "Whoa. Is that the clove oil lotion I gave you for your pruritus? It's *strong*." She stepped away, waving a hand in front of her nose.

Ethan lifted the collar of his sweater and sniffed, smelling only a faint spiciness. "Are you messing with me or being serious?" The oil worked much better at treating his scar's itchiness than the shea butter lotion she'd bought him before. "I smell bad?"

"No." His sister shook her head, yawning into her forearm. "Not terrible. Just takes some getting used to. It's like having a simmering pot of spiced cider standing next to me."

While the server returned with a tiny white cup on a saucer for Paige, an onslaught of images kicked him in the kidneys. He was on their balcony again, watching Haley tilt her pale-blue eyes up before telling him he smelled like Christmas.

"Ethan?" Paige's eyes were wide over her espresso. "We can be outside in ten steps. Do you need some air?"

It was unlike other times when he'd needed to flee a room without explanation, in that, this time, his chest felt like it was exploding for another reason entirely. His, "Yes," was a gruff whisper.

"Let's go." Paige threw back her coffee like a shot of tequila and set her cup on the mantel of the unlit fireplace on their way out.

Like usual, his sister gave him his space. Ethan strode aggressive circles around the intimate outdoor courtyard, trying to dissipate the dread cinching his muscles. Paige kicked off her shoes and perched on the tiled edge of the three-tiered fountain, letting her fingertips dangle in the water.

"Ethan, hey." His dad slipped outside, catching him mid-circle. "Can I do anything to help?"

Damn it. Not only had he ruined his own day by allowing himself to kiss Haley, but now he was screwing up his mom's birthday celebration by having three-fourths of her family outside.

A deep inhale filled his lungs. "I'm fine. You should head inside and be with Mom. Paige, you too. I'll be there in a minute."

"Wow, that's cute," Paige said to the water between her fingers. "You think you can tell me what to do."

"Is it too much after being at Centennial Hall last night?" His dad's face was already ruddy from his first glass of champagne. "You looked so calm with your friend. Happy, even."

"It's not the room. I just need a minute," Ethan said, running his hand over his shortened hair.

"What friend?" Paige bounded over with unnecessary enthusiasm. "You finally reconnected with them? About time. Who'd you bring? Zane? Rowan?"

"No, it was someone new. A woman." Dad tilted his head, staring off into the eight-foot-tall hedges that lined the well-manicured garden space. "Hazel? Holly?"

Ethan cringed at the memory. It'd been stupid introducing Haley to his parents, though not as tragic as breathing in her skin this morning.

"A *woman*? Dad, how could you not have mentioned this on the ride over? Or when I was falling asleep at the kitchen table? Or the minute you met her?" His sister squinted up at their father. "Seriously! Ethan doesn't have friends, let alone lady friends."

"I didn't think about it. We were busy with the lecture and the gathering afterward, and then I was making sure everything was settled with this." Dad gestured to the noise spilling from the slightly ajar French door. "Lady friends seemed irrelevant."

"Lady friends are most definitely not irrelevant." His sister crossed her arms.

Ethan tilted his face toward the blinding sun with a noisy exhale. "Please stop using the term *lady friend*."

"Who is she?" Paige spun her fury toward him.

"She's nobody." The words came out too forced, like jagged gravel spilling from his throat.

Paige arched a single eyebrow. "Doesn't sound like nobody."

A sheepish grin peppered his father's flushed cheeks. "You're right, son. I should check on your mom. I like the new look, by the way." Dad patted his elbow before returning to the party.

"Spill." Even barefoot, his sister was a force.

He ran a hand over his jaw. "Can we drop it? Please?"

Paige simply waited.

"It doesn't matter. Dad's right. It's irrelevant."

He had to give up this hallucinatory state he kept sliding into whenever Haley was around, making him think things were possible. Making him think that maybe she wouldn't mind that he was ruined. That maybe she could look past it.

Ethan shook his head, and some of his newly cut hair slipped over his eyes.

No. People like him couldn't have normal relationships. That was the *truth*.

Simple. Elegant. Finite.

Devastating.

Paige's expression softened. "I'm sorry."

Ethan focused on the massive flagstone pavers beneath them to keep himself from completely falling apart.

"I'd really hoped your next relationship would've worked out."

His teeth held their unrelenting grip as several beats passed. "Let's just go celebrate Mom."

"Okay, big brother." Paige patted his back with a gentleness that somehow made it worse. "Okay."

◊◊◊

Though Ethan had distractedly pushed his food around his plate at brunch, Paige had polished off her entire entrée and was now devouring a family-sized bag of chips on their parents' patio. Hummingbirds zipped by with annoyed chirps that he and his sister were occupying their territory. The day had warmed fully, prompting Ethan to shed his sweater and roll up his sleeves. Paige abandoned her party outfit altogether, opting for an oversized T-shirt and boyfriend jeans.

"Don't look at me like that. You know I don't eat when I get stressed about work," she said over a mouthful. "I need to catch up for the last six weeks."

He held up his hands. "I'm not judging."

Paige rearranged the pillows on the wrought-iron chair next to her and propped her feet up. "It'd be bad if I went to sleep right now, wouldn't it?"

Ethan checked his phone. "Seeing that it's three-thirty, yeah. I'd say that would mess you up. Try to make it at least until seven. Eight would be better."

His sister groaned and slipped further down in her chair. "Entertain me so I won't pass out."

"Of course, your majesty. Juggling or storytelling?"

"Storytelling." Paige tossed the open chip bag on the table, snuggling into the cushions.

"Let's see . . ." Ethan searched for some nonsense story to satisfy Paige until she eventually fell asleep. Since her eyes were already fluttering, it wouldn't take long. He'd let her nap for an hour and then wake her so that tonight's sleep wouldn't be ruined. "Once upon a time—"

"Mmmm. All the good ones start like that."

He cleared his throat as if annoyed, but his heart squeezed. When they were little and his parents were working on their research, he'd often be the one to put Paige to bed.

"Once upon a time, there was a yeti . . ." His temple twitched. This wasn't the story he was going to tell. This wasn't the story he was *ever* going to tell. Ethan had already decided over hollandaise-covered eggs that he was going to bury this whole chapter of his life until it suffocated.

"He . . ." As much as his mind tried to change the subject, his mouth kept talking. "He was used to his icy, solemn lifestyle and thought he was content until, one day, a bunny came into his territory. The bunny was noisy and joyful. Even when she was sad, she somehow radiated sunshine. Then, she started doing annoying things, like bringing the yeti homemade muffins, keeping him company when he needed it, and making fun of him."

"I like this bunny," Paige said through a yawn.

An unhumorous chuckle escaped him because Paige would have.

"They became an unlikely pair of friends, having various adventures, until the yeti did something tremendously stupid.

He fell in love with her." His ribs seized until breathing was painful. "The bunny would be obviously chatting about anything and everything, and Yeti would dream of impossible futures where they would be together."

His fingers fisted as his forearms tensed. "But he knew it was best if she returned to the land of the bunnies. He needed to stay where he was, in his cave. Alone. Because bunnies don't love yetis"—a hard swallow swept his throat—"even if she did kiss him back like everything flooding through his body was reciprocating through hers."

The memory he'd decided to destroy presented itself in over-saturated technicolor. For a few precious seconds, Ethan allowed himself to relive the kiss—the texture of her skin beneath the pads of his fingers, the way she molded to him, her tea-stained tongue, her sighs . . . the impossible way her heart seemed to converse with his.

"Ethan?"

He pulled his unfocused gaze from the low stucco wall surrounding their parents' xeriscaped backyard.

Paige took one look at him and sat up, toppling a pillow to the cement floor. "You're not telling a story. Was this the woman Dad mentioned? Does she know you love her?"

His palm covered his eyes, exhaling.

"Ethan!"

The despair that had taken residence in every cell in his body flipped to irritation. "Like I said before, it's irrelevant." He yanked at his unbuttoned collar, exposing the top of his scar. "No one can love this."

Ethan expected his sister to be understanding, to support him like she always did. So, the swiftness with which she rose from her chair and walloped him in the head with a pillow was a surprise.

"Are you saying she's never seen it?" Her hands fisted on her hips. "You love this woman, but you don't trust her enough to show her your scar."

"Just let it—"

"So, you took her choice away."

"There's no choice to make. No one wants this."

Paige hit him again, her swing sending the remaining contents of the chip bag sprawling over the ground. "Not every woman is Amber. She was a garbage"—whack—"human"—Ethan grabbed the pillow mid-swing—"who didn't deserve you." His sister's shoulders heaved. "That's it! I'm telling Mom."

His brows pinched as his mouth flew open. "What?"

"You call yourself a feminist," she grumbled, marching toward the sliding glass door.

One step was all it took to swing Paige over his shoulder, belly up.

"Ha ha!" The satisfaction in his sister's voice should have been a warning. "That won't work anymore. I've been taking Pilates."

She sat up so fast Ethan lost his grip around her waist. Paige slid to the floor triumphantly, but not before knocking a large tin star from the porch's rafter. The twelve-pointed star slammed onto the metal tabletop with a crash before tumbling to the ground.

Through the floor-to-ceiling glass windows, Dad rushed into the room that led to the porch, saw the two of them staring menacingly at each other, made his *I'm-not-getting-involved* face, and turned back toward his study.

"You go fix this right now," Paige demanded.

"There's nothing to fix. It's over."

Paige's eyes widened as her mouth pinched. "I love you so much, but sometimes . . ."

Everything sagged as the words slipped through his lips. "I'm infuriating?"

His sister's fingers slowly unfurled as her jaw softened. "Yes." Two heartbeats passed before she pulled him into a lung-squeezing hug. "It's your life, your decision, but Ethan . . . what if she's different?"

While a lizard darted down the wooden porch column to sneak a tortilla chip, only one thought chiseled at his temple.

There is nobody like Haley.

Chapter 22

"Okay, Haleybaley. I'm heading out." Her coworker, Cole, grabbed his coat from the back of his chair. The last scheduled donor had just waltzed out the front door, clutching two packs of Oreos. "You sure you don't want me to wait with you?"

Normally, Jana, their manager, would've closed the center, but she'd left an hour ago when her teenage daughter needed to go to urgent care after potentially breaking her foot during an impromptu soccer game with friends.

"No. Go home, and kiss those cuties of yours," Haley said, knowing Cole had three kids under three to get home to. "I'm just going to wipe everything down and be out of here myself."

Truthfully, she'd been debating spending the night to prevent accidentally running into Ethan at the apartment complex. Though the Red Cross surveillance cameras made an impromptu sleepover on a donation chair out of the question.

Cole raised a dubious eyebrow at her. "You sure? You've been off all day. Are you feeling okay?"

Since she'd received the kiss of her life followed by the crushing blow of Ethan walking away mere moments before getting into an Uber to work her shift, no, Haley wasn't okay. She probably wasn't going to be for a while.

"I'm fine. Promise." She plastered on a convincing smile, shooing him. "Now get. I'll see you next weekend."

As soon as Cole was through the glass door, her lips dropped. Haley pulled her hair down from its ponytail and let it sweep over her face, curtaining the emotions bounding through her.

Her body worked mindlessly. Only the nasal sting of the astringent wipes alerted her to the fact that she was still at the Red Cross Center. She could have been on the moon, sitting in piranha-laden water in a sweltering jungle, or trapped in a soundless room.

The swooping of the door opening yanked her from her misery.

"You forget something?" Haley tossed the wipe in the trash and glanced up.

Ethan—not Cole—stood in the entry. His hair was mussed, like he'd been running his hands through it all afternoon, and he looked even better than this morning with his white shirt unbuttoned at the neck and rolled to his elbows.

Her pulse jumped into her throat as she turned her back to him, her shaky fingers gathering up the folders she needed to put away.

"We're closed," Haley managed over her straw-coated tongue. "You can make an appointment for another day at Redcrossblood.org."

"Haley." His voice was a cement mixer full of broken glass.

The way Ethan said her name was completely unfair. He shouldn't be able to do that. He shouldn't be the one to sound devastated.

He'd walked away.

Haley traded the folders for a bundle of tubing as an idea flashed in her mind. As the soft, rubbery plastic slithered between her fingertips, some semblance of control trickled through her bloodstream. "If you're going to stay, then you can at least donate and do some good. There's a critical shortage right now."

His dress shoes slowly clicked closer as the implications of what she'd just suggested dawned on her. She'd have to run her fingers—albeit glove-covered fingers—over the soft, innermost nook of Ethan's arm. She'd have to feel his warmth. She'd be unable to avoid his clove scent at the proximity needed to draw his blood. Then, she'd be unable to work here without thinking of Christmas. It was already bad enough that memories of him made her want to avoid their complex.

Her shoulders caved in on themselves.

"*Haley.*" This time, her name was a desolate rasp.

"Please leave."

She'd never heard herself sound so small. Even after Jason had berated her over and over. Even after she'd apologized for messing up another one of his family's functions by playing on the floor with his younger cousins. Even after she'd muttered,

"I understand," after listening to his elongated explanation for their breakup.

It didn't make sense why she would feel this destroyed by someone she'd met only a month ago, but Haley's stomach twisted and snarled, anyway.

Ethan's exhale flowed from behind her, but she didn't turn around.

Haley was superb at emotional chicken. She'd been playing it her whole life. Too many long, silent dinners had passed with her dad growing up. She could sit in this stagnant, stilted silence as long as it took. Ethan obviously came from a loving family, so there was no way he'd win this battle. Sooner rather than later, he'd give up and leave.

He'd already proven he was good at that.

"You wouldn't be able to do it through this."

Through? Her gaze automatically turned over her shoulder, following his pointing fingers to the crook of his left arm.

Ropes and pocks of healed burn scars criss-crossed over an area that usually held some of the tenderest skin. Her head snapped up, and so much pain shone back at her—more than had ever been layered under his familiar, melancholic gaze.

Ethan dropped his head, and a slight line of scars along the left side of his neck, just barely peeking over his loosened collar, snagged her attention. "Haley, I . . ." His chest rose and fell with a shaky breath. "I . . ."

"Is—" Haley cleared her rough voice. "Is it from when you saved Paige?"

"Yeah." He bent his elbow, obscuring the scar as he touched the notch between unmarred collarbones. The back of his forearm was smooth and muscled, with a light amount of hair.

"Did she—Did she get burned too?"

"No." Ethan's eyes drifted back up, but he kept his arm bent over his chest. "I got us both out, but then she thought Rosalind Franklin was still in the house, and—"

"Rosalind Franklin?"

He grimaced slightly. "Paige's cat."

Her breathy gasp resonated in the vacant room.

"That was when I got trapped inside. When the firefighters got me out, Paige noticed Rosalind had already been outside."

Haley could feel her head shaking. That was so *incredibly* unfair. The cruelty of him suffering such injury without even getting to be the cat's hero seared a hole through her stomach. "I'm—I don't even—"

She was dumbfounded by her inability to speak. None of the frenzied words flying through her mind seemed enough, seemed worth the grandeur of what Ethan had been through. Her fingers itched to touch him, but she clenched the blood bag instead.

"As much as I wouldn't wish this"—his hand roughly gestured to his chest—"on anyone, I'm glad I was there." Ethan blew out a tense breath. "I hadn't been the best person right before it happened. I'd slipped into someone I wasn't, and Paige had been trying to set me straight. She'd tricked me into visiting her in an attempt to knock some sense into me." A dry chuckle left him. "I was so pissed, but she convinced me to stay the night, that we'd hammer it all out in the morning. Only, that morning never came."

The creaking of the air conditioner turning on sounded like a fighter jet screaming over her head.

"It's just—" Ethan's lips pressed into a firm line. "I haven't done anything like this . . ."

Understanding dawned. "You haven't been with anyone since you were injured."

His jaw twitched. "No, um. I was with someone at the time"—a tendon jumped in his neck—"but the healing process was really extensive, and I was in and out of the hospital a lot, and . . . you can't expect that anyone would want . . ."

Numerous invasive medical questions peppered her brain. Like, what was the total surface area of his wound? Was the whole thing third degree? How long did it take to fully heal? Did it still hurt? Who the heck was this woman who rejected him in the midst of recovering, and where did she live so Haley could give her a piece of her mind?

The scowl that had been pinching her lips loosened as another thought rushed to the forefront. "Is this why you keep rejecting me?"

"Rejecting you?" His near-perfect brows raced together. "This has never been about you. You're amazing. I just—" Ethan glanced at his scarred forearm. "It gets worse."

It was as if a great wizard had pulled back a velvet curtain with an enthusiastic *Ta-da!* Ethan had been pushing her away before she had a chance to run on her own. He'd probably been doing it for years. This was why he lived the way he did—had isolated himself.

Twin emotions braided down her spine. On some level, Haley understood why he'd protected himself, but the fact that he didn't trust her to be okay with something like a scar gutted her. She'd seen people missing half of their skull, others armless, sightless. But it was who they were *within* that mattered.

Tension pinched at her nose as moisture gathered at the corners of her eyes. "What do you want, Ethan?"

His gaze never wavered. "I want you."

It was another broken admission, like the truth couldn't help spilling out.

"But I need you to be honest with me." Conflict resounded in his muscles, his body stiffening as he spoke. "Don't tell me it's fine when it's not. Don't pretend to be okay with it when it disgusts you. Don't stay when you realize you don't want to be with someone who's ruined."

Haley flinched at his words. It took everything in her not to pull Ethan to her chest and hold him.

"Then you'd have to trust me." She forced herself not to move an inch, to show him she was as serious as he was. "You'd have to trust me to tell you the truth. To mean what I say. Can you do that?"

His chest rose with a shaky inhale, and time suspended for a few trembling seconds before he nodded.

"Okay." The word took all her energy with it.

"Okay," he repeated, stepping forward.

Several floundering heartbeats slammed against her ribs before she blurted, "What about what I want?"

Ethan froze.

Her stomach pinched, seeing despair trickle back into his beautiful cheekbones, but she needed to say this. She needed Ethan to understand that *this* was part of the deal.

Thinking back, it had always been her goal. The reason she'd consistently poked and teased. She'd been fueled by the relentless desire to achieve the same reaction, because on a fundamental level, even if he couldn't admit it to himself, Ethan needed this.

"I want you to smile more. For you to laugh."

Another slow step closed the distance between them. Both of his hands wove through her hair at the base of her skull, cradling her head.

"Will you be the reason for me to smile and laugh?" The tone of his raspy voice dropped.

Haley only managed a sedate nod. Her body felt as pliable as a warm piece of saltwater taffy, and part of her silently begged him to pull and stretch her to her limits.

"Then I will."

Ethan's words washed over her face as his nose slid down hers. Haley thought she'd been prepared for the radiant sensation of his lips on hers—after all, she'd already experienced it—but she'd been wrong. This time was infinitely better than the first. As her mouth parted, one of his hands flattened against the small of her back, bringing her body flush to his.

Heat bloomed inside her like a desert wind whipping through, tossing her organs like weightless tumbleweeds. She'd always been an open book, but Ethan's tongue seemed to be able to search within her and discover intimate details even she didn't understand.

Haley could have spent the next fifty-seven minutes memorizing the subtle intricacies of Ethan's lips, but her duplicitous stomach had other ideas and grumbled—*loudly*.

"Can I feed you?" Ethan gave her another decimating kiss. "I love feeding you. You make all these happy little noises."

Haley couldn't help but chuckle at his words.

Ethan leaned back, and the sincerity in his eyes stole her breath. "Officially this time. A real date. Please."

Her heart clenched when uncertainty sprinted through his expression, even though she'd just attempted to kiss the lips off his face.

A wide smile lifted her mouth, and she watched Ethan soften. "I'd love that."

Chapter 23

"This doesn't look like Thai," Haley said as a vest-wearing valet opened her door.

"It's not." Ethan pocketed the ticket from another valet. "We'll have to save that for another night."

She had continued needling him on the way here about where they were eating, and finally, with a playfully frustrated sigh, he'd said they were getting Thai food, expanding to state that tasting all the cuisines was an essential part of his plan for world domination.

Now, however, as the valet drove Ethan's Audi away, they were left outside what looked like a *very nice* restaurant. Haley's fingers fidgeted with the skirt of her dress to dissipate some of the twitchiness pulsing in her stomach.

After he'd driven them back from the Red Cross Center, Ethan had asked her to knock when she was ready. Skittering jumping beans had trampolined through her veins when Haley put on the dress she'd bought two weeks ago—the same day as the fire alarm.

When the blue-and-white, diagonal-striped dress with clusters of bright, graphic oranges had peeked out of the rack, Haley had known she'd found something special. The thrift store gods had smiled upon her that day because the bateau-neckline, high-waisted, knee-length beauty fit like it was stitched to mold her body. It even had *pockets*.

There'd been no valid reason for her to buy such a nice garment. No occasion she could have imagined wearing it during her brief stay in Tucson. But now, a rhythmic, steady tapping resonated beneath her collarbones.

She'd unknowingly bought it for tonight.

"Shall we?" Ethan offered her his sweater-covered elbow like he was a duke in the 1800s.

He was all manners and poise while speaking to the host, weaving her through the large restaurant and pulling the chair out for her at their table.

"Holy—" She cut off the second part of her commonly used phrase just in time.

The intimate table for two was situated against a floor-to-ceiling window overlooking the entire valley. Nighttime Tucson sparkled below an ombre sky. The warmth of many miniscule lights nestled in orderly intersecting rows. In the distance, the uneven purple outlines of the surrounding mountain ranges contrasted with the last of the sun's rays. Haley watched the familiar glowing orb disappear beyond the western border of the city.

"Good evening. My name is Sean, and I'll be taking care of you this evening." A server in a crisp black Oxford and apron pulled her attention. "Can I start either of you off with a signature cocktail or perhaps a bottle of wine?" The textbook-size wine menu sat untouched between them.

"We just need a few more minutes," Ethan answered.

Once the server was gone, he asked, "Would you like wine?"

That familiar drowning feeling began to overtake her. Everything had been fine, but now the heavy scents of the tarragon, cilantro, and sage felt like they were gagging her. She'd expected dinner out with the man she'd already shared several enjoyable meals with. Even though Ethan was almost blindingly handsome now, that hadn't made her nervous. This place, however, brought up bad memory after bad memory.

The handful of times Jason had taken her to the nicer restaurants in Baltimore, he'd always criticized her ability to be a good dining guest. Afterward, she'd pour through YouTube videos, trying to fix what was wrong with her, learning the difference between a table fork, salad fork, and dessert fork. Haley knew to pass the salt and pepper together and circulate the bread bowl to the right, but it never mattered how much she studied, because each time they went out, Jason would find something wrong with her, something to pick at.

Like wine.

No matter how nice the vintage, wine left her with a pounding headache. Would Ethan be disappointed if she preferred margaritas to Pinot Noir?

As her inhales became more scattered and frantic, her eyes ticked down to the menu. There was a paragraph about how the

French-inspired Southwestern restaurant locally or responsibly acquired their produce, meat, dairy, and seafood. *Southwestern cuisine*. Maybe ordering a margarita here wouldn't be "childish and irritating." Didn't the server say, "signature cocktail"? Maybe one of them was lime- and tequila-based.

"Haley."

Her mouth opened to answer, but her gaze began darting around the beautifully decorated restaurant. Nothing was out of place. The music was at the perfect decibel. The temperature of the room was sublime. The cushion of her chair, cloud-like.

The only thing out of place was *her*.

"Haley," Ethan said more forcefully.

Her eyes snapped to his.

"Come with me."

He rose so quickly his chair made a slight squeak across the carpeted floor, but all Haley noticed was that his large hand was outstretched to her. She clung to it like a lifeline and allowed him to pull her through the crowded restaurant. How many rooms had they passed through to get to their coveted window seat? Now it felt like a labyrinth.

When they entered the last dining room, Haley finally saw salvation—the exit. But before they could cross the room, a man dropped on one knee beside his companion at the table. Ethan stilled, tucking her to his side and flattening them against the nearby wall. He obviously didn't want to disturb this man's proposal by walking through it.

Though the sweet words of espousing love diverted Haley's brain from its tailspin, they didn't stop the first thought from popping out of her mouth. "Don't propose to me like that."

Ethan blinked down at her.

What did I just say?

This was their first official date—which she was *RUINING* by the way—and now she was instructing him on how to propose to her.

Her brows must have touched her hairline, her eyes opened so wide. "I mean. Don't ask anyone to marry you like that. Whomever you pick. A long time in the future. If you want to. Marry someone, that is," she said in a rushed whisper.

Her shaky hand fluttered over her lips so no further idiocy would tumble out.

A grin flirted with the corner of his mouth as Ethan leaned down to murmur softly, "What's wrong with the proposal?"

"It's just—" Haley smoothed her hand over her dress, trying to ignore how the heat of his body was seeping through the fabric. "It's too public. Asking another person to spend the rest of their life with you should be done in private."

The smirk on his lips continued to deepen. "But what if the person I'm asking loves attention?" Ethan gestured to the woman now showing off her ring-dazzled hand to every person within a ten-foot radius. "She doesn't seem to mind sharing this moment with others."

Haley watched the overjoyed bride-to-be nearly leap out of her seat to show off her sparkly gemstone. No, that woman certainly didn't mind receiving a request for marriage in the middle of a busy dinner service.

His lips brushed her ear. "Come on. I think we can leave now."

While Ethan made their excuses to leave, blaming their abrupt exit on his sick and vomiting imaginary dog, Haley was torn in two. Half of her chided her inability to function like a normal human being in a nice establishment. And the other half couldn't pull her attention away from the still-hovering sensation of Ethan's lips on her ear. She kept wondering how it would feel to have that hot, searing softness translated to other, more sensitive parts of her body.

Only when they were driving down the mountain toward the main grid of the city did Haley compose herself enough to stitch the two sides back into a semi-functioning person. "I'm sorry." She turned her body, pulling her knee up and twisting toward him in her seat.

"For what? Being uncomfortable and needing to leave?" Ethan said, like it was nothing, like he wasn't, in the least, disturbed by the fact she'd pulverized his plans for their evening. "That's not a big deal, Haley. Do you have any idea how often something like that used to happen to me?" His laughter bounced around the car.

Ethan *laughed* at the colossal inconvenience she'd created.

"I was the king—the king—of freaking out in normal situations and needing to be anywhere else. It happened so often that it became easier to stay at home." His eyes darted to hers for a breath, and Haley understood the deeper subtext.

Silence filled the car for a long while before that half-smile tugged at his mouth. "Besides, I promised you Thai, anyway."

When he whipped his Audi into the parking lot of a microbrewery with three food trucks parked out front, Haley almost wept. She almost cried stupid, ugly tears over being able to sit at a wooden picnic table with a paper plate full of noodles and a cold draft. Because Ethan hardly knew her, but he somehow *understood* her.

The brewery had an indoor seating space, but since today had been warmer than expected, almost everyone was outside on the large paver patio. The exterior walls of the building were huge industrial garage doors flung open to the evening air. With two orders of pad thai and two IPAs on the table, Haley's stomach and shoulders settled.

"What's your last name?" she asked.

Ethan slurped up a lingering noodle. "Pérez-Tremblay. My parents thought it was best for us to have both of their names."

"Ethan Pérez-Tremblay. That's a mouthful," she teased.

A husky chuckle was her reward. "You can see how Yeti was much easier."

Haley grinned over her raised glass of hoppy deliciousness.

"But"—Ethan paused as he wiped his chin with his napkin—"there's more."

"Oh?" She tweaked her eyebrows. "It gets worse?"

A guitarist in the patio's corner strummed the beginning chords to an old Dave Matthews Band song.

Ethan's eyes seemed to shine under the outdoor string lights that zigzagged above them. "Three guesses to figure out my middle name. I'll give you a hint: it's unusual."

"Lacy."

She was rewarded with another laugh, sending sparks zipping around her insides.

"No, try again."

"Hmm." Haley placed her chin in her palm, thinking. "Rutherford."

"Another valiant try." His mouth was set with that full smile again. She was becoming a little addicted to the way Ethan's face looked when he grinned like that. How had she been surviving on half-smiles for this long? "But no. One last try."

Her eyes bounded around the outdoor space, looking for inspiration, or maybe avoiding how Ethan's affectionate gaze made her feel like she was melting through the slots of the picnic bench. Names of constellations raced through her mind. Maybe his parents would've picked something celestial since they were both astrophysicists.

"Andromeda?"

Ethan's smile only rose. "Good thinking, going with a constellation, but no. It's Herbert."

Haley let his name roll through her mind before saying it out loud. "Ethan Herbert Pérez-Tremblay. *Okay*," she said the last word slowly.

He snuck a sip of his beer. "Told you Yeti was easier."

She shoved a swirl of spicy noodles in her mouth to keep her from saying something impulsive. After she'd fully chewed and swallowed, she asked, "Do you still want me to call you that?"

"Maybe every once in a while. I kind of got used to it." He poked at his dish with an unexpected shyness.

She nodded. "I can absolutely do that."

They ate in silence for a little while, listening to the brassy sounds of the guitarist's voice.

"Aren't you going to ask my last name?"

"Kineman," Ethan said to his plate, picking up a piece of chicken. When his eyes met her shocked ones, he asked, "What?"

Her brows dove together. "How did you know that?"

"You told me after your car accident. Remember?"

She didn't.

Wait . . . that's right. He'd asked what day it was, and she'd given him the typical person-place-date orientation answer.

"Okay, smart guy," Haley said, trying to recover from the reeling inundating her. "What's my middle name?"

"Sunshine?" The word came out with complete, endearing sincerity.

Trying to recall that vital function called breathing again, she plastered a teasing twist to her lips. "*Yeti.*"

His unexpected laugh overpowered the lyrics to "Grace Is Gone" and caused a few patrons at the nearest table to glance over.

Then Ethan muttered something in Spanish, shaking his head.

Haley couldn't help the ribbon of peace that wove through her. Hearing Spanish reminded her of a time when she'd felt loved, when Mama Nena's rapid, soothing lilt as she chatted with her sister on the phone had been the backdrop to Haley's kitchen table homework sessions. The soft blur of unknown words had been as comforting as freshly baked cookies.

Even still . . . Haley wanted to know what he'd said. "In English, please."

That wide grin fully curved his mouth before he stuffed it with noodles. "Maybe someday."

Chapter 24

"Wait, so if Paige is a geneticist working on pancreatic cancer, and your parents are brilliant astrophysicists, that makes you the black sheep of the family . . . or rather, the black yeti." From in front of him, Haley took her hand off their handrail to slap her forehead. "The clothing choice makes so much sense now."

"Ha. Ha. Very funny." Six more steps and he'd make her pay for poking at him.

Haley spun to face him, teetering a little in her retro white booties. Instinctively, Ethan steadied her with a hand to her waist.

"I guess I wasn't too far off with the genius joke. Seems like a family trait." That look was creeping over her features again, the one that had transformed her face at the restaurant.

"We're just people, Haley."

Her shoulders crawled up, an action that probably irritated her neck. "Incredibly intelligent people."

His palm smoothed up her back, his thumb drawing soothing circles just below her shoulder blades. "If it makes you feel better, Paige had the stomach flu last winter. I can one-hundred percent guarantee she had diarrhea."

The joke about unpleasant bowel distress should have made Haley laugh, but her lips downturned.

His eyes ticked to the hovering concrete slabs beneath them, trying another strategy. "The stair trolls are going to get us if we stay here much longer."

When she didn't tease him, when her body firmed with a rigidity that sent alarm corkscrewing through his stomach, Ethan wove both hands through her hair. "Hey. Talk to me."

Haley opened her mouth, but none of her beautiful, tumbling words came out.

Her silence punched the air out of him in one resounding swoop.

This was it.

He would have been lying if he hadn't been grimly anticipating this exact moment all evening. Though he'd covered his scars with his sweater and tie before Haley had arrived at his doorstep, the revolting memory of them had probably made enjoying her pad thai a challenge. Maybe that was why she'd struggled at the first restaurant. He'd interpreted it through his lens, thinking she was uncomfortable in that situation, but . . .

It had to be him.

His eyes pressed closed as the excruciating detonation made its mark.

Stupid.

He knew better than to want something like this, to think this was possible. And since Haley was one of the kindest people he'd ever met, it was probably knotting her up inside thinking of the nicest way to let him down, to tell him she regretted her decision.

His pin-pricked fingers pulled from her warmth. "I'm sorry." He pushed his hands into his pockets and receded a step.

"It's like . . ." Haley sucked in an uneven inhale, but Ethan couldn't look up.

He didn't want to see her face contort while she told him. He wanted the last memory of her to be the wry twist of her lips as she teased him while "Shake It Off" played softly through his speaker system moments ago.

"You know when your mind is stuck in a tailspin of catastrophic images? An asteroid hits the complex in a fiery blaze, a tsunami drenches the staircase with its incapacitating force, the earth quakes and opens up beneath us, swallowing us whole."

Ethan forced himself not to wince. This one time, he would have preferred her not to be hyperbolic.

"I only have a high school diploma and trade training. I mean, sure, I've educated myself with the best the internet and audiobooks have to offer, but that can't stand compared to the obvious brilliance and formal education of your family. Even with our varied backgrounds, there's the simple fact that you live here, and I live 2,264 miles away. And yes, I might have looked that up when I went to the restroom earlier."

His gaze snapped up to catch her somber sigh. "Aren't we doomed?"

Ethan frowned. "Doomed?"

Haley looked as desolate as he felt. "Yeah. How can this work?"

The action happened before his brain had processed it—bracketing her ribs and carrying her to the safety of their apartment landing. "You want this to work?"

He couldn't help that the words were rushed over her stunned and gaping mouth, that he'd pressed her frame onto the narrow space between their doors, that he was losing his mind waiting for her answer when all he wanted was to crush his lips to hers.

Her chest seesawed against him. "What—Did—Did you just carry me like a sack of potatoes?"

"You were trying to sacrifice us." His hands slid to her hips as his nose brushed hers.

"I will not be picked up and lugged around at will." Even though Haley tried to make her words sound firm, her eyelids fluttered closed.

Ethan was a second from covering her mouth with his own when the slap of sandals at the base of the stairs interrupted.

"Glad to see that turned out. Now, if you don't mind, I require assistance." Aster's scratchy voice ripped through the air like lightning, shattering the intimate moment and springing them apart.

"Um, hi," Haley said with a little wave. "Can I help?"

Aster looked her up and down, scowling. "Not in that thing, but that's fine. Muscles here can probably do it himself."

"Muscles?" Haley muttered under her breath.

"It's a long story," he whispered back before heading down the stairs.

Aster had learned his name, among other things, during the interrogation he'd unwittingly attended last night. Since she'd been wielding razor-sharp scissors with dangerous precision, Ethan had deemed it best to answer her questions.

The tap of Haley's heels kept time behind him as he followed Aster toward the pool area. Most of the complex's mesquite trees weren't taller than a one-story building, but the one outside the pool fence stretched an impressive twenty feet into the sky. Its thick, scratchy bark had been fortified by overflowing water from raucous cannonballers.

"You no-good, stinking rascal. See if I'll let you back in the apartment after this," Aster shouted her words toward the sky.

There could only be one person—or rather, creature—she was yelling at. The dim light of the nearby lamp post illuminated a satisfied-looking Sebastian stretched out on the topmost branch.

Ethan rubbed his temples.

"This is because I wouldn't buy those crickets he likes." Aster took one hand off her hip to gesture an arm toward the rebellious reptile. "They're too expensive. You don't need gourmet crickets. I spoil you enough as it is."

Haley stepped beside him, eyes lifted to find the green iguana amidst the dark tree bark.

"Well?" Aster gruffed at Ethan. "Go get him. I might be fit, but I'm well past tree climbing. And he can't stay out here. He'll get too cold when the temperature drops overnight." She craned her neck again, raising her voice. "Didn't think about that when you started this little tantrum, did you?"

With Aster's *humph*, Ethan turned to give Haley an apologetic look, but Haley was not only entertained by this entire exchange, she was practically vibrating with delight.

"The upper branches probably won't support his weight," Haley said.

"I was worried about that too. Here." Aster picked up a pair of floral palazzo pants from the sidewalk. "They'll be short on you, but they'll cover all the necessary bits. Just tuck your dress into them." Aster shuffled over to Haley, expanding the waistband.

Haley gripped his upper arm for support, lifting a foot toward the awaiting fabric.

"No." The rough word escaped like a bullet. He cleared his throat and softened his tone. "That won't be necessary. I can get him myself."

Haley had run her hand over the fruit-covered fabric with a satisfied smile no less than six times during their date. There was no way Ethan was going to let her tear up what must have been a favorite dress.

"Bossy," Aster quipped.

"Only in the best way." Haley softly shouldered their cantankerous neighbor.

Aster laser-surveyed Haley again, *mm-hmmed* her approval, and swung an impatient arm at him. "I haven't got all night."

Ethan sidestepped a baby barrel cactus on the way over, weaving through the sporadic patches of dry bushes. Mesquite trees weren't made for climbing. Their trunks were gnarled and abrasive, and their branches were covered in radial spines. Like everything in the desert, they managed to stay alive by protecting what water they held within and preventing themselves from being eaten. How Sebastian got that high without puncturing himself was mystifying.

A pursed exhale left Ethan's lips.

The trunk picked and scraped at his hands and sweater, snatching little gray cashmere souvenirs as he traversed. He'd expected Haley's voice to chase him up the tree. A part of him had been looking forward to it, knowing her conversational nature would irritate Aster. Instead, the incessant whooshing of his own scattered heartbeat kept him company.

Once his feet had lifted him ten feet off the ground, Ethan had to close his eyes and press his forehead against the coarse bark. His lungs strained to pull breath after tight breath, never quite filling all the way. The rhythmic whooshing in his ears had turned over to a high-pitched ringing. Strange places began squeezing with pain—his earlobes, the backs of his vibrating knees, the insteps of his feet.

"I thought yetis were close with the reptile community."

One of his downcast eyes reluctantly cracked open, and there she was—her tea-length skirt brushing against the tall dry grasses at the base of the tree, her cardigan-covered arms hugging herself, her lips curved into that devilish little smirk. Looking down from this height should have sent him into a tumbling spiral, but all Ethan could think about was, once he survived this impossible endeavor, he was going to kiss that smile off Haley's lips.

"Come on, then," Aster commanded. "You've been through worse than this. Get him. Get down. Then you're done."

Ethan ran a sweaty palm over his hip, and it came back sticky with sap. A smattering of stars glimmered beyond the shadowy branches above. The scaly creature must have taken pity on him while he was hyperventilating, because Sebastian was now closer to the trunk of the tree, only two feet away.

The next few motions were so quick it was almost an out-of-body experience. There was a push of a calf muscle, an extension of a foot and hand, a securement of a—gratefully compliant—reptile by the belly, all followed by a brisk, blind repel down the tree. Somewhere in there, a needly spine scratched at his ear and another ripped a hole in his slacks, but Ethan couldn't care less.

Subduing the shaking of his fingers as he extended Sebastian to Aster was futile. His brain was too busy processing the fact he was alive and how amazing the firm sidewalk felt beneath his dress shoes.

Aster cradled Sebastian over her shoulder with one hand while the other gave Ethan's cheek a not-so-gentle pat. "Not bad." Then she spun on her heel and marched away, scolding her cold-blooded friend.

"Interesting," Haley mused, joining him on the sidewalk.

"She's something."

Aster aggressively opened her apartment door and disappeared into the jungle beyond.

He shook his head, turning to find Haley's studious gaze fixed on him with that unnerving focus.

"I don't mean her. She's *fabulous*. I mean you. You're clearly afraid of heights, but you helped her anyway. Why?"

A small shrug lifted his shoulders. "It wasn't a choice."

"It wasn't a choice *for you*. There's a difference."

A few heartbeats of cricket song settled between them. Haley's contemplative expression softened when her focus snagged on his hair. She plucked a piece of bark away before slowly laying his disheveled locks back in place.

"There," she said with a final sweep. "You're presentable."

"I look okay?"

When her faded-blue eyes settled on his, Ethan was certain she understood the question beneath his question.

Her fingertips ran the line of his jaw, the sensation jumbling his barely settled heart rate. "I was attracted to you when you were in sweats with a beard and long hair." Her gaze quickly draped over his disheveled clothes. "It's honestly a little intimidating the way you look now."

His mouth moved to argue, to remind her that she might be disgusted by what was under his newly acquired finery.

Haley pressed her thumb over his lips. "You said you'd trust me."

When her other hand settled over his chest, an erratic breath stumbled into his constricted lungs. Two layers of clothing separated her palm from his scarred skin, but it'd been a lifetime since a woman had touched him like this. His eyes darted over her face, and her small smile only grew.

"Why don't you walk me home, make me forget about gravity for a minute or two, and then we'll say goodnight."

As relief poured through him, the words he'd muttered in Spanish at the brewery flitted through his brain again.

It's like you were made for me.

Even that sentence was impossible—had escaped unwittingly. He didn't deserve this, didn't deserve her, but it was undeniable how Haley filled every somber, empty hole within him.

Her lips grazed his cheek before she released him, leaning back. "Besides"—that twist was playing with her mouth again—"tomorrow is a busy day. You've got lots of heroes to foil. I've got a shift to work. And then we've got margaritas to drink."

Chapter 25

As Haley slid the bolt of her front door securely in place, she couldn't think of a better first date. If there was a First Date Hall of Fame, she could've submitted this one and won—even with the iguana retrieval.

Especially because of it.

All her cells were oscillating from within, having their own little dance party. Haley kept her feet in place on the chance that Ethan could hear the tap of her booties on the linoleum but allowed every other movement to be uninhibited. There was The Sprinkler, good old-fashioned fist pumping, and some strange waggle she'd just invented. She even threw in the YMCA.

Her dress skirt billowed around her almost artistically when Haley collapsed on her couch. A smile rose as she ran her fingertips over the fabric. This beautiful garment would always be associated with Ethan's supple lips.

It was odd that so much had transpired in a mere forty-eight hours.

It *felt* like two lifetimes.

With every positive thing that happened this evening, insidious spikes slithered down Haley's spine because, on the other side of the country, Remmy was suffering. Her best friend had become unhealthily obsessed with Marcus's every move, subsequently stewing over the possibilities for his weekly Thursday absence.

"Call girl with a tight schedule?"

"The only night the other woman's ex has her kids?"

While Haley had been working at the Red Cross earlier, she'd tried to rein in Remmy's fears with more logical answers but had a hard time coming up with plausible excuses. She'd been so focused on keeping Remmy from a tailspin that Haley hadn't even mentioned the kiss with Ethan that morning.

Her fingertips ran over her swollen lips as her phone rang from within her purse. Haley must have telepathically summoned her best friend's call. When Marcus's smiling face glowed on the vibrating screen, her nose scrunched.

Haley sucked in a deep breath, calming herself so she didn't bark, *"What do you want, you unfaithful scum?"* instead of, *"Hello."*

"Hi, Marcus," she said as she strode to her bedroom, taking off her earrings.

"Hey. I know it's late, but I'm worried about Remmy." Tension ran through Marcus's usually velvety voice.

Worried you'll get caught, jerk bag?

Haley swallowed, trying to keep her tone even. "Oh? How so?"

"It's really late, and she's not home. When I call her phone, it goes straight to voicemail."

It was past midnight on the East Coast, and Remmy was an in-bed-by-ten kind of girl if she had work the next day. The last time Remmy had texted was around 4 p.m. EST., saying she couldn't listen to Marcus breathing and was going to work out.

A ribbon of worry poked Haley in the rib. "She didn't come home after the gym?"

"No, she did," he said. "But then she said she needed to drop something off at Aunt Tara's and never came home."

Internally, Haley laughed as she perched on her bed and began unlacing her boots.

"I'm sure she just lost track of time while visiting." The lie sounded fake, even to her ears, but there was no way she was assuaging Marcus's fears if he was cheating on her best friend.

"I'm worried. What if she was in an accident on the way there or back? I don't have her aunt's phone number. Do you?"

The escalating panic in his voice made Haley pause. "Marcus?"

"Maybe I should drive by and see if her car's there," he said, not hearing her. "Yeah. She has to be there. If not, I don't know what I'll—" Haley could hear his uneven swallow. "I guess I'll call the hospital?"

Her heart wrenched.

"You know what? I'm going to head over there. I've got to see for myself. I need to know she's okay."

Haley's arm shot out as if to grab him. "Marcus, wait."

"Why?"

A cautious breath filled her lungs. "What do you do Thursdays after work?"

"Oh crap. She noticed. She had to have noticed if she said something to you." His sigh flowed over the phone. "Okay, just don't say anything. I was going to call you anyway with a heads up, but I wanted to talk to her dad first."

"What are you talking about?" Her forehead wrinkled.

"I'm going to ask Remmy to marry me. I've been taking dancing lessons on Thursdays after work because she always makes fun of me." Remmy *had* been particularly vocal about Marcus's lack of rhythm and the fact that every time they went out, he was "all elbows."

"I didn't want to embarrass her when I asked her to marry me. I planned on taking her on a trip Valentine's Day weekend and going the whole nine yards. Fancy dinner, show her my new moves, and—"

"You need to ask her now," Haley interrupted, gripping her comforter with her free hand.

"But I've got it all planned out. I'm going to put the ring in a champagne glass and everything."

Haley shook her head until lingering neck pain tweaked. "Do you have the ring now?"

"Yeah, I picked it up at the jeweler's yesterday. I had it custom made, so I had to drive to Baltimore to get it."

Her forehead fell into her palm. *That* explains his three-hour absence.

"She's worried you're not interested." Haley didn't want to fully betray her best friend's trust, but she didn't want Marcus to wait two weeks and give Remmy three ulcers in the meantime.

A choking sound echoed over the phone. "I love Remmy more than I ever thought possible. I can't imagine my life without her. She's *everything*."

Haley's eyes misted over, but she kept the emotion out of her voice. "Then go tell her that right now."

"Okay . . . okay." Haley could see him nodding along, mentally adjusting to the change in plans. "Thanks, Lee."

Haley was in her llama-print pajamas, scrubbing off makeup, when her phone pinged with a text. Remmy's tear-streaked face was smushed up next to Marcus's, her fully fanned-out hand below their chins. On her ring finger was the most gorgeous antique-style engagement ring—just the thing Remmy would have picked for herself. *He proposed!* captioned the joyous image.

Haley was typing congratulations when the phone rang in her hands, so she told her best friend congratulations instead.

"You're going to be my maid of honor. You know there's no discussion about that!" Remmy squealed, prompting Haley to hold the phone away from her ear.

"Of course!" she answered, her cheeks pinched from her humongous grin.

A small part of her wanted to share her own joy but knew this wasn't the time. Her relationship with Ethan wasn't going anywhere—not on her end, anyway. He might decide that their differences or the distance was too great, but witnessing a terrified Ethan climb a tree to help a neighbor solidified the twitching racing up and down her spinal column.

Haley knew better than to let go of a good man.

After a little more conversation, an ecstatic Remmy ended their call. As Haley lowered her phone from her ear, she grinned at the mascara smudges in the sink—each its own wispy mark on the otherwise unremarkable porcelain. Her thumb was scrubbing away the one that resembled a miniscule bird when her phone pinged again.

A tiny, formidable-looking yeti glowered at her from the small circle to the left of Ethan's text message. Haley tucked her bottom lip between her teeth, remembering his rumbly laugh when she'd saved the image to his "Ethan Herbert Pérez-Tremblay AKA Yeti" heading. The entire time she searched for the accented é to perfect his long name, Ethan had laughed and swiped unsuccessfully for her phone, insisting she label him "Yeti" instead.

Ethan: *When do you need to leave for work tomorrow? I'll drive you.*

Haley: *You can't be my personal car service.*

Ethan: *Why not? You like my car, called it "hot" even.*

A blush crawled up her neck and warmed her ears, but her forehead pinched with indignation.

Haley: *Because I said so.*

Ethan: *Now who's the two-year-old?*

She sent him a tongue-out emoji and could almost feel his exasperated sigh through the wall.

Ethan: *If you don't let me drive you to work, I'll break into your apartment and fix that drawer to the left of your range that the manager said he was too busy for. Then I'll put everything away backward just to thwart you. Forks mixed with spoons, knives fraternizing with reusable straws. It'll be chaos. Mwahahaha.*

Though Ethan's lengthy threat should have brought forward a bursting laugh, saliva caught in her tight throat. Haley had mentioned spilling her silverware all over the place at dinner—she complained about it often—but she hadn't mentioned the drawer's location. Her brain racked through each memory, each conversation. She hadn't mentioned the specifics about the drawer since she'd delivered him apple muffins—weeks ago.

Haley: *Meet me on the balcony.*

Dots hovered and disappeared, hovered and disappeared.

Haley knew Ethan wasn't ready for their relationship to be more physical, that had been apparent the second his chest shuddered when she placed her hand on it. Ethan also didn't believe that she could want him. She'd seen it wash over his gorgeous eyes, twitch the corner of his jaw, and tighten the muscles of his shoulders.

Fortunately, she had time—a whole month, in fact—to convince him. Though Haley wasn't particularly good about being patient, the tugging deep in her stomach told her that this would be worth it.

Haley: *Just to talk*

Ethan: *K*

"Hey." He opened his glass door a few seconds after she closed hers. One of his navy sweatshirts topped off his flannel pants. "What's up?"

"You want to fix my silverware drawer?" All her blood rushed to the surface of her skin, though her bare feet began freezing on the cold concrete.

Ethan blinked and then tucked his hands into his sweatshirt pocket. "Yeah. It bothers you."

Haley nodded, suppressing her desire to act until she received the answer to her next question. "It does. Especially with how I have to open it."

His brows quirked like she'd lost her mind. "*Right.*"

She crossed her arms over her chest to hide the vibrating sensation shaking every cell in her body. "And how's that, exactly?"

"Up, down, and to the left." He frowned. "Are you mad at me? I was joking about breaking in. I'd never violate your privacy like that."

Her step forward was so quick Ethan startled slightly. "I know I asked you out here just to talk, but would it be okay if I kissed you?"

His perplexed expression dropped as eager hands wove around her waist. Her mouth was on his in an instant, the taste of spearmint mixing pleasantly with his clove scent. Ethan groaned as his tongue spun around hers like they'd been separated for months instead of minutes.

"Why do you remember those tiny details about my apartment?"

"Because you told me." His hands traveled up the sides of her thin pajama top to bury into her hair.

Her head automatically dipped back into his fingers. "But nobody listens to everything I say. Even Remmy checks out after a while. Half of it is insignificant."

"Nothing you say is insignificant." Ethan's lips traveled down the column of her neck. "I feel like every time you speak, your words etch into my skin."

A rasp broke from her mouth.

If Ethan would've let her, Haley would've backed him into his apartment that second. She would've shown him how transcendent it felt to be heard, how much that sentence meant to her.

Then the tip of his tongue teased her collarbone, and arguments for holding out lost the debate raging in her veins. Haley grabbed his front pocket and yanked his firm body against hers. Her fingers burrowed inside, flattening against his hardened abdomen through a soft layer of cotton.

"What do you keep in there?" Ethan's erratic breaths puffed over her skin as she spoke. "Nuclear codes are obviously out, but maybe the secret recipe for Coca-Cola? A way to make puppies never age? A key to a time machine?"

His husky chuckle sent sparks sprinting to her toes. "You're the perfect amount of trouble, you know that?"

When he leaned forward and nipped the crook of her neck, a pliable moan fell from her slack lips. Everything in Ethan tensed as a stifled growl resonated against her. With a heaving exhale, he used his hip-filled hands to separate their bodies.

"What time—" He cleared his rough voice. "What time am I driving you tomorrow?"

Every cell in her wanted to pout, but her scattered lungs managed a coherent answer. "I work at seven, but I like to get everyone donuts on Mondays."

"Of course you do." His words weren't poking or jarring. They were said with uninhibited affection, making her heart thrash in her chest.

"It's hard to have a case of *the Mondays* with a cruller between your teeth."

Ethan's smile only widened, sending that shimmering sensation sweeping her body again.

"Six-twenty, please."

"I'll see you then." Then his hands framed her face, and Haley saw him get lost, witnessed the struggle to set a simple kiss on her lips and turn his body away. Each inch in the opposite direction felt like pulling magnets apart. Only when his hand held his door handle like it was a rope keeping him from being sucked into quicksand did he look back.

"Goodnight, Haley."

"Goodnight."

The instant his door closed, the world came rushing back in. Everything was overstimulating.

The coyotes yipping and barking in the neighborhood beyond, telling the others where they were, was earsplitting. The tendrils of cold that'd been tapping at her toes spun up her calves beneath her pajama leggings and buried into her bones. The dryness of the desert was stuffy and overbearing in the loss of Ethan's scent. Even the remaining mint on her tongue turned sour.

Once returned to the warmth of her apartment, Haley's unsteady feet tread over the utilitarian carpet and dropped her on the bed.

There was only one place she wanted to be tonight, and that was unattainable.

An impatient inhale filled her lungs to the brim, and she forced herself to count to three before letting it out.

Haley snatched her phone from its tossed, mid-bed location and stretched out on her stomach. Remmy had sent close-up pictures of her ring while Haley had been outside. After responding with an exorbitant amount of heart emojis, Haley pulled open OnlyApp and re-read Zach Abrams's response from yesterday before typing her own.

Hey, Zach Abrams. That's cool. I'm partial to Audis. Black ones. Full disclosure, I never thought you'd text me back—or that your assistant would text me back. If this is your PA—what's up? I hope he treats you well! But back to what I was saying . . . I never expected you (anybody) to see these. Embarrassing, I know. But since you have, I feel like I should let you know I appreciate your time and won't be bothering you with my ramblings any longer.

Her index finger hovered over the send button, frozen.

If I'm REALLY being honest, I might have initiated these messages with some far-fetched notion that, in some alternate timeline, we'd meet, you'd fall in love with me, and well . . . roll credits. Happily ever after, etc. But . . .

Haley paused, biting her thumbnail.

I'm pretty sure I'm already living some version of that with an infuriating, yet incredible, man who somehow understands me. All of me. Even the messy, annoying parts. I'm not sure if you're aware, since women (present company formerly included) fling themselves at you daily, but that's pretty rare. So, I'm going to hold onto it as tightly as I can.

Before she could second-guess anything, Haley clicked *send*. A rushed exhale sailed over her teeth, but regret didn't infiltrate a single cell in her body. Instead, a buoyant giddiness simmered beneath her skin as she flopped on her back. Now, all she had to figure out was how to calm down enough to get some sleep.

Chapter 26

"The usual?" Zane asked his eight-year-old daughter, Caroline. She nodded without a word, perching on the edge of a cafe chair. "And a flat white if memory serves?"

"No. Please. I can get it," Ethan said.

His friend's disarming, lopsided grin did nothing to quell the swarm of angry hornets stirring beneath Ethan's skin.

"You got dinner last night. I insist. You can help me out by keeping Caroline company."

Before he could argue, Zane kissed his daughter's crown and loped away. Caroline pulled a pencil from the front pocket of her starchy navy pinafore and began drawing faint lines over the blank page in her green, ringed journal.

Ethan got the impression she didn't *need* company.

His memories of Caroline had been of a child who refused to wear shoes. She was often covered in chocolate and, occasionally, cholla cactus spines. The cheerless girl in front of him was an entirely different person, more like a perturbed fifty-year-old administrative assistant than a third grader. Even her short blonde hair was yanked into a severe pony at the nape of her neck, her spotless white polo fully buttoned. The only childlike thing about her was her coral, sequined shoes.

Ethan attempted to swallow the discomfort clawing up his throat and let his gaze wander. Ground Street Coffee looked familiar and different at the same time. Multi-colored umbrellas adorned the new tables, but the burnt-orange exterior, the hand-carved wooden sign above the entrance, and the purple, nicked door remained the same.

Over a dozen road bikes leaned against the metal railing separating the business complex from the walking path that followed the Rillito River. Cyclists wrapped in brightly colored spandex relaxed at various tables, their cycling shoes clicking on the cement when they went back inside for a refill or another fruit tart.

Though Ethan had stopped coming to visit several months before his accident, many memories were imprinted on the cement slab beneath his feet. When he'd been in town, he and his friends often gathered here. In college, Kevin and Kyle had worked as baristas before Kevin began dating Becca, the part owner and head pastry chef. A smile ghosted Ethan's lips, remembering how Kevin had denied their involvement initially, even after he'd come back from his lunch break with flour handprints on his backside.

Of course, that was before Ethan had screwed everything up, and fate decided to punish him for his poor choices.

"What are you drawing?" Ethan leaned over Caroline's sketch, attempting to quell the surging memories.

Two elbows flung over the page as Caroline glared with pinched eyes.

"Sorry." Ethan stepped back, collapsing into the chair across the sun-warmed table.

Gratefully, the awkward silence sitting between them wasn't silent. The boisterous voices of the cycling group peppered over "Quelqu'un m'a dit" crooning through patio speakers built into sandy false rocks.

Zane returned with a small tray containing a mug of black coffee, a hot chocolate with whipped cream and rainbow sprinkles, and his flat white. Ethan half expected his friend to keep the sugary drink while giving Caroline the mug filled with bitter blackness. When Caroline dropped a finger full of whipped cream into her mouth, Zane smiled.

"Can I pet the dogs?" Caroline was already rising, cupping her purple mug with both hands—her sketchbook secured beneath her arm.

"Sure thing. Say hi to Liz and Tina for me."

Three white bichons were tying their leads into knots next to the cafe-provided water bowls. At the nearby table, two women with cropped gray hair rocked with laughter, sharing pound cake and a porcelain pot of tea.

Both men watched Caroline's small form become enveloped in two lavish, maternal hugs. When Caroline cracked a smile, Zane rubbed his chest with his knuckles, crinkling the sepia band image of his The Verve T-shirt.

The ease that perpetually accompanied his agreeable friend melted away. For the first time since he'd been in Zane's presence, Ethan witnessed the effort he'd been exerting to make everything appear tranquil.

"I'm sorry." Ethan had said it four thousand times during dinner last night, but he'd never be able to say it enough. There'd been so much that he should've been there for.

Zane adjusted his glasses, causing some of his messy blond ringlets to rearrange themselves around his frames. "No. It's not you. It just takes her a while to warm up to new people."

Ethan winced. He wasn't a new person, but the last time he'd seen Zane's daughter, she'd been three, and her life hadn't been decimated by a sick mother and divorce.

Caroline opened her sketchbook to the supportive *Ooohs* and *Ahhs* of the older women, and Zane let out a staggered sigh.

Ethan's stomach felt like it was trying to digest itself. "I don't know how to make this up to you."

His friend glanced up, almost surprised to see him there. "Oh, no. No worries. Seriously."

"Zane, knock it off." His hand fisted on his thigh. "I was terrible to you and everyone. And then, when you all tried to help me, I selfishly wallowed. I couldn't even be bothered to notice that there are other people in the world with their own problems. I've been a self-centered jerk. Let's call it as it is."

"One-hundred percent agree." Kyle's voice rumbled over Ethan's shoulder. "I'm assuming, by being here, you're taking steps to rectify that?"

Wisps of steam from his mug rose over Kyle's maroon *Art is for Everyone* T-shirt. Kevin tromped up beside him with a reusable tumbler, wearing the same shirt.

"Where's *Haley?*" Except, Kevin sang *"Haley"* like Frankie Valli sang *"Sherry."*

"Who's Haley?" Zane leaned back and crossed a leg over his knee, assuming his casual, unaffected pose.

"A woman who has Ethan flummoxed." Kevin grinned, taking a sip.

"Really?"

"You could see his heart beating in his eyes when she sang." A dramatic hand slapped Kevin's chest. "Adorable."

"Why didn't you mention this last night?"

Ethan's focus had been on making up for all the time he hadn't been there for Zane. He'd listened to the story of Tessa's diagnosis, treatment, and recovery; his genuinely overjoyed, proud-dad stories of Caroline; and allowed his friend to omit the details of his recently finalized divorce.

"It's new," Ethan hedged.

"Did she ever end up making it into Zach Abrams's film?" Kyle asked.

A bubble of bile splashed over Ethan's tongue. He'd been itching to ask Haley if she responded to the movie star but was afraid of the answer.

Over the week, they'd fallen into a comfortable rhythm. He'd drive her to and from work, then she'd change out of her scrubs and meet him on their shared balcony. Eventually, Ethan would convince her to let him take her to dinner. Each night ended the same, with a reality-shifting kiss.

His twitchy muscles misfired in strange places—triceps, shins, lower back—thinking about the way Haley melted each time their lips met. Even though their last kiss had been moments before he'd arrived at Ground Street Coffee, when he'd dropped Haley off at the auto shop to retrieve her car, it already felt like twelve years.

Ethan rubbed the back of his neck. "No."

Kevin's shoulders bounced. "It was a hard gig to get."

"Where's Rowan?" Ethan glanced around the busy courtyard, looking for the fifth 'dorm bro.'

"Group," his friends said in unison.

When confusion flooded Ethan's cheekbones, Zane explained, "He's combined group therapy with rock climbing on Mt. Lemmon. Every once in a while, that schedule overlaps with us getting together."

Zane asked Kyle a question, and they dissolved into easy chatter about the theater youth workshop Kevin and Kyle were leading this afternoon. His friends' voices wove under and over each other like an often-read letter, the paper softened at the creases. When Ethan shared that he no longer worked for OnlyApp and, instead, developed apps for various school systems to share information with parents, Kyle's gaze lost its frosty edge. Each teasing jab and subsequent bout of laughter settled the buzzing in Ethan's spine. Just one thing kept picking at him like a spiny thistle.

He could've been here.

What would the last few years have looked like if Ethan could've had this level of connection every other Saturday?

"I'm done." Caroline stepped beside Zane, journal hugged to her chest.

His head dipped toward his daughter. "Which cyclist did you use today?"

"I used him." Her brown eyes fixed on Ethan with a guarded expression.

"Oh." A slight glint of surprise crested and then waned on Zane's brow.

Caroline's vision narrowed as she frowned. "I got your cupid's bow wrong." She flicked open the book in her hands, readying her pencil against the page.

An incredibly intricate pencil portrait laid on the seven-by-ten-inch page. It looked as if a skilled adult had sketched it, not a barely four-foot-tall girl. Caroline's nimble fingers erased and then retraced Ethan's upper lip, glancing up only once as she drew. All the while, his friends regarded the entire exchange as commonplace.

"That's better." Caroline's shoulders settled with her words. "Do you want it?"

"Um." Ethan's eyes darted briefly to Zane's. "Yes, please."

A small smile shifted over Caroline's lips as she tore along the sketchbook's perforated edge.

"Don't forget to sign it." Kevin bent to affectionately elbow her in the ribs. "That way, if he's ever down on his luck, he can sell it for millions."

Caroline looked like the child she was when her eyes rolled, but she signed the page in looping, messy cursive.

"Thank you," Ethan said, accepting the drawing.

Acid pulsed through his veins instead of blood. He didn't deserve a gift like this without earning a place in his friends' lives first.

Caroline looked at her neon, houndstooth-patterned watch. "We have to go, Dad."

"Right." Zane moved to pick up their dishes, but Kevin waved him off.

While Caroline explained to Kyle that, as checker team captain, it was unacceptable for her to be tardy, Zane enveloped Ethan in a hug much like the one he'd received last night—uninhibited and comforting. "It's nice to have you here, Ethan."

Zane was tucking Caroline into his Volvo fifty feet away when the question that had been poking at Ethan all morning refused to stay quiet any longer. "What happened? Zane filled me in on everything about his life over the past few years, except for why he and Tessa separated."

Kevin and Kyle shared a look.

"It was a heart-wrenching decision for Tessa," Kevin began. "Almost dying made her reevaluate what she wanted. She wanted that all-encompassing, firecracker love before it was too late. For herself, but also for Zane." He frowned. "They're still incredibly close, but it's like they've always been. Friends and partners. The whole divorce proceeding was one of the most zen processes I've ever seen."

A heavy pause settled between them.

"But after working to keep his best friend alive and his family together for two years, Zane hadn't seen that coming," Kyle supplied.

"Damn."

"Yeah," Kevin and Kyle said in unison.

"Check in on him." Kyle's words were as taut as a steel bridge cable.

"I will." Ethan tried to infuse his voice with the sincerity vibrating his muscles.

His friend surveyed him for several beats before nodding, smoothing a hand over his beard. "Okay. If you keep this up, I might consider inviting you to my wedding."

A slab of concrete bashed his skull. "You're engaged?"

"You've missed quite a lot." Kyle waited a beat before continuing, "Her name is Dani. Maybe someday you'll get to meet her."

"I'd really like that," Ethan said, determined to prove to Kyle he was here to stay. "Congratulations." Another thought occurred to him. "Is Rowan married too?"

"No." Kevin snorted. "He was in a long-term relationship for a while, but that ended six months ago. I think, deep down, he's still waiting for Claire to come home."

"She's still traveling?"

Claire had left Tucson to hike the Pacific Crest Trail after their junior year. Since Rowan had been smitten with his sister's best friend since he'd been thirteen, he'd taken her absence hard.

At least Ethan had been there to help Rowan nurse that heartbreak. He resolved to help Zane through *this* one.

"I think so. He doesn't bring her up much," Kyle said.

"Ah."

"We've got to run, but . . . this was nice." Kevin smiled, his eyes crinkling at the corners. "Next time, bring Haley to say hi."

Haley would be overjoyed to join them for their coffee ritual. She'd already informed Ethan that she was following Kevin,

Kyle, *and* All World Theater on OnlyApp. Ethan's mind did a quick calculation. He could bring her in two weeks, but the Saturday following that, she'd be back home in Maryland. The beat of the catchy house music mimicked the ticking clock Ethan felt in his chest.

Chapter 27

It was déjà vu. Haley was standing outside the auto shop with the ubiquitous scent of tires accosting her nose, but what the kind auto-shop manager had just explained made absolutely no sense. Her right hand cradled her phone while she stood in front of her loaned car, its pristine bumper glinting in the sunlight. She should have been diligently capturing pictures of the beautiful, fully repaired car to send along to its owner—who'd yet to respond to Haley's email about the accident—but her thumb clicked through her contacts instead.

Her dad picked up on the third ring. "Lee." He paused. "Everything okay?"

"You paid for my repair?" Her voice shouldn't have sounded so skeptical. It's not like he was a horrible man who never provided for her, but there was a strong expectation that once Haley became employed, she should pay for herself. He hadn't helped her financially since she graduated high school.

"I did. I hope that's okay."

Haley rubbed her brow with her wrist, the saguaro keychain of her keys dangling into her field of view. "Yeah, it's fine . . . but why?"

A motorcycle ripped down the nearby main street, the sound of its noisy engine trailing. "You said you were concerned about the cost."

She had, but Haley never expected that he'd been listening.

"Also, I felt guilty, and it gave me some way to help you."

Her forehead pinched. "Guilty about what?"

The sound of a cabinet closing was layered over her father's noisy exhale. "About a lot of things. I . . . uh . . . I've been reading this book about improving relationships."

Haley couldn't stop her lips from separating in a confused ellipse. The man who never spoke about anything but work, and occasionally baseball, was reading self-help books? It made sense that she had poured through dozens in the aftermath of Jason's cruelty, but the idea of her father cracking open a Brené Brown book was like someone telling Haley she'd been breathing syrup instead of air.

"It's helping me realize I haven't been the best father. I—" He sighed. "I was too caught up in your mom leaving. I figured since I wasn't good enough for her, I'd never be good enough for you."

Ringing in Haley's ears reverberated in the space her father had left open with his pause.

He cleared his throat. "The book showed me I was too focused on my feelings of worthlessness, and because of that, I was an absent father." Her pulse slammed the sides of her neck as another pause settled over the line. "I'm sorry."

Haley's back hit the side of the car before she slid to the uneven, pebbly asphalt below. All this time, her quiet father had been doubting his own value, not finding *her* lacking.

"Maybe," he continued, "if it's okay with you . . . we could, uh, talk every once in a while."

A jagged stone stuck to her left palm as she brought her fingers to bracket her forehead. The earth lurched, dizzying, to the left. "S—sure."

"Good. Good." Haley could picture him nodding, running that nick raw in the kitchen counter. "How's work?"

A thonk accompanied the bursting laugh as the back of her head rested on the door. After that impassioned, unexpected speech—the one she'd never dreamed she'd receive—Haley should've predicted he'd start on familiar ground.

"Work's good," she said, the beginnings of a smile curling her lips.

"Did I miss something?"

The sun felt like it was shining from within, each ray streaming through the spaces between her ribs. "No, Dad. Everything's fine. Do you want to hear about what I've been doing between shifts?"

For the first time in years, she heard her father's small grin in his words. "I'd like that."

Haley's heart somersaulted as her smile broadened. "For starters, I've eaten more cilantro than I thought humanly possible . . ."

◊◊◊

The wind gave Haley's cheek a not-so-affectionate pinch, challenging her perched position atop her car's hood. Though the air had been calm when she'd left the auto shop, it had rattled her windshield wipers as she drove up the single-lane road to her current location. Ethan had estimated that coffee with his friends would take about an hour or two, leaving her plenty of time to explore "A" Mountain.

From her vantage point, the disjointed, silky wisps of cirrus clouds crowding the sky almost took on a playful quality. Cherubic. Spiraling. Though the twenty-two-mile-per-hour wind thrashed at the low-lying foliage, the creosote branches squeaked when they rubbed against each other. If this wind had been ripping through Maysville, the stately oak and hickory trees would have launched a much louder protest.

Beyond the neat squares of glass and beige stucco, the Catalina Mountains blended seamlessly with the Rincons—like two friends clasping hands over the horizon. Haley's eyes traced each granite ridge and depression. The tan etched hollows reminded her of a cartographer's depiction of ranges she'd been forced to memorize in middle school.

Haley let a contented sigh join the gale as her mind replayed her recently disconnected phone call. Not only had her father listened to her, but he added a few modest details from his week as well. She didn't have a framework to fully explain the conversation she'd just had, but it felt like being snuggled in warm, fluffy blankets.

When her hair whipped around her face and slapped her on the lips, Haley reluctantly retreated to the shelter of her sedan and dialed Remmy. Her best friend had been swamped with work and the fact that she was soon to be a *Mrs.*, so although they texted daily, calls had been relegated to the weekend.

"Hello, Mrs. Hughes." Haley smiled, putting in her earbuds before shifting into gear so another sightseer could enjoy the view.

"Jones-Hughes. Or maybe just Jones." Remmy gave an exasperated huff. "I don't know if I'm going to change my name."

"You don't have to." Haley waved a thank you to the car, letting her into traffic.

"Yeah, I know. Only one of ten thousand details I need to decide on between now and next summer." Another sigh bounded over the line.

"Take it day by day. I'm sure everything is being thrown at you right now because your family's overjoyed, and everyone has an opinion." Remmy's snort lifted Haley's lips. "When I get home, I'll help you. Remember how good I was with binder organization for school? We'll get you a wedding binder and break the whole thing into little digestible bites."

"Seriously, Lee. What would I do without you?"

"Cease to function," she deadpanned. "You'd just lie there in a puddle of your own urine."

Remmy made a *gah* noise. "I'm not helpless."

"No, you're not, and now you've been reminded of that." It was hard to keep the cheeky smile out of her voice.

"Jerk."

"You *love* me," she sing-songed.

Haley could feel the eye-roll.

"Should I put Zach Abrams down as your plus-one?" Remmy asked.

Her friend texted daily, asking if the movie star had messaged her again. Haley answered each question truthfully—no—but hadn't explained the valid reason *why*.

Memories of Ethan swirled. The way her scalp ached until his fingers burrowed in her hair. The way his smile and laugh were easier and easier for her to attain. The way her chest settled whenever he was near, sighing with contentment.

Haley wove down the mountain road, the skyline view disappearing into a neighborhood. "No. I don't think he'd want to attend after I told him I'm not interested."

"You did what?!" Haley winced at Remmy's ear-splitting question. "*Why?*"

"Because I kissed Yeti."

"Explain. Now. On video call."

"I'm driving," Haley said through a laugh, turning on her blinker. "You'll have to settle for a verbal recounting."

By the time she'd satisfied Remmy's need for specifics, Haley was in her parking spot and had converted the call to video. Marcus tried to look busy in the background but gave himself up when he began dusting a glass of water.

"I'm not *surprised*, surprised." Remmy paused, tapping her lip. "I'm surprised, but not surprised. You know?"

Haley suppressed her grin. "No, because it sounds like I broke you, and now you're only allowed to say the word *surprised*."

"I don't like that I don't know him." Remmy scrunched her nose, leaning back against her white tufted couch.

She let a sprinkle of hope whizz through her veins. "He might come to visit."

"And when would that be?"

"I don't know. It's all very new." Haley shifted in her seat, trying to see Ethan's parking spot. When shiny blackness peeked out from in front of a beaten-up conversion van, her lips lifted on their own.

"Hmmm." Remmy's non-verbal comment pulled her gaze back to the screen.

"What?"

"Nothing," she scoffed. "Just be safe, and use protection, and—"

"Thanks, *Mom*." Haley let her eyes fly wide. "But I'm twenty-seven, not seventeen. I know how condoms work."

Not that she and Ethan had gone further than a sweeping goodnight kiss. Haley would have happily spent their evenings tangled up in each other, but Ethan was still holding back.

Remmy put a hand up in surrender before her face sobered. "It's just . . ."

"What?"

Her shoulders heaved with a sigh. "Long distance is hard, Lee."

An invisible hand punched Haley in the ribs. "I know that."

"Like, really hard. That summer Marcus did an internship in New York was rough, and we were only four hours away, not a day's worth of air travel."

Marcus had given up trying to not eavesdrop and leaned his elbows on the back of the couch, coming into view. "It was worth it, though." He kissed the top of Remmy's head.

"You're right." She smiled up at him. "Never mind me." Remmy waved a hand. "You should have fun and see where this goes. And even though I don't know him or his family, I'm sure he's a great guy."

Haley almost reminded her that Remmy *had known* Jason and his family but kept her mouth clamped.

"What's his name again? His full legal name?" She reached for a yellow pad on the end table.

"*Remmy.*"

"What? There's nothing wrong with a little light online stalking. Make sure he doesn't have any priors, that sort of thing."

Haley ended up rattling off Ethan's name because she knew Remmy's heart was in the right place. "What movie are you two watching tonight?" she asked, trying to change the subject.

"*Sabrina!*" A happy Marcus beamed through the screen.

Remmy rolled her eyes and thumbed in Marcus's direction. "It's a good thing this man makes perfect popcorn, or I wouldn't be able to sit through sloppy Harrison Ford struggling to breathe."

"He's love-struck. Don't you remember those early days?" Haley asked.

The corner of Remmy's mouth lifted as her gaze tilted to Marcus's again. "I guess."

Effervescence tingled her shoulders, watching her friend's happiness. "Why don't you enjoy the afternoon with your *fiancé?*"

"You don't mind?" Remmy's eyes reluctantly drifted back to hers.

Her smile widened. "Not at all. Talk to you soon?"

"You bet."

The second Haley opened the car door, a gust of wind attempted to forcefully remove her coat. Then, as a one-two punch, swirls of dust coerced her eyes closed and invaded her nostrils.

"Ugh. I get it. I get it. It's a bad day to be outside."

The wind died down instantaneously, almost as a *thank you* for listening. Haley scrubbed her forearm over her face to dislodge any remaining debris and strode toward her apartment. It was a silly, juvenile thing, but she ran her fingers over the trunk of Ethan's car as she passed it.

A palo verde tree's branches swayed momentarily into the path as she traveled, stopping her. Then, her feet were right back on their way. The rest of her body had already decided, already reasoned that if *please* always worked so well for him, why in the world wasn't she asking?

So, when beautiful Ethan opened his door, she said, "Hey, Yeti. Mind if I come in?"

Chapter 28

Ethan was an ossified version of himself as Haley whisked past him. Though her whole body seemed to light up at his mumbled, "Sure," his stomach churned restlessly. There were at least six things he wanted to quickly obscure from her observant eyes, but he was trapped, setting his front door back in its frame.

Haley was immediately drawn to his desk setup and, thankfully, not the sink full of dirty dishes. "So, this is where the magic happens. And by magic, I mean nefarious plotting, of course."

Ethan wanted to fall into their easy, teasing repartee, but seeing Haley in his apartment punched the air out of him.

Her blonde hair was a mess around her shoulders, as if someone had put her in a wind tunnel. Incandescence flickered in her eyes and around the corners of her mouth as she waited for his answer. Ethan almost shook his head at it. How could she be so calm when his heart was thrashing in his chest?

Haley's fingers carelessly caressed his keyboard, and it glowed in response. "I meant to mention it earlier, but I like that shirt," she said to the backlit keys. "The brown in it matches your eyes."

He'd selected the tan flannel with caramel squares and thin burgundy stripes mostly because it felt slightly softer than the black, blue, and green one. Though Ethan knew he'd eventually wear that shirt, too, since Paige had meticulously selected both. Most of the week, he'd worn his hoodie atop jeans, but meeting with his friends this morning had warranted something nicer.

Though she'd brought her gaze up, Ethan remained speechless. He couldn't get over the fact that Haley was standing here. With him. *Alone.* They'd been spending every evening together, but they'd been keeping their living spaces separated.

Haley being here crossed a line he was certain she wasn't aware of.

Why should she?

She had normal relationships with normal people. He, on the other hand, hadn't had anyone but his family inside his apartment. The tiny space seemed to shrink with every second he shared its air with Haley.

Hugging her elbows, Haley glanced at her purple sneakers. "Do you want me to go?"

"No." The word was a harsh avalanche scraping from his throat.

That little smirk lifted the corner of her mouth as she turned and surveyed his simple home. "I've got to say. I wasn't sure what to expect. With your pots and hammock, I thought I might be walking into an interior designer showcase."

"That was Paige."

Haley's muscles flinched like she wanted to look back at him but was resisting. Instead, she surveyed the apartment-provided photo of a sunset on the wall that separated his bedroom from the main living area. "I see."

He rubbed his neck. "Disappointed?"

"No." She tried not to be obvious, peeking into his bedroom, but failed. "It sounds weird, but this feels more like you. You put details into the things that you care about. I wouldn't have expected you to care about decor."

"How do you mean?"

"You've never talked about it. But your car, on the other hand"—the smirk deepened—"I feel like I could describe all those custom adaptations myself with how meticulous you detailed them. Your desk looks exactly how I pictured it when you spoke about work, even though you were convinced I wouldn't enjoy learning about 'computer stuff.'" Haley winked before surveying his hammock again. "It was nice of Paige to build you a little oasis."

"She thinks I spend too much time inside."

"You do." Haley grinned, and his muscles tensed in succession—calves, thighs, abs, chest.

When she started walking toward him, Ethan realized he'd never left his position near the door. The soles of his boots squeaked on the cheap patch of linoleum as he shifted his weight.

"It's really crappy outside. Like hide-your-chillens, a-storm-is-a-comin' bad. I don't want to fight the wind again. Could we order delivery for lunch and watch a movie or something? What do you feel like? Pizza? Chinese? My treat."

She was inches from him, her faded-blue eyes flicking over his hair, shoulders, lips.

A halting inhale lifted his chest. "Haley . . ."

"Please?"

The woman had the gall to add a little pout to her seductive lips, to soften her eyes at the corners, to weave her hands up his shoulders and fasten her fingers around his neck.

"Chinese."

The second he croaked out the word, Haley pecked his lips with a jubilant, "Yay!" and bounded away, slipping out of her coat and draping it over the back of the couch before setting her purse on the kitchen countertop and pulling her phone out to search for restaurants.

Ethan exhaled hard, rubbing his hand over his chin. "I've got a place." He picked up his phone from the wireless charger on his desk. "Most everything is good. The lo mein is great. Moo goo gai pan's a little insipid, though." He fought the trembling in his fingers, then surrendered to the need to place the mobile order with two hands.

"Lo mein sounds great."

Keeping his eyes on the screen dotted with over-saturated images of noodles and sliced beef, he asked, "Chicken with extra vegetables okay?"

"Sure."

"The app says it'll be here in forty minutes." Ethan finalized the order before registering that Haley's "Sure" had been muffled, like it'd been said through a wall.

Hurried steps brought him to his bedroom. Haley's fingers were resting on the black paper just below the small space he'd pulled open to allow him to shave every morning. "Oh, Ethan." The soft way she said his name sliced at his ribs.

"I shouldn't be in here." Haley spun, pressing herself against the counter. "This is rude and graceless, and I'm sorry. I was just curious, but I should have been more respectful." She paused to swallow. "Actually, would you prefer I leave? Or we could go to my apartment and crack the door open to watch for the delivery person. They've got to come up the same stairs."

Each tumbly word propelled his feet forward. "No. Stay."

"I'm sorry." The steadiness of her gaze made his breath catch. "It's okay."

Haley frowned. "It's not." They weren't talking about her being in his bathroom anymore.

"I know." Ethan paused as his heartbeat sprinted to the point he might pass out. "Stay anyway?"

Haley being here shifted everything in his mind, reorganizing and reshuffling what he thought was possible, what wasn't.

When she stepped in front of him, Ethan let his fingers carefully twine into her wind-knotted hair. A puff of air left her lips as she softened. She always did that when he touched her, like she was molded to fit his hands, like everything that was rocketing through his body was mirrored in hers.

"Haley," he breathed her name over her mouth before claiming it as his.

Frantic energy followed Haley's hands as her tongue tangled with his. They were everywhere—his hair, his back, his waist.

They impatiently pulled at her cheerful blue cardigan, flinging it from her body.

When the soft thud of its landing echoed in the silent room, everything in him froze.

Haley mirrored his posture before dropping her forehead to his sternum, pushing a pearled button into his scar. "I'm sorry." She leaned back, catching his gaze. "Me being here doesn't have to mean anything different. We can just watch a movie and have Chinese. I just like being with you."

Ethan should've been able to see his reflection in the mirror over her shoulder but could only see Haley. She was mesmerizing, the way her delicate chest rose and fell, her dilated eyes sweet with remorse she shouldn't have been feeling, her tongue nervously wetting her lower lip.

His jaw bunched as he lifted her with an inhale, placing her on the vanity. Initially, Haley's eyes widened, until he leaned back, and his trembling fingers fumbled with the button she'd just pressed her head against.

Ethan halted before he moved lower, before he let his hands shift and what was hidden beneath the fabric would be exposed. His chest shuddered, breathing harder than he had while kissing.

A soft caress cradled his jaw as Haley's reassuring gaze drew his attention. Her eyes never left his as he stumbled to unbutton his shirt. Only when he'd finished and a narrow area was open did she delicately tilt her head, asking an unspoken question. Ethan's throat worked with a tight swallow as his chin dipped.

Breathing completely ceased as Haley surveyed the chaotic whirls he'd left exposed. Her hand came forward, hovering millimeters from the center of his chest.

"Will it hurt if I touch you?" she whispered, her eyes finding his again.

"No. Parts of it are more sensitive than others, but not there. There are several patches where I can't feel anything at all."

Her fingertips traveled over the subtle hills and valleys of the scar directly over his heart. "Where is it most sensitive?"

Ethan pulled back the left side of his collar. "Here," he said, pointing to the skin under his collarbone.

Rationality ceased to be a guiding principle when she leaned forward and brushed a delicate kiss over the area he'd just identified. Haley was not only touching his tortured skin like it wasn't blotchy and hardened, she was *kissing* him.

"Where else?"

He was lost to her now. She might not know it, she might never know it, but he was *hers*. There would never be another second in his life where he wouldn't be hopelessly, desperately in love with Haley.

Ethan mutely pointed to two more locations, and she covered each in a soft kiss: the side of his right lowermost rib and the very top of his left bicep. He pulled his left sleeve partially down to show her the last spot, and she gingerly took the fabric in her fingers, removing the rest of the sleeve. His whole body went rigid as Ethan allowed her to do the same with the other sleeve.

A horrible, arresting pause settled between them as Haley's gaze scanned his upper body, his scar in its entirety.

"This is me." He tried for an impassive shrug, but a frown pulled at his lips.

"I like you." The sincerity in her eyes made his throat clench. "Can I?" she asked, hands poised over the jagged criss-crosses covering his abs.

Ethan nodded.

His flinch was reflexive when her hands flattened against his skin, fingers spread wide. Haley pushed upward slowly, touching everything, reverently tracing every inch of his scar, finding and exploring the borders. His muscles quivered in response, his chest struggling with breath after insufficient breath.

"You're sure I'm not hurting you?" Her eyes darted up again. "Not with this."

Inside, he was being slowly and painfully flayed. How was he ever going to hold onto her? It would be more agonizing than the entirety of his burn care to have Haley walk out of his life now.

Her hands wove over his collarbones, framing his jaw as her thumb barely brushed over his parted lips. Seconds elongated in a tortuous way until Haley's eyelashes fluttered closed, and she pressed her mouth to his.

This final touch restored action in his body. Electrical impulses seared as he palmed the back of her head to deepen the kiss. Haley moaned against him, widening her legs so he could fall between them. Three languages' worth of expletives ripped through his mind. He'd never been so frantic to kiss someone, never felt that it was absolutely necessary to his survival.

Pain whispered in the background as Haley twisted his hair, but all of his focus was on the sensation of her snug white T-shirt against his chest, the relentless grip of her thighs against his waist, and the taste of her saturating his tongue. Her greedy fingers fell to his back, smoothing over every mound of muscled skin until she reached the base of his spine.

"Haley, wait," he murmured, separating their bodies slightly. "Are you sure?"

Her eyes fluttered open, absolutely confused, until her gaze fell to her hands. Haley's thumbs were against the brown belt over his hip bones, but the rest of her fingers had stealthily dipped beneath the fabric of his jeans.

A guttural growl left her, her hands strangling the leather and denim. "Yes."

Relief was a tsunami sweeping through every cell as his hands slid under her thighs, picking her up and carrying her to his bed.

Chapter 29

"I'll get it!" Haley hastily threw the gray sweatshirt strewn atop Ethan's dresser over her naked frame and raced to his door to receive their lunch. After being worshiped like a goddess, the need to pay for this meal bounded like a feral animal within her. The delivery person had perfect timing as her and Ethan had just collected their breath mere moments ago.

The second Haley tossed open the door, it dawned on her that, though she was completely covered—the hem of Ethan's hoodie coming to her mid-thigh—she probably looked thoroughly tumbled.

The teenager on the other side of the door barely looked up from his phone as he handed her a plastic bag with a, "Thanks for the tip."

Her shoulders sank as the bag with a receipt stapled to the side sagged onto the kitchen counter. *Darn that stealthy Yeti.* Her discouraged sigh was followed by a deep inhale, bringing the clove scent of Ethan's sweatshirt, of his skin, deeper into her body.

Haley ran a hooked index finger back and forth across her lips. Every cell was still twitching with awareness. Being with Ethan had been different than anything she'd ever experienced, and her brain was struggling to process everything—especially the one memory that kept cycling on repeat.

How earlier, when Ethan pressed his forehead to hers, this relieved exhalation had tumbled out of his mouth and into her gasping one. It had all been too overwhelming—his heat surrounding her, the effervescence bubbling through her body, the way his eyes fell closed and his dark lashes seemed to beat against his cheek at the same cadence her heart had been hammering in her throat. Then, his lips had fallen to hers again, and the rest had been a blur until this streaking, blinding light tore through her limbs at the same time her name tore from him.

"Hey."

Haley nearly stumbled, pivoting to see Ethan standing in the doorway to the bedroom. He was back in his Yeti garb—black sweats and a hoodie—and somehow, the sight of it sent a sharp slap across her chest.

"Hi." She cleared her sandpaper voice and tried again. "Hey."

"Hey," he repeated.

The sudden awkwardness flooding the room and the fact that Ethan had the hood over his beautiful hair set something ablaze in her. In less than six longish strides, Haley was within a foot of the doorway. Everything in Ethan seemed to expand at her ascension. His eyes widened. His chest drew in a large breath. His shoulders rose.

Her hands paused for a beat on their way to the fabric wreathing his face. He watched her diligently, almost as if frozen against his will. When soft cotton hit her fingertips, Haley swallowed and pushed it back slowly. Ethan's halting exhale brushed a strand of hair out of her face.

Her gaze dropped automatically to the swirled skin along the left side of his neck. The impulse to gently touch his scar pulsed through her body, but before Haley's brain could issue the command, her heart gave another one.

Rising on her tiptoes, she pressed her lips against his skin, over what she knew held one of the largest superficial veins.

Haley wanted her message to have a direct line to Ethan's heart.

He didn't move—didn't breathe—and her action felt insufficient. Infinitesimal. So Haley tried again, this time laying her face over his skin and wrapping her arms around him.

When her eyelashes fluttered against his scar, his muscled arms almost squeezed the oxygen from her body. Ethan's chin burrowed into her hair, tugging errant strands as his short, inefficient breaths expanded against her.

Haley got the distinct impression that it had been a long time since Ethan had been held. Willing her aching calves not to quiver from her toe-lifted position, she settled in for the long haul. She tightened her arms, let her whole body press against him, and simply waited.

Somewhere in the distance, a clock ticked, his various computers hummed, but it wasn't until the contents of the plastic bag shifted with a flop that Ethan finally, reluctantly, loosened his grip.

"We should eat." His words were murmured against her temple.

"Yeah."

Neither of them moved for several seconds until Haley allowed her cranky calves to release their position. Once her feet rested on the ground, she wove her hands under Ethan's arms and laid her check over his chest, snuggling back in. If the size of his exhale was any indication, she'd been right in thinking he wasn't quite done being held.

Time pulsed steadily on until he whispered Spanish into her hair.

"English, please."

Ethan's grip tightened before releasing her. "Maybe someday."

She rumpled up her nose and poked him in the chest. "That's getting really annoying."

"Not infuriating?" The corner of his mouth kicked up. "I'm losing my edge."

Haley couldn't stop the irked growl that left her.

Ethan's widest grin lifted his lips as he tugged at her hand and led them to two non-apartment-supplied stools beside his kitchen counter.

The entire time he portioned out the wor wonton soup, egg rolls, lo mein, and two other dishes he'd purchased, Haley tried to feed the flames of irritation over him keeping things from her but failed. Freshly ravished and relaxed, Ethan was simply too adorable. This subtle pink swept just below his jaw whenever he caught her staring.

Ethan pushed a bowl and an overloaded plate toward her and settled himself on the empty stool, nearly folding himself in half to perch upon the small seat.

"How about some music while we eat?" He tapped on his phone, and a cello version of Ed Sheeran's "Perfect" reverberated from a soundbar beneath his computer setup.

Haley's inhale was noisy. "This song is on—"

"The 'Running through a castle as my lover and I pine for each other' playlist?" His shy smile splintered what was left of her intact organs. "It's great background music for work. I've been listening to it since you mentioned it."

Her face didn't know if it should scrunch, or slack, or try to kiss the lips off his.

Ethan aimed his grin downward as he picked all the broccoli and relegated it to the edge of his plate. She was about to ask what made it an offending vegetable when he spoke again.

"How did picking up the car go?"

Plum sauce and cabbage were currently occupying her tongue, so she quickly chewed before answering. "Easy peasy."

Ethan nodded to his food. She could have left it at that, but after everything he'd shared with her, Haley wanted to open up about the one topic she never glibly rattled about.

"Actually"—she covered her mouth with her forearm to obscure her latest tasty morsel—"my dad paid for the repair."

"That's nice." He shoveled another impossibly large bite into his mouth, his plate nearly half empty already.

Ethan always paced her when they ate at restaurants, but he was inhaling his food like he'd missed meals for a day. A flush pinked her cheeks as the *reason* for his hunger bumbled into her mind.

"Uh, yeah." Haley put her fork down, shaking heated memories from her mind. "It was nice, so I called him to thank him, and . . . and he wanted to talk."

When she glanced up, Ethan had stilled. "And that's different."

"Yeah." She rubbed her upper arms. "Dad and I don't . . . talk."

It was almost as if she could read his thoughts passing over his amber-brown eyes. "I know, right? Imagine me, Miss Chatterbox, not talking to someone, but it's not something that we've ever done."

Ethan smoothed a strand of her hair behind her ear. "I'm glad you're getting a chance now."

"Yeah." Her saliva felt trapped in her throat. "I think I made a lot of choices in my life because I wanted his approval, for him to show me he loved me. Dating Jason was one of those things. I think, deep down, I knew he wasn't good for me, but Dad liked him. Jason's dad is a lineman like my father, and Dad was emphatic—as emphatic as my dad gets—about us dating." She sighed. "Honestly, it should've been six weeks, but it lasted two years and ripped me up in the process."

His fingers covered and squeezed hers on the countertop. Haley let herself get lost in the perfect vasculature of Ethan's strong, reassuring hand.

The real reason she'd stayed with Jason was because Haley didn't think she deserved better. But now, she'd found a man who she was completely in sync with, who seemed to fill all her empty, anxious spaces, who grounded her.

The pressure started in the pit of her stomach and then spread outward in noxious spirals.

How long could she keep this? Keep him? She was only here for three more weeks.

She couldn't give up what she'd just experienced. Not when she didn't fully understand it. Not when whenever she thought about Ethan, or talked to Ethan, or kissed Ethan, or made love to Ethan, her chest felt like it was vibrating with a fierceness that could produce its own sound frequency.

"Hey."

Haley blinked when Ethan's fingers gently raised her chin.

"Sorry for rambling."

A noisy exhale left his nose. "You know me better than that."

She did. That was the problem. They'd spent the last week closing down restaurants, talking. What she didn't already know, she was thirsty for. Haley wanted every droplet of information about him, from the important to the minutiae, to wash over her skin.

"Tell me something," she said. "Big, small, anything."

Ethan surveyed her for several heartbeats. "Broccoli tastes like feet."

It was reflexive, the laugh that punched out of her.

A smile flirted with the corner of Ethan's mouth, and Haley's blood hopscotched along in her veins.

"Is that all?"

Ethan squinted his eyes, thinking. "Valentine's Day is Arizona's birthday."

"Oh, really?" She settled her elbow on the counter, placing her chin in her palm.

He nodded, picking up his fork. "February 14th, 1912, thereby becoming the 48th and last contiguous state in the Union. Followed by Alaska and Hawaii. Of course, there are the inhabited territories, like Puerto Rico and the Virgin Islands." Ethan swallowed a mouthful of noodles.

The deliciously nerdy tone of his voice soothed the nervous twitch still lingering in her stomach. "What else?"

"I think the beach-or-mountains question is stupid. They're obviously both ideal for different reasons."

It was a challenge to subdue the grin wanting to dance on her mouth. "Maybe you're just indecisive."

A single eyebrow arched. Ethan could do that this whole time? How dare he be able to pin her with such a look when both of her eyebrows doggedly stayed together. "Do I seem indecisive?"

"No." Cautious. Protective. Not indecisive. "What do you want to do after this, Mr. Decisive?"

He pressed his lips into a line, but his discontent didn't match his playful glare. "I'm going to make you watch a tech documentary if you aren't careful."

"Fine with me." Haley pinned him with a cheesy grin. "I *love* computer stuff."

"Pain," he mumbled.

She batted her eyes dramatically. "Someone once said I was 'the perfect amount of trouble.'"

"I can't imagine what misguided soul said that about you," Ethan said, returning his attention to lunch.

"I've also been called other things, like delightful, charming, perfectly quirky—"

"A fluffy bunny."

"Hey." Haley pushed his shoulder. "I reject that adjective."

Setting down his fork, Ethan rotated toward her, his black-sweats-covered knee slipping between her bare ones. "You shouldn't. There's nothing wrong with radiating sunshine. I love that about you."

His hand fell slightly above her kneecap, almost absentmindedly, but the instant his fingers made contact, her nakedness beneath Ethan's oversized hoodie pricked at her consciousness.

A shuttered inhale drew into her lungs as everything hummed into awareness.

Ethan's gaze traveled to his fingers as that same realization flickered over his face. The tendons in his neck jumped as he swallowed. Heat radiated up her thigh, even though he hadn't moved a millimeter. Any second now, she was going to lose her balance and keel over.

"I don't want to watch a movie." His words rumbled deeper than a volcano about to erupt.

"Okay," Haley managed from her dry throat.

Ethan's eyes found hers. "Can you answer one thing?"

She nodded.

Ethan could ask her any question right now, and she'd tell the raw truth.

Did he want to know that the first time she thought about kissing him had been when he wrapped his impossibly large fingers around her aching neck after the car accident? Did he want to know that, right now, her heart was hammering at her ribs with such a force she was afraid they'd shatter? Did he want to know that if he didn't slide his hand up her leg this instant, she'd probably implode?

His shoulders raised with a largely drawn breath. "I promise this will be the last time I ask, but . . . you're sure you're okay with this?" His eyes flicked to his chest and back. "With me?"

"Yes." Her brow quirked. Hadn't she been explicit with her actions?

"Okay, good." Ethan nodded for a long while, his gaze dropping to the ground.

Her mouth opened to reassure him the second his thumb started tracing expanding circles on her skin. Haley forgot what vowels and consonants were.

The languid pace with which Ethan leaned over felt like it took seven and a half years. She was nearly hyperventilating when his lips brushed the shell of her ear.

"In that case . . . run, little bunny."

Haley's eyes widened as her pulse attempted to reach the upper limits of tachycardia.

How many various sides did this man have? And why did it feel like she was clicked into each one like a personalized puzzle piece?

The devious lift of Ethan's mouth as he pulled back was enough to reduce her to steam. Forget melting into a puddle—she went straight to vaporization.

His eyes darkened, and instincts took over. A yip fled her mouth as she bolted from the counter, nearly knocking over her stool. Once Haley cleared the couch, she turned to see his shoulders shake with a rumbly chuckle as he rose from his stool. Before she could react, Ethan vaulted over the couch, tossed her over his shoulder, and was striding through the doorway to his bedroom.

Chapter 30

Stepping out onto the balcony, Ethan was sure the aching sensation in his chest was his heart bursting with joy. The last of the day's rays were bending artfully between the homes and stubby trees in the distance. As breathtaking as that was, it was Haley's blonde crown barely peeking above the fabric of his oversized hammock that stole his attention. Her sporadic humming prompted his head to tilt, trying to identify the tune as he moved closer.

The white cords of her earbuds traced down her neck and over her pink sweater, disappearing beneath a circle of beige fabric that Haley was jabbing with a threaded needle. Her phone was nestled between her and a pillow at her hip. Wearing orange corduroy pants, Haley was a mirror image of the sunset herself—golden hair, downy pink, and cherubic tangerine. Even her wiggly toes were covered with fluffy red wool.

Haley didn't stir when he stood directly above her, so Ethan gently cleared his throat, not wanting to startle her while she was holding a sharp object.

The way her face lit when she glanced up incinerated his heart a second time.

This last week had been the best of his life. He'd foolishly thought the previous week—taking Haley on dates and kissing her goodnight—had been heaven on earth. But also having her fall apart in his arms while they made love before holding her until she twitched with sleep . . .

Ethan wasn't one-hundred percent sure he wasn't back at the hospital in a medically induced coma, dreaming all of this.

Haley popped out an earbud with a Cheshire-cat grin. "I commandeered your hammock."

"I see that." His mouth curled up. "What are you making there? A green fork?"

When her lips dove into a frown, alarm slicked over his skin.

"It's supposed to be a saguaro." She tilted the embroidery hoop, surveying her handiwork. "You'd think my expertise with needles would've made this new hobby a piece of cake, but I'm like a blind narwhal over here. I mean, look at the back." The opposite side of the hoop was a messy jumble of lime-colored strings. "This shouldn't be that hard."

"I'm sure it just takes practice, like anything."

"Yeah." That grin that always splintered him brightened her face. "Happy Arizona's birthday."

Haley had said that formally celebrating Valentine's Day when their relationship was a tenuous two weeks old would be silly. He'd agreed with her, though he secretly would have relished the opportunity to spoil her.

"Happy Arizona's birthday."

Ethan couldn't resist any longer. Bending at the waist, he met Haley's lifting lips in a satiating kiss. Only . . . what settled the buzzing at the base of his spine apparently wasn't sufficient for her. Haley clenched his dangling hoodie strings, pulling him closer. A chuckle left his lips as she tossed her craft project on the cement and used the other hand to tug his shoulder toward her.

The hammock dipped and swung, hitting the railing with a bounce as it accommodated his weight. Haley nearly upended the both of them when she flung her body on top of his, pinning him against bending fabric.

"I thought you'd never come outside." The fevered words were hushed over his ear before her lips trailed down the left side of his neck. "I missed you."

Given that they'd seen each other this morning, showering together at her apartment before she left for work, that sentence made his pulse thud in his ears.

"Can we skip Margarita Monday?" Her hands were sneaking beneath his sweatshirt at the same time his fingers skirted over the velvet skin of her lower back.

"Absolutely."

Haley pushed all the way up, grinning at him in a way that made his brows quirk before an ominous snapping rose over the hushed sounds of the quieting desert. The back of his head hit and broke one of the gray pots, sending soil and an aroid palm smattering over the floor before his shoulders and back crashed to the ground. He firmly braced Haley to keep her from ending up face-first in the crushed plant.

"Ethan! Oh my goodness, are you okay?"

They untangled their legs from the half of the hammock still attached to the balcony's crossbeam, spilling pillows into the scattered soil.

Ethan winced as he rubbed his head, sitting upright. "I'm all right."

"Let me look." Her fingers were exploring his scalp, tenderly displacing his hair. "No cuts, but you're already getting a goose egg."

"If that's the worst of it, then we got off lucky."

It only took a few minutes to rescue the palm by repotting it into a small trash can, gather the shards of pottery, and sweep up the rest of the mess.

"I'm sorry for breaking your hammock." The crestfallen look on Haley's face as she wrung her hands hurt him more than the throbbing of his skull. "Let me cook you dinner to make up for it."

"You don't need to—"

Soil-covered fingers wrapped around the base of his neck, tugging his lips to hers. Ethan all but dropped the broom in his hand. When Haley finally released him, a breathy, "Okay," was all he could manage. The shy smile flickering over her mouth didn't match the seductive kiss he'd just received.

The second Haley opened her balcony door, "Walking on Sunshine" sang into the cool winter air. Haley dropped the trash bag into her kitchen can before picking up her phone.

"Crap. Crap. Crap."

Pinpricks needled his intestines. "What?"

"It's Remmy. I've missed fifteen calls from her." Haley answered the call. "What's wrong?"

Ethan knew that Haley's best friend was away for a long weekend with Marcus, celebrating their engagement. He hoped that both of them were safe.

"Zach Abrams shared your post!" Remmy's voice shouted over the line.

Momentary relief over Remmy and Marcus's safety was swiftly followed by cramping. It started in his quads before bounding to his ribs, shoulder, and jaw.

Haley placed the call on speaker, dropped her phone on the countertop, and opened OnlyApp. She had several thousand new followers and hundreds of direct messages. A clenching hand compressed his stinging ribs. In a desperate attempt to soothe the sloshing sound in his ears, Ethan laced his thumb through Haley's belt loop as he looked over her shoulder.

"What post? What are you talking about?" Even as she spoke, Haley toggled to the post that now had thousands of likes.

"I can't believe this is happening. You could actually meet Zach Abrams. That's what you've wanted for forever."

The picture of the Red Cross center that Haley had posted several weeks ago stared back at them. Zach Abrams had given her reposted credit and captioned the photo with, "Everyone should help out. Making my donation tomorrow."

The phone vibrated as Haley's still-dirty hand covered her gaping mouth. *Jana-supervisor* blinked over the photo as Remmy's sprinting speech continued.

Haley shook her head. "Remmy, hold on." She answered her second call. "Hello?"

"Haley, I just got off the phone with Zach Abrams's personal assistant. He'd like to donate blood tomorrow to raise awareness for the national shortage. He'll be accompanied by his team, and the local news channels will be there to get some video clips. But—and here's the crazy part—Zach Abrams personally requested that *you* be there. Apparently, you know each other? How is that possible? And why didn't you tell me? And why don't I already have his autograph framed on my desk?" Though her boss's voice was professional at the beginning of the call, it quickly dissolved into a high-pitched, fan-girl tone.

When Haley began to tremble, Ethan smoothed a palm between her shoulder blades, even though it felt like acid was eating away at his insides. The corrosive liquid worked through his organs first before excruciatingly dissolving his bones.

"I—I, um—I don't understand—" Haley glanced up at him, shock vibrating in her eyes.

"His donation time is at ten, and they've asked for everything to be ready two hours before. So, I'll see you at eight. Actually, make it seven-fifteen, just to be safe." Jana's voice had returned to its previous no-nonsense state.

"S—sure," Haley stuttered.

"I'll need you to stay for the rest of the shift in case the news outlets want to ask more questions, etc. Now, you'll have to excuse me. I have to text my stylist to see if she can open her studio for me this late." The call disconnected.

Haley's fingers clawed through her hair as Remmy's call bounced back to life.

"How *dare* you put me on hold at a time like this?" Remmy boomed, mock-upset.

"I'm sorry. It was my boss from the Red Cross," she said, her words and breaths short.

"What did she say?"

As Haley relayed the quick conversation to her friend, Ethan's skin began to itch. Even though he was still touching Haley, even though she pressed her body back into his hand, he couldn't help thinking this was it.

There was no way he could compete with Zach Abrams.

It didn't matter that, four days ago, after looking at the bank account he hadn't touched in over a year, Ethan decided to anonymously donate two-hundred thousand dollars to The Red Cross. It was too little, too late.

Ethan was *trying* to be the right kind of man again, but Zach Abrams already was.

Knowing compressed into a heavy metallic mass that settled at the base of his stomach. Though it pained his fingers, Ethan let his hand drift back and shifted a few inches away.

Haley was going back and forth with Remmy, oblivious to his movement.

At least he'd gotten to kiss her. At least he'd been able to love her. He'd stepped out of his comfort zone for the first time in five years and been rewarded with the two most blissful weeks of his life. Maybe he could live off these memories for the next five.

Even as these thoughts raced through his mind, the truth was a responding smack to the jaw.

There was no positive way to spin this.

It was going to hurt like hell.

Unlike when he'd been blindsided by heat and flames, seeing Haley gush on the phone was like being under a paralytic and watching fire slowly creep toward him.

"No. Wait. I don't know. Let me check," Haley said to Remmy before toggling to her text conversation with Zach Abrams.

Ethan averted his gaze. He didn't want to be reminded that it was his creation—*his damn app*—that took away the woman he loved. He didn't want to see whatever Haley had written that had been perfectly witty and enigmatic and obviously captured Zach Abrams's heart.

"No, nothing. He never responded to my last message." Haley bit her thumbnail. "That's weird, right?"

"Maybe not. Actions speak louder than words," Remmy said. "And him essentially demanding your presence is a *pretty big* action."

Haley's gaze flicked to his. It quickly bounced from his shoulders, to his chest, to the pocket of his sweatshirt, which obscured his hands.

"Albuquerque," Haley blurted, instantly stilling.

"Got it." Remmy's voice was even, understanding what Haley had meant with that one word. "Text me later." She hung up.

Before Ethan could wipe the confusion off his face, Haley weaved her hands over his shoulders, buried her fingers in his hair, and brought her lips to his.

This kiss was its own form of torture.

Every pass of her dewy lips over his was excruciating. Every sweet swirl of her hungry tongue sent spines shooting through his muscles. Even so, he held Haley like a dying man gripping the last tendrils of life.

His fingertips attempted to memorize the dip of her spine, the gentle roundness of her modest curves, the texture of her hair. Meanwhile, his brain laid a wax recording of her sensual sounds, capturing the unique hum vibrating in her throat when he pressed their bodies together.

The urge to tell her, to let her know what beat in every cell of his body, screamed in his head. He'd been able to quiet it over the last week—barely. He'd gotten away with whispering that he loved her while she was out of earshot or telling her a version of it in Spanish, relishing in the playful scrunch of her nose when he refused to translate.

But doing so now and having Haley walk away would only leave him more flayed than he'd been after the accident.

"You said you'd trust me," she whispered to his lips.

It was the sadness in her voice that made Ethan pull back, seeing the new hollowness swathing her eyes.

"Haley." He tucked a strand of hair behind her ear.

She caught his hand and pressed her cheek against it, squeezing her eyes shut.

Ethan didn't want to do this—to be the one causing her pain. He needed to pull himself together. If she chose Zach after meeting him, then Ethan would accept his fate and move on—at least, in appearances so that Haley wouldn't feel guilty about making the better choice.

It was time to dust off the skills he'd learned in the *Introduction to Acting* class Kevin and Kyle made him take sophomore year. Ethan smoothed out his face.

"Haley, look at me." His breath hitched when those pale-blue eyes centered on his. "I do trust you. Am I a little threatened that Zach Abrams personally requested you? Sure. I'd be stupid not to be. But just as my Tuesday is going to include making sure the world is constantly on the brink of collapse, yours is going to revolve around meeting your favorite movie star." He forced his lips up. "It'll be fun. Then you can come home and tell me every single detail."

The amount of effort it took not to cave under her observant gaze was gargantuan. When Haley softened, when that wobbly smile lifted her lips, it made everything worth it.

If all he had left was tonight, Ethan was going to make the most of it.

"Let me love you." His lips found hers again, drinking every detail in. "Let me love you, and then let me feed you. You're too frazzled to make dinner."

"I'm not frazzled," she countered, tilting her head back when he cradled it with his hands.

"You are." Ethan soothed his words down her neck. "Let me soften your nerves, order your favorite pad thai, and you can process the fact that you'll be meeting an idol tomorrow while I listen."

Haley's murmured, "This is a dream," reverberated as he backed her into her bedroom.

He knew she meant meeting Zach Abrams.

But for Ethan, Haley was his dream.

Being with her was something impossible. Something he never could've imagined. A dream that, in twelve hours, he might have to wake up from.

Chapter 31

"There's no way this is real life. Nope. No way," Haley muttered to herself as she and her fellow Red Cross employees waited in an antsy line for Zach Abrams. On Sundays, four phlebotomists and two front staff could easily handle a six-hour blood drive. But today, over thirty employees crowded the donation center, each vying for the first glimpse of the celebrity.

The waiting staff wore smiles in various states of nervousness as news cameras filmed B-roll. Though the white perforated sunscreens that shielded donors from the harsh Arizona sun were rolled to the ceiling, it was impossible to see anything through the crowd that had taken over the parking lot. Several of the people waiting were actual donors, those who'd had appointments *before* Zach Abrams announced he'd be the first stick of the day.

When Haley was certain the anticipation in her bloodstream was starting to poison her, Zach Abrams breezed through the door. Cheers and shouts followed his team of six—two personal-assistant types and four behemoths you'd expect could guard the gates of hell. Zach pulled off sunglasses and tossed his dark locks with an affable grin. A snug black T-shirt hung to every trainer-earned muscle as well-worn-but-presentable jeans sat on his trim, limber hips.

Sludge had replaced her saliva, and Haley was having a hard time swallowing it down as Zach went from twenty feet, to ten feet, to—*Holy crap!*—three feet away, clasping hands with a bouncy Jana. Her supervisor was tittering about the honor of having him at their facility and what a helpful and important thing he was doing for the country, when Zach's gaze drifted to Haley and stopped. Then, his award-winning, red-carpet smile spread across his face as her name left his picture-perfect lips.

Haley had to have been hallucinating.

Zach Abrams was saying *her name* like they were old friends, like he was pleased to see her. Remmy was going to pee herself, hearing the retelling of this.

Beside her, Sabrina, a coworker she'd worked with only once before, was near seconds from fainting. Cole swept a snug arm around her shoulders to keep her from unintentionally inspecting the freshly buffed floor tiles.

Haley's hand looked like a leaf quivering in the wind as it extended to be engulfed by Zach's large fingers. "Nice—" She cleared her throat. "Nice to meet you."

A million thoughts, observations, and sensations jumbled together. Flushing, cooling, and tingling mangled her body at once. *Wow, soft fingers, but* wide *shoulders. Lavender? I wouldn't have expected him to smell like lavender.* Her jackknifing heart tried to escape through her nose as a chorus of *Oh my goodness, it's Zach Abrams!* shouted over everything.

"Likewise." His broadening grin interrupted the thought-tornado Haley was trapped inside.

"Mr. Abrams—" Jana began.

"Please"—he held up a modest hand—"call me Zach."

Jana shivered before she pulled her twitchy lips into a professional smile. "We'll have you over here in this chair."

As Jana led Zach to the nicest of their donation chairs, he nodded to his staff. Everyone understood the rules of the morning. There were to be no cameras and complete privacy during donation, but when Zach was done and the line was clamped, he'd smile for the cameras before they removed the needle. After donating, everyone's phones would be returned to them, and they'd be given an opportunity to take a picture with the star. Boom mics lowered and news cameras were turned off as Jana called her name.

Haley's purple sneakers scuffed on the way over. "Yes, ma'am?"

"We already did his intake in the car to make the process faster, so he's all yours." Jana winked as she handed Haley the donation supplies.

Her stomach dove to her toes. "All mine?"

Haley had assumed that Jana would draw Zach Abrams's blood. Since she'd been in her supervisor's presence for *hours* without Jana mentioning this crucial detail, betrayal crept up Haley's spine like a scorpion.

Jana's pointed stare before ushering the remaining staff back confirmed Haley's fate.

"Crap," she mumbled to herself.

The familiar featherlight weight of the triple bag bundle felt like an anvil in her fingers. Zach hoisted himself up on the chair, relaxing back. He might as well have been on a beach lounger in Bora Bora. Haley's throat tightened as six-foot-high medical partitions surrounded them.

Within seconds, it was just her and Zach Abrams. Though dozens of people could be heard shuffling beyond the mauve border, it felt very private.

Intimate.

Cement flowed through Haley's veins as she pulled her handheld computer from her red scrub pocket. She went through her routine without lifting her eyes, mindlessly babbling with an uneven voice about each task, scanning the barcode on the tubing, preparing the collecting machine, and tabbing through the screen in her vibrating hands.

She always overspoke in general, but Haley did it more at work because explaining the minutiae of her job usually soothed whomever she was about to stick. This time, however, it was hard to ignore that it was Zach Abrams's expensive boots right next to her setup.

"Name?" She asked this of everyone. It was a simple and crucial step to confirm identity, but now it seemed ridiculous.

He let out an amused chuckle. "Zach Abrams."

Haley bit the inside of her cheek. "Arm preference?"

Normally, they'd have established that first, but he was in a double-armed chair, so Haley could easily switch from one side to the other.

"That's actually why I asked you here." The smooth timber of his voice wavered for the first time since he'd arrived. "I hate getting my blood drawn, but I wanted to do something good before I left Tucson."

Haley nodded. Zach was well known for helping out local charities when he was shooting on location in addition to his usual work with The Humane Society. His speckled half-greyhound rescue, Jax, was often the focus of his OnlyApp posts when he wasn't working on a film.

Zach's fingers brushed over the juicy median cubital vein in his left arm. "My veins roll a lot. I often end up looking like a horror-movie extra by the time they get them to cooperate. Lucky for me"—he paused, raising those perfect eyebrows with a playful smile—"I heard you were a vampire."

The backs of her knees started pulsing. "Ha. I said that, didn't I?"

"Among other things."

A burning flush crept up her neck.

Haley drew her gloves on with a stern mental shake. *Just another person. Just another vein.* Her fingertips examined his arm. The vein was thick and spongy, perfectly complementing his musculature, but Haley understood that, sometimes, even the flirtiest veins were hard to get.

Ignoring how his warmth snuck up her forearm, she said, "All right, let's get you clean and give this a shot." Haley broke the antiseptic open and began the one-minute scrub of his inner arm.

"I also wanted to thank you," Zach said after a few seconds. "For your last message. That really shook something loose inside me."

"Oh?" Everything was too noisy all of a sudden. The coughing, laughing, chatting of the people on the other side of the border. Her incessant heartbeat echoing in her ears. Even the sound of the swab over Zach's skin was deafening.

"Yeah. It made me happy to read that, even though I don't know you."

Haley glanced up to catch Zach's slight smile fade to a firm line, his eyes trained on where she was circling alcohol.

"It made me realize that I had something like that once, but I let life . . . excuses really, get in the way." His frown deepened as he stared at the partition.

"Alina?" she guessed.

Alina Ivanova was a gorgeous Ukrainian-born actress whom Zach had recently been in a year-long relationship with. Notably his longest, the tabloids loved to remind the public. The couple had called it off in an amicable split, citing scheduling conflicts, about five months ago. It shamed Haley to think that, at the time, she'd been delighted by the prospect of Zach Abrams being single. Her messages to him had begun shortly thereafter.

"Yeah." A palpable sorrow swept over his features as the cool air dried the antiseptic on his arm. "I'm going to fly to Aspen after this, instead of returning to LA, and see if Alina will give me another chance."

When his shoulders sank, Haley saw Zach for what he was: a man aching for a love he once had.

Ethan had been right.

Zach Abrams was just like everyone else.

Careful not to contaminate her insertion site, she laid a reassuring palm on his forearm. "I'm sure she'll be happy to see you."

Zach's grin was wary. "Seeing how it was me that broke it off, I'm not sure. I used every plausible excuse under the sun, but really, I was terrified of how much I loved her. Of how good we were together. When that year mark hit, I freaked out. One year is like ten in the film industry. Nothing is meant to last there. Everything is finite and fickle, sand slipping through your fingers. But Alina always felt permanent. Like she was my other half." He shook his head, and his black locks swept over his eyes. "Sounds stupid, I know."

"It doesn't."

He blew out a big breath, looking like a nervous man instead of a confident, multi-million-dollar celebrity. "It seems like fate that I wrapped this film at the same time she finished hers. That's never happened before. It was always hard to find time for each other, to eke out what seconds we could before our demanding careers pulled us apart. I read your message right before her most recent post popped up on my screen."

Haley had seen Alina's picture, having followed the Oscar-winning star when she started dating Zach Abrams. Alina had posted a snow-covered mountaintop photo, taken out of a private jet window, captioned, *Looking forward to enjoying a few weeks in the snow.*

"It was kismet. I'm certain of it. The only thing I'm not sure of is whether she'll be willing to forgive an idiot." He flattened his lips with another heaving exhale. "I guess we should get this over with so I can find out. I'm ready when you are."

A smirk tweaked Haley's cheek. "Already done."

Zach's brows rushed together, noticing the 16-gauge needle in his arm, blood flowing freely down the tubing. While he'd been talking, she'd swiftly secured his vein using the two-finger technique Melinda had taught her when she first started at the hospital in Maysville, inserted the needle, and taped up the site.

Haley popped the tourniquet she'd applied while he'd been distracted and handed him a dog-shaped squeeze ball. "Squeeze this every twenty seconds or so."

He continued to stare at his arm. "You weren't kidding. You *are* a vampire."

"That's why you asked for me specifically, right?" she asked, luminescence sweeping her skin.

Zach's surprised laugh bounced between the partitioned walls. "Are you interested in being my personal phlebotomist?"

Haley shook her head. "You just have to find a good one near you. There are hundreds of us out there."

Then Zach Abrams pinned her with his full-wattage smile. "No. I've got a feeling you're one of a kind."

Chapter 32

Ethan's heel bounced so hard against the base of his office chair that a staccato beat quadruple-paced the cello version of "Moon River" coming from his speakers. Twelve minutes ago, he'd received a photo of an ecstatic Haley beside Zach Abrams. The star was beaming, a red Coban dressing around his left elbow. His right elbow couldn't be seen, but his right fingers were loosely draped over Haley's hip—the same hip Ethan's teeth had nipped earlier this morning.

His jaw clenched as he let out a noisy exhale.

The lines of code on his screens were starting to look like hieroglyphics instead of intentional, artistic prose. Ethan grabbed his phone to head outside. The air was already warm when he stepped onto the balcony. February weather usually hovered in the seventies, but since the last week had consistently been ten degrees warmer, the management had relented to oppressive community pressure and opened the pool early.

Ethan let his hands grip the railing and stared, unseeing, trying to dislodge the retina-burned image of Zach Abrams touching Haley. His mind was a whirling maelstrom of *what-ifs* when something tickled his pinky. A large black ant crossed his knuckles, using his hand as a bridge. Its legs coordinated in an effortless pattern, swiftly traversing Ethan's veins like hills before returning to the even landscape of the metal railing.

A desolate sigh left his open mouth. Since his hammock was still incapacitated, Ethan slumped onto one of Haley's patio chairs and dialed his sister.

"What's up, chicken butt?" Paige said instead of hello.

His head shook, the corner of his lip lifting against his will. "Do you think you could make it work with your schedule to come home this weekend?"

Paige hummed as some lab device pinged in the background. "No. I could make next Saturday work, I'm pretty sure. Why? You miss me already?" The last question was asked in an irritating baby voice.

Ethan ignored the bait, waiting a beat.

Haley had asked him to trust her. There was no way in hell he'd ever trust Zach Abrams or any other man, but Haley, he knew. If the same woman came home that had wrapped her legs around his waist before she'd left for work, they could weather this.

Maybe they could weather anything.

"I want to introduce you to Haley."

"Finally." Irregular beeping followed her word like she was punching buttons. "I'm the reason you two are an item in the first place, don't forget. Without my pillow intervention, you'd still be alone in your sad hermit hut—wait, no. What did you call it? *Yeti cave*."

A heavy exhale accompanied the hand pulling down his face. Ethan would never live that particular storytime down. If Paige had her way, she'd recount that entire afternoon during his and Haley's wedding toast. Fluttering ticked at the base of his chest, prompting Ethan to clear his throat before continuing.

"If you get here in the afternoon, we can have dinner at Mom and Dad's, and then . . ." He wasn't sure what they should do. It'd been a lifetime since he'd been intentionally social. "Ah . . . drinks? A movie?"

"We'll figure it out," Paige said. "I'm excited. Ugh, I wish I was alone in the lab so I could do a happy dance."

Ethan laughed. "When has having others around ever stopped you?"

Her voice dropped. "We've got people from The Broad Institute working with us for the next few weeks, and I don't want to scandalize them . . . *yet*."

"No reason to hide that crazy. It's going to come out whether you like it or not."

"Yeah, I guess." A door closed on Paige's side of the call. "Hey. You got a sec?"

"I called *you*."

"Oh, yeah." A hesitant, humorless laugh left her mouth.

The swift change in his sister's voice sent tension zinging from his collarbones to his fingertips.

"I'm just going to say it." Paige paused again, perhaps to torture him. "I met someone."

His head tilted, eyes narrowing. "Why are you saying that like it's a bad thing?"

"It's not bad. It's . . ." Paige sighed. "We've been dating for a while."

"How long is 'a while'?"

"Not long. Six months maybe." Paige's voice climbed an octave.

"Six months?"

"I know. I'm sorry. I didn't want to tell you about Julien because I didn't want you to feel like I was abandoning you. But you've got someone now, so—"

"Is that why you've been single for so long?" A spiky boulder rolled down his spine, thinking about the fact that Paige hadn't had a serious boyfriend since the accident. "Not because work took up all your time?"

The idea that *he* was the one that had kept his sister from happiness was eviscerating.

"I—" Paige's voice cracked. "I just love you . . . and I want you to be okay."

Ethan's heart squeezed, hearing the tremble in her words. "Paige, I *am* okay."

That sentence sent a high-energy wavelength streaming through every cell, vibrating and rearranging as it zipped through.

He was okay. He would be okay.

Losing Haley was definitely not ideal, but he'd already been through hell and *survived*. With Paige, his parents, and now his old friends by his side, Ethan could do it again. It would decimate him a second time, but he'd still go on breathing.

He was pretty sure, anyway.

"I don't want you to think you can't be happy in front of me. I'm not going to fall apart because you have a boyfriend." When Paige didn't automatically answer, he added, "Why don't you bring him down with you next Saturday? I'd love to meet him. I'm sure Mom and Dad would love to as well."

"Uh . . ." She hesitated.

"They've already met him, haven't they?" His voice dropped as shame threatened to suffocate him. "Why is everyone still treating me with kid gloves? You did it at Mom's party, and now you're doing it with this." Agitation crept into his words, flushing the skin beneath his sweatshirt. "I'm *fine*. You having a boyfriend is *fine*. I don't like you keeping things from me. You know I hate that."

"No, you're right. It was stupid of me." He could imagine Paige deflating in her ancient blue office chair, the one that had been around before DNA was sequenced. "I'm sorry."

Ethan sat in silence, his muscles twitching inconsistently, before Paige said *"brother"* in tortured French.

"I'm here. I love you. Nothing will change that," he answered in Spanish.

His sister's relieved sigh blew through the line before someone knocked on her office door, and they had to end the call.

Forty minutes later, Ethan was still on the patio, his brain spinning from Paige's confession. Whether or not Haley came home and chose him over Zach Abrams, he needed to get his affairs in order. He was no longer clinging to life at the whim of fate and the best efforts of medical professionals. He was whole. Scarred, yes, but whole. Healthy.

It was about time he began acting like it.

Ethan rose with a determined spine when Haley burst out of her balcony door.

"There you are." Flushed, breathless joy accompanied her words, like she'd just run up their apartment stairs.

Ethan attempted to suppress the instant bliss surging through every cell but failed tremendously. "Haley, hey. I thought you wouldn't be home until later."

"I wasn't, but fans tried to mob the center after Zach left, so Jana canceled the rest of today's drive."

He nodded, waiting—waiting for her to let him know if her time with the celebrity had changed things between them. Ethan tightened his abs and worked to keep his face from showing how his throat was closing off.

After three lurching heartbeats, Haley took a large step, molded herself against him, and sealed her lips to his in a long, soul-encompassing kiss.

"I had an epiphany while talking to Zach," she whispered against his mouth.

Haley leaned back, leaving her hands intertwined behind his neck. "We were chatting like old friends. He was telling me stories about his ex-girlfriend, Alina, and all I could think as I listened and drew his blood was how I'd recount the entire conversation for you." Her eyes took on that hyper-focused quality. "Because you're the person I want to tell my stories to."

Everything in Ethan lit up. He was a power source, fueled by the look on Haley's face. But oxygen stubbornly refused to stagger into his stiff, rigid lungs, making it impossible to answer.

Haley continued, undeterred. "Have you ever done that thing where you got what you wanted and freaked out and started self-sabotaging?" She smoothed a hand up his neck to play with the edges of his hair. *"Thirteen, thirteen, thirteen,* I kept thinking as I drove. It was like an earworm ticking an annoying beat."

His brows pinched.

"Thirteen days left until I have to fly home, until this"—her eyes flicked between them—"ends."

Even though Ethan had been preparing himself for this conversation all day, the pain squeezing his collarbones was insurmountable.

"So . . . I've made a decision for us. We can argue later about how it's rude of me to decide on your behalf, but . . ." Haley took a deep inhale. "We're not going to be scared and push each other away. We're going to be terrified together." A determined nod brought her chin down.

The clarifying question singed his tongue like red-hot chili sauce, but Haley beat him to it.

"We're going to keep dating. And when the month winds down, we can decide what that means, specifically."

Ethan had never felt relief so completely. So profoundly. The tension he'd been holding in unknown places—the side of his neck, his triceps, the tops of his thighs—loosened as a held breath finally shook free of his exhausted chest. He was a second from telling her everything, that he was in love with her, that he'd figured out the perfect solution to their two-location problem, but Haley's ringing phone interrupted him.

A dry laugh punched from her. "Patrick Aldrich," she said to Ethan as if it was an explanation. "I haven't spoken to him since he tried to get out of doing work for our group history project senior year. You wouldn't believe how many people messaged or called me today, asking about Zach. Folks are really coming out of the woodwork." She chuckled again and went to cancel the call but accidentally swiped up. "Oops." Haley shrugged and put the phone to her ear. "Zach Abrams isn't interested in your latest scheme, whatever it is."

Haley froze, her fingertips fluttering to her lips. "What?"

Ethan frowned as he watched her previously buoyant body slump, her lower back sagging against his interlaced hands.

She listened and nodded, quivering. "No. Thank you," Haley said, her voice uneven. "Thank you for telling me."

By the time she'd disconnected the call, Ethan's heartbeat was thrashing like a mountain lion caught in a cage.

Her red-rimmed eyes lifted. "It's my dad." A violent shudder shook her. "He had an accident at work. One of the D-rings on his climbing belt snapped." She hiccupped, tears falling to blot her red scrub top. "Pat said he hit his head on the pole on the way down, snapped his femur, and . . . he hasn't woken up. They're taking him to surgery for his leg and the swelling in his brain."

Ethan's arms gripped her as steadily as humanly possible, but impotence laced an invisible hand around his throat and choked him. Though his eyes were fixed on the stucco wall of their balcony, his mind bolted from one possible solution to the next.

He backed her through the open glass door to her apartment. "Pack a bag. I'm going to look up flights." When Ethan moved to step away, Haley held on with a fierceness that sucked the air from his body.

"Okay," he whispered. He tucked a hand around her hip and propelled Haley to her bedroom, delicately setting her on the edge of her bed with a kiss to her forehead. Haley quivered, biting her thumbnail.

It didn't take long for him to find her luggage and fill it with bright clothes. Ethan wondered if Haley even owned a black dress, hoping with his entirety that she wouldn't need it.

When she didn't respond to him calling her name, he knelt in front of her. Haley blinked, surprised to see him there.

"He's all I have." The words scraped from her throat.

"I know." His hands framed her face, his thumb brushing a tear-soaked blonde strand out of her eye.

Now wasn't the time to remind Haley that, as long as she wanted him, he'd be with her always.

"Let's get you home," Ethan said instead.

Chapter 33

Ethan had secured her luggage in the back, helped her into the passenger seat, and was rounding the car when Haley's brows furrowed on their own. When he flung himself into the driver's seat and reached for the ignition, she grabbed his wrist.

"Wait."

Ethan's mouth popped open, but she spoke first.

"D-rings don't snap. They can take thousands of pounds of force." Haley let go of his arm, but her hand hovered in mid-air, transfixed. "And I'm pretty sure Pat's still on suspension. I remember overhearing at my dad's poker night while I was packing to come here that he'd been drunk on the job."

An expletive—the *worst* one—rushed from her mouth as she fished her phone out of her purse. When her dad didn't answer, Haley left a quick voicemail before calling the hospital operator to ask if he'd been admitted. The kind operator reported that no one by the name of Robert Kineman was at the hospital and asked if there was anything else she could do for Haley.

"No, thank you so much."

"Your dad's not in the hospital," Ethan said, his voice tightening as her phone dropped to her lap.

"Doesn't look like it." Haley pressed her lips together with a harsh, nasally exhale. "That no-good piece of—"

"It was a prank?" Ethan had fully turned in his seat, bald anger etching into the hollows of his cheeks, the muscles of his jaw.

"I don't know, but I'm—"

Remmy's contact lit up the screen. Haley rolled her neck with a groan before answering. "Did Pat call you too?"

"Pat? What? No. I called to—" She cut off her sentence when Ethan sneezed, and Haley said, "Bless you."

"I thought you were still at The Red Cross."

Haley's stomach was lassoed to an anvil and tossed off the side of an eighty-story building. It was one of those telepathic best-friend things. Remmy was calling with bad news. Haley could *feel* it. Her vision spun, the black dashboard in front of her looking more like a turntable.

Maybe it hadn't been an ugly prank. Maybe her father had been rushed to surgery so quickly he hadn't populated into the hospital's computer system.

A dry heave propelled her to fling her door open and double over.

"I need to tell you something, but I'd prefer if you were alone," Remmy said.

Ethan followed Haley outside, eyeing her over the hood. He looked as wrecked as she felt, concern for her flooding his beautiful features.

I need a minute, she mouthed, then turned and walked away. Her footsteps stumbled over the slight bump between the edge of the parking lot and the wild land beyond, but Haley managed to follow the narrow strip toward the main road. Scraggly desert chicory threatened to nip at the ankles of her jeans as she passed.

"Remmy," she said once she'd gathered her breath. "Patrick Aldrich just called me and said my father had been injured on the job and is now in surgery."

"Oh my—okay, hold on."

Haley could hear her friend pick up her desk phone and dial. "Mama? I need to know if Mr. Kineman is in surgery. Pat just called Haley and told him he was hurt . . . uh-huh."

A metallic taste stung her tongue before Haley realized she'd bitten her lower lip. Her phone was pressed so firmly to her ear that it was heating despite the cool, cloudy day. When a notification sound rang in her ear, she nearly tripped into the hovering buckhorn cholla cactus.

Tears flooded her face, dripping onto the screen.

Can't talk now. Call after work. Dad

"Mama says he's not in the system." Remmy's voice came from her shaking palm.

Haley slapped the phone to her ear, the back of her free hand swiping at her cheeks. "Okay, thanks."

"Oh, honey," Remmy said to Haley's watery response. "I'm sorry. I should have realized something was up when you said his name. Pat has been palling around with Jason. He probably did it to ruin your day. Everyone in town's been talking about you meeting Zach Abrams today." Her best friend muttered a colorful description of Pat under her breath. "That's it. I'm going to add Pat to the list of jerks that need their insides rearranged."

"Make sure you leave a scar," Haley said after a shaky inhale.

"You know I will."

"I miss you so much." The words escaped on their own.

This day had already been too much. The highest of highs followed by the lowest of lows left Haley exhausted and dizzy. In the absence of her best friend's fierce hug and a round of margaritas, Haley would need her fluffy monster blanket and at least four hours of *The Big Bang Theory* to recover from the last twenty minutes. Or maybe Ethan could rub her neck—that was equally soothing.

Haley glanced back the way she'd come but couldn't see him or his car. "Wait." Her left eye twitched. "If you weren't going to tell me about Dad . . ."

"I'm not sure how to say this."

Goosebumps trailed up Haley's forearm. Remmy was the queen of blunt, often annoyingly forthright. Her hesitating was a bad sign.

"You know OnlyApp?" Her friend paused, stalling.

Haley passed the sand-colored stucco sign for their apartment complex, pivoted onto the sidewalk that ran along Sunrise Drive, and began walking west. "The most popular social media app and the way I was able to meet Zach Abrams this morning? Yeah, I'm familiar."

"How'd that go, by the way? Give me all the details."

"Remmy."

"Fine." Her best friend sighed. "For the record, I only called because on the heels of meeting your favorite celebrity, this isn't that bad. Perspective is everything sometimes."

Haley rubbed between her eyes. "What are you talking about?"

"Ethan created it. OnlyApp."

That slipping, forty-five-degree sensation made Haley's vision gray. "What?"

"Him and two other prominent developers in Silicon Valley. It says right here on Wikipedia . . ." Remmy began reading from the page, but Haley stopped listening.

The speed at which her and Ethan's past interactions flew through her mind was whiplash-inducing. She crawled over each conversation, analyzed each detail. Over the past week, they'd begun revealing the sticky, gritty details about themselves. He'd described some of the worst days after the fire, how cruel he'd been to his friends, and how worried he was that they wouldn't take him back. Though she'd always been an open book, Haley admitted how lonely she'd been as a child—even with Remmy and her family there—and how all she wanted growing up was not to burden her father.

When Ethan had spoken of his life in California, he'd mentioned that he had headed some big projects before the fire, but that, in recovery, he'd realized he was happier working on smaller ones. Ethan had neglected to tell her that his 'big project' was an app that most of the world used daily.

Haley's forearms tensed as her stomach tried to evacuate her body through the soles of her feet.

There'd even been the one night Ethan had explained what he was doing on all his screens. She'd tucked herself onto his lap, fingers playing with his hair, while he'd detailed every keystroke. Haley had loved the way Ethan lit up when he spoke about coding, about solving problems.

That moment had felt so genuine. Honest. She had created all these perfect scenarios with a fictitious version of Zach Abrams, but nestled against Ethan as he dropped computer jargon like sugary treats, Haley had realized she'd somehow found the thing she'd always wanted.

A *real* love story.

There was no longer a reason to create a fake, imaginary relationship. Not when she could have the silly, playful one that somehow had its own heartbeat. Whenever Ethan poked at her, or she pushed back, or they fell apart in perfect synchronicity, those moments *breathed*. Every wink or laugh or stumbly mistake was something you could pick up and hold. It existed. And it existed with a flawed and imperfect man. Someone like her.

Or so she thought.

Haley's pulse galloped in her chest, thumping at her temple.

The reason Haley had always reveled in the smaller things in life was because she needed to prove that those things were important. Because *she* was small. She was just one person, living a seemingly insignificant life.

Sometimes, after working an incredible shift at the hospital, Haley would drive home numb. The steady sounds of the road would hold space in her ears as a heaviness pressed at the apex of her spine. Haley helped dozens of people every day, but if she didn't work, if she didn't contribute . . .

What was she worth?

She wasn't a talented, benevolent celebrity with the reach of millions, nor the founder—*the creator*—of the most successful social media app of all time.

She was just Haley, a quirky woman from a small town who happened to be good with needles.

Bile roiled up again, and an unearthly noise escaped her throat.

"Lee?"

"I need a minute," she said, stopping to brace a palm on her kneecap.

"I couldn't find any OnlyApp accounts for him, but it's probably one of those prince-in-plain-clothes type of situations," Remmy continued, not giving her the minute she'd requested. "He wanted you to like him for him before letting you know that he's loaded. I mean, programmers can easily make six figures, but this . . ." A low whistle sounded over the phone.

"Not helping," Haley squeaked.

She hadn't even considered how much money Ethan had. A sour taste overwhelmed her tongue, scratching at the insides of her cheeks. The road ended at an intersection, and Haley jerkily shot right, heading north.

"I don't think it's so bad. It's like you stepped down from an A-list celebrity in Zach Abrams to B, C-list with Ethan. Either way, you were destined to be on some list." Remmy was trying so hard to make her laugh, but *oof* . . . crickets.

An oversized diesel truck roared past Haley, making her jolt away from the sidewalk into the dirt.

"Just don't do anything drastic. I think he's a good guy . . . just misguided."

Haley's entire abdomen clenched so hard she involuntarily leaned into herself. How many times had she and Remmy made excuses for the men in their lives? How many times had Haley done that for Jason? How much had she suffered because of it?

"Lee, promise me."

"I promise," she said automatically.

"Your fingers better not be crossed behind your back like you used to do when we were little."

Haley pulled her free hand from behind her back, uncrossing her fingers. The action had been subconscious, and Remmy calling her on it made Haley feel like her best friend was walking beside her instead of thousands of miles away.

"Why wouldn't he tell me?" The pitch of her voice was unnaturally high.

Remmy sighed. "I don't know. You're going to have to ask him."

That was the last thing that Haley wanted to do. It already felt like thin, thread-like strands of her soul were fraying, being pulled by the slight arid breeze. What she thought was real—what she thought could've been her future—was another fabrication. Had her over-indulgent brain imagined the whole thing? Over-interpreted his words, his actions? Made something out of nothing?

Haley's heart fought against the worry dissolving the remains of her internal organs, reminding her of how vulnerable Ethan was with her. How, when her affection for him would pulse through every cell in her body, his expression was an identical mirror. Haley's shoulders slid away from her ears until a sentence echoed in her skull.

Whispered Spanish.

The thought jolted her to a stop.

He'd always held part of himself in secret. Haley had constantly asked for an explanation, but he'd always quirked that half-smile and refused. She'd thought it a game, one she'd partially enjoyed, but now a solitary idea over-crowded the rest.

Haley wasn't sure she could handle whatever else Ethan was hiding.

Chapter 34

It was a strange sensation, experiencing full-body understanding. It was almost like a shakedown at the cellular level. Dizzying. Disorienting. Ethan had known pain, but not knowing if Haley was safe at this moment trumped even the worst days of recovery. His skin itched with an intensity that didn't seem possible.

Two more minutes. He was going to wait one-hundred-and-twenty seconds before he got in his car and started searching. Haley had asked him to give her space, and at the time, he'd figured she'd simply pace the windy apartment sidewalks. But he'd walked those pathways over and over. The complex wasn't so large that he could've missed her. Haley had to have been somewhere else.

Ethan's calves tensed, and he spun in a half circle to return to their building. *Best to check her door one more time.*

"Why didn't you tell me about OnlyApp?" The question peppered his back when he was halfway up the stairs.

The sound of Haley's voice ameliorated most of the venom poisoning his bloodstream, but Ethan knew he wouldn't feel completely settled until her skin was beneath his fingertips. He made it down one step before her outstretched palm made him freeze.

"Don't." Her voice cracked, splintering his ribs. "Don't touch me. I can't think when you touch me."

Haley folded her arms over her shuddering chest, visibly attempting to regain her composure. "Explain."

Ethan sagged into himself, resisting the urge to tuck his hands into the pocket of his sweatshirt and, instead, settled them along the seams of his jeans. "I was ashamed. That's a time in my life I don't like to think about."

"Why?" It was slight, but Ethan caught the sorrow sweeping below her narrowed brow, staining her irises a darker blue.

"Because that's not who I am. It's not the real me. I was wrangled into that project by my two partners because I was the best at what I did. To me, it was a big puzzle to solve, something to conquer. Initially, I couldn't have cared less about being liked or making money . . . until I cared too much." A breath left his open mouth. "Ultimately, the fire was a blessing. It wiped me clean and forced me to start over."

He hesitated only a second before forcing himself to verbalize the thoughts that had been racing through his mind for weeks. "I thought the life I'd built afterward was a good one—until you moved in, and I realized how much it was lacking."

A heavy swallow snaked down Haley's throat. Seeing it, his feet propelled forward automatically, but Ethan forced himself to stop when she backed up slightly.

The midday sun beat down on their shoulders, warming their hair. Haley's golden locks practically ignited. Every cell in his body ached to touch her, but Ethan finally understood there could be no more hiding. He'd hidden his scar initially, and then his past, but now he had to be completely transparent.

"What else, Haley?" He rooted his shoes to the rough cement stair. "What else do you want to know? I'll tell you anything."

"What are you always whispering in Spanish?" The wince accompanying her sentence, like she thought he'd been saying something negative, flayed him.

"'It's like you were made for me,'" Ethan said, his voice husking. "That's what I'm saying. Or sometimes, 'I can't believe you're here,' or when you're farther away because I was certain you'd memorize it and translate it . . . 'I love you.'"

Her eyes widened as a trembling began in her fingertips.

"I know. We've only known each other a short while." He exhaled. "But you make me want to wring every drop of sunshine out of each day. You make me feel like I was never fully awake until you burst from your apartment, muttering about house clothes and asking about tamales." His heart beat frantically against his throat, but Ethan kept going. "It's overwhelming, like I'm inside out half of the time. I kept pushing it down, trying to ignore it, telling myself we were friends, that you can't love someone you just met, but I did, Haley. I loved you right from the start, and there's no way to assign intellect to that. It just was. It just is."

If there'd been any doubt over his ability to stun the verbose Haley into silence, Ethan understood now that he was more than capable. Her shaky fingers covered her lips, pressing hard against them as twin lines of tears streamed down her cheeks.

"Haley." His palm attempted to crush the metal stair railing into dust. "Please."

Her slight nod was all the encouragement he needed to fly down the remaining steps and gather her to his chest.

"I'm sorry," he whispered to her crown. "I know it's too much."

When her forehead rocked a *no* against him, Ethan froze.

Those pale-blue eyes locked on his, promising to shatter what was left of him. "It's the same." Haley pressed her palm to the space over her heart.

Wordless.

His body felt like it was malfunctioning as her thumbs skirted up his neck and over his jaw, holding him firmly. "I love you, Ethan," she whispered.

Haley didn't hesitate. She eagerly pulled his mouth to hers, sighing when they made contact. The same relief ricocheted through his body, soothing every edgy twitch, calming the undercurrent of his soul.

This. This was what he needed for the rest of his days.

Her.

A pliable moan vibrated against him when his tongue attempted to communicate these thoughts to her. He'd done a decent job explaining how he felt, but Ethan could speak every day for hours and never be able to fully detail what Haley meant to him. His fingertips slipped under her white Henley, and joyous expletives shot through his brain at the sensation of Haley's skin beneath his palms.

Haley tugged at his back, pulling herself flat against him. His response was instinctual, automatic. Rushing, churning energy surged to the base of his spine, lighting his skin from the inside. His hands repositioned, framing her ribs, but . . . there was no surface to back her into. All Ethan wanted was to feel every inhale, every ripple of her muscle beneath him. Out of options, he nudged her up one stair.

Haley's fingers slid through his hair and gripped, separating their lips. "I was prepared to repetitively listen to the ten-minute version of 'All Too Well' over you," she rasped. "I had it planned out and everything. Darn you, Yeti."

Ethan couldn't suppress the rumbly laugh bursting from him. "I love you." His head shook on its own. "I love you so damn much."

The corner of Haley's lips twisted, and the impulse to seal them with his was uncontrollable.

Haley softened with the sweetest sound when he kissed her again. Then, the movement of her hands grew hungry and wild, pushing against him so roughly he nearly stumbled backward. Ethan growled when her teeth tugged at his lower lip. Their progress up the stairs was headed in the wrong direction, and he was half a second from sliding his hands under her thighs and picking her up when a familiar voice interrupted.

"You know you have an apartment? Two of them, in fact. Right next to each other with an adjoining balcony to share.

Lots of space that isn't in the public eye." Aster's words somehow conveyed disdain *and* amusement.

Haley's mouth made the most delicious popping sound as it separated from his that Ethan had to fist his hands at the small of her back to keep from snapping at their neighbor. He turned around, pulling Haley down to the safety of the cement slab and securing an arm around her waist. If he had to stop kissing Haley, he was at least going to keep touching her.

"Hello, Aster," he managed between ragged breaths. "You need help, I assume?"

Ethan expected a quip or her standard *humph*, but Aster's smile broke wide over her teeth. That was when he noticed the scarf secured over her tight ponytail and the fact that she was wearing teal pants and sneakers beneath her practical brown coat.

"How do you know what our balconies look like?" Haley asked.

Aster's chin gestured up the stairs. "The left one used to be mine. The right, Loraine's. We knocked down that pesky wall on the balcony so we could drink tea on a big wicker couch in the mornings."

Ethan struggled to imagine Aster sipping tea. Ghost pepper sauce or straight lighter fluid, maybe. Her admission explained why Aster had been on the stairs that night, why she always seemed to hover nearby.

Aster stiffened as unmistakable sorrow swept her face. "It worked out. I'm getting too old for stair climbing, anyway."

Haley tugged out of his grip and rushed to swallow Aster in a hug with such speed that he and Aster stood shocked, staring at each other.

"I'm sorry," Haley whispered to the paisley-patterned silk wrapping Aster's ears.

Their neighbor blinked, then patted Haley's shoulder like a wrestler tapping out.

Only Haley wouldn't let go. "I can't imagine losing my best friend."

After a long while, Aster spoke, her voice cracking. "It's no cakewalk."

Ethan's jaw tweaked, hearing anything other than bossy confidence in their neighbor's words and took a page from Haley's book. When he wrapped both women in his arms, Aster groaned.

"Why are young people so emotional all the time? Isn't it exhausting?"

"Yes," Ethan and Haley answered at the same time, prompting everyone to burst into unexpected laughter.

When their chuckles simmered down to satisfied sighs, Haley asked, "What can we help you with today?"

"I need a jump." Aster dug keys from her coat pocket. "I used to drive Loraine to her appointments, but it's been over two months, so my battery's dead."

Ethan rubbed a hand over his chin, remembering how they met. "Does someone get groceries for you?"

"No. I get them myself." Her eyes flinted with stubbornness. "I walk to Safeway every Tuesday."

"That's dangerous," he balked, thinking of Aster crossing six lanes of traffic on her own.

The irritation in her *humph* was undeniable. "Cardiovascular disease is dangerous. Walking is good for you."

Haley had her arms crossed and eyebrows raised with a smirk. Since he obviously wasn't going to win this argument, Ethan focused back on the task at hand.

"Where are you parked?"

Aster spun on her heel and marched away.

Ethan should have expected his feisty neighbor to stride up to the 2013 bright-blue Mustang GT convertible—the only other flashy car in their parking lot—but his jaw still dropped. Though Aster stated she hadn't driven in two months, the car had been recently washed and buffed. Since new layers of dust were constantly covering every surface in Tucson, keeping a car clean required diligence.

"I've got cables in the back." Aster began rummaging around in a very cluttered trunk.

"After we're done with this, how about we all go to lunch? Rosa's?" Haley's eyes flicked to his, the light in them decimating his automatic objection.

Ethan already had plans for after this. Plans that involved only Haley, closed doors, and an obscene amount of nudity. He barely suppressed the punched sound wanting to escape him.

The corner of Haley's mouth tipped up, reading his expression.

"Sure, fine," Aster said, still bent and searching in the trunk.

Haley laid her hand on his bicep, raising on her tiptoes to whisper her words against the shell of his ear. "Relax, we'll get to that after." Her eyes linked with his as she pulled away, a smile stretching wide on her lips. *That* smile. The one that seemed to be just for him.

"We've got time," she said, and Ethan fully understood that she meant the rest of their lives.

Chapter 35

Haley couldn't resist stopping mid-stair to sneak a kiss from Ethan. Like always, he met her eagerly. After a thoroughly satiating kiss, his gruff voice teased, "Why are you determined to torture me by keeping me on these stairs?"

"I can't help it. I'm being sentimental. It's the last time we'll be on them."

Ethan chuckled, his hands winding through her hair. "You know we'll be coming back to the complex to see Aster. We can make stair visitation a thing if you need it."

"Really?" Her exuberant question pulled his smile wider.

"Of course." He grazed and nipped down her neck. "Now, back to the task at hand. Move." Ethan encouraged her up another stair. "Not that I didn't thoroughly enjoy the afternoon with my sister, dinner with my family, Kevin and Kyle's *Urinetown* production, and"—Ethan paused to lift a single eyebrow, driving home how much time they'd spent with other people today—"coffee with the cast and my friends afterward, but I need some *Haley time* now."

Though the low, masculine way he said *Haley time* made her spine tingle, she planted her feet. "You had 'Haley time' first thing this morning before we finished packing."

An annoyed growl accompanied Ethan's lips as he worked his way back up to her mouth. "I need a lot of Haley time. It's an addiction. You've replaced my need to topple successful governments by destabilizing their infrastructures. Besides, I don't foresee us getting a lot of alone time once we get to Maysville."

They'd be staying—*temporarily*—at her father's house, in separate bedrooms at Dad's request. He wanted to "get to know" Ethan before they found a place of their own, something Ethan completely understood and agreed with. The protective, shotgun-on-the-table tone of her dad's voice when he'd asked them to stay with him had sent unexpected warmth sailing through Haley's body.

Ethan's lips pulled her attention back to the present, and Haley relented her fight for the stairs. She let him carry her to the landing, her heart smiling as his tongue played with hers. A breathless sigh escaped her when Ethan pinned her to his door and efficiently unlocked it. Then, there was that weightless, freefall feeling the instant the wood gave way before his strong arms caught her.

His apartment looked identical to hers. Empty. Suitcases were tucked against the wall next to the kitchen table. Ethan's desk, patio plants, and hammock were gone, temporarily relocated to his parents' house. When they came back to Tucson in November, Ethan would collect them for the winter home he'd buy them.

The memory of their conversation, the one they had a week and a half ago after they'd had lunch with Aster, popped into her mind.

"I think I'm going to keep one of these," Haley said, wrapping her gray sweatshirt arms around herself and taking a deep inhale of Ethan's lingering clove scent. "Aren't girlfriends supposed to steal their boyfriend's clothing?" Her pulse sprinted faster than it had during sex, worried she'd overstepped boundaries by dropping the G-word.

The languid pace with which the corner of Ethan's mouth curled up didn't help her nerves.

He gathered her foot into his palm, massaging his thumb strongly into the center. Ethan had put his black sweats on but, for the first time, remained shirtless. Haley's heart simply sung—belted loud, messy words of joy—over him feeling confident enough to be so comfortable with her.

"If we're going to be adding labels to our relationship, I've got one." Ethan's demeanor was casual, his gaze focused on his task.

Haley attempted not to groan with pleasure when he worked his way to the arch of her foot. "What's that?"

"Snowbirds."

Her eyebrows furrowed. "Snowbirds?"

"It's a popular term for people who live here part time. They use Tucson to escape the cold and then go somewhere that isn't the surface of the sun in summer. We'll spend summers in Maysville and winters here. Six months each. This year will be a little more in Maysville

because I'll be heading home with you in March." When he took a breath, Haley could see the break in the façade. A slight trembling trickled into the sure hands smoothing strokes over her toes. "The people who snowbird are usually retired, but I can work anywhere. Is that something you could do with your job? Something you'd be interested in?"

Ethan finally brought his eyes up. The uncertainty in them slashed at her soul, sending ice careening through her bloodstream.

She pulled her foot back to kneel in front of him with a bounce. "You mean besides being a fluffy bunny in love with a yeti, I get to join the fowl community?"

This time, when he shook his head and muttered Spanish, Haley knew exactly what he was saying.

◊◊◊

"What do you think about driving back in the fall instead of flying? It might be fun. We can even take different routes during different seasons. North in the fall. South in the spring," Haley said, playing with Ethan's interlaced fingers on the airplane armrest. "Not that I don't enjoy flying *first class*." She wiggled her eyebrows.

As much as she'd envisioned elaborate fairy-tale endings with Zach Abrams, the reality of dating someone who possessed this much wealth had initially made Haley want to jump out of her skin. Jason had always thrown his superior income in her face, but Haley reminded herself that this was *Ethan*—the man who wore holey moccasins and years-old sweatshirts.

Still, she couldn't help but bluntly bring up the subject last week. Ethan had pinked adorably, which helped settle the bees that had taken residence in her stomach. As expected, Haley had needed a drink of water after hearing the sum total, but it made sense. He'd sold his stake in the company but continued to amass money from his invested stock, which naturally was doing phenomenally.

When Ethan had taken her in his arms and asked if it was a deal breaker, she'd paused only a second before shaking her head no. He had nodded and then told her one truth further. Except for paying for his medical care and wiping his family's debts clean, he'd only accessed that money one other time—to donate to The Red Cross.

"I want to set aside enough for the future, but the rest, I'd like to donate. That's one thing Zach Abrams has right. That and being amazed by you."

Oddly, Zach Abrams had sent her a message last Wednesday with the incredible news that Alina had taken him back. Haley had responded with the same exaltations and celebratory emojis she'd sent Remmy after her engagement. It was unlikely that she was going to maintain a connection with the celebrity, but Haley wasn't about to ignore a spontaneous message.

The seatbelt sign dinged above them. "Though, next time I fly"—Haley paused, lifting her chin and laying a delicate hand on her collarbones—"I'm bringing a derby hat and gloves so I can give this section the respect it deserves."

Ethan rolled his eyes. "Haley, if I wanted to, I could have chartered a private jet for us."

Her stomach pitched like they were roughing through turbulence. "Oh."

He brought the back of her hand to his lips. "Driving sounds better, but I'm only going if you pick a road trip playlist with at least twenty Taylor Swift songs."

"Done." Haley beamed.

Since they'd dropped his Audi at the car transporter prior to catching their flight, Ethan would have to slum it with the radio in her crossover for the next few days.

The captain's crackly voice requested that the flight attendants cross check. Even though she and Ethan had spent this last flight snuggling with each other while watching the same movie, tension tip-toed up her vertebrae. The plane dipping in altitude only compounded the nausea building in her stomach.

"Maybe we should rent first instead of buying. You might not like Maryland or living in such a small town." An uneven swallow squeezed down her throat. "Plus, Trudy from the Stop and Go is going to be inappropriate with you. That's how she is. She's going to grab a fistful of biceps the first time you meet. Probably every time. And Dad . . . that's going to be its own hurdle. He might warm up to you after a while. Oh heck, what am I saying? He just warmed up to me after twenty-seven years." Her breaths began to speed and shorten. "Crap. This isn't going to work."

"Haley."

The low, patient tone of his voice shot straight to the back of her neck, slithering downward in a soothing motion.

"Whatever and whoever comes our way, we'll deal with it together." Ethan's fingers slipped behind her head, encouraging her to meet his expressive amber eyes. "As long as you'll have me, I want to be with you. Whether that's in Tucson, or getting felt up at the Stop and Go"—an unexpected laugh broke from her tight chest—"or wherever in between."

Ethan paused, sincerity skating down his sharp nose. "All I know is, it doesn't feel right not being with you. It's like you set off a glitter bomb in my life, making an impression that's impossible to remove. But that's exactly what I want. I *want* to be picking up a shoe ten years from now and dump out a handful of golden glitter. I want you, Haley. Whatever that means."

Haley had to bite the inside of her lip to keep from crying.

"I'm sorry," she whispered.

His head shook subtly. "Don't be sorry."

"I was freaking out."

Ethan's half-smile hit his mouth. "It's okay."

Her chest oscillated with a shaky inhale. "I just want us to make it."

He brought her forehead to his before kissing her softly, sweetly. "Keep talking to me, and we'll make it."

Haley tugged on his sweatshirt strings, drawing him closer. She loved when he dressed like this, like a half-Yeti/half-Ethan hybrid—a standard black hoodie topping dark jeans and black leather shoes. "I love you."

"I love you too." Ethan smiled as he leaned back, tucking her head into his shoulder and holding her.

When the plane bounced on the tarmac, he dropped a kiss on her head and relinquished his steady grip. "You ready for this?"

Her mouth twisted. "The question, good sir, is are you ready for Remmy? Because you're going to get the cross-examination of your life. She's going to rake you over the coals the entire drive home."

His eyes glinted playfully. "I'm ready."

Bright-pink bubbles trickled up her chest. *Together*, they were ready for anything.

Epilogue

A year and a half later

Four pelicans sailed overhead as Ethan pushed up to sit on his rented surfboard, just beyond the wave break. For the forty-seventh time, he patted the small zipper pocket in his long-sleeve rash guard. When Ethan felt the small circle against his deltoid, the muscles in his back loosened—*slightly*. He'd been a ball of nerves all morning and had even Charlie-horsed his left foot getting out of bed at their quaint Pacific Beach rental home.

Haley pulled up to him with a tiresome *wooh* sound. "These waves keep getting stronger. I need to catch my breath."

They'd been surfing for almost two hours. Though it was Haley's first time, she'd taken to it almost instantly, cheering like an exuberant three-year-old the first time she stood up. Now, most of her hair had fallen out of its ponytail, the wet strands sticking and unsticking to the top of her T-shirt.

"Yeah," Ethan said absentmindedly, staring at the shore they'd just worked like crazy to get away from.

Any minute now, Paige would meet them here with her fiancé, Julien—the two of them playing hooky this Thursday afternoon. After a few hours in the sun, they'd all be going out to dinner.

Hopefully, to celebrate.

"Are they here yet?" Haley asked, her gaze following his sightline.

"Doesn't look like it." He glanced over, trying not to get distracted at how amazing Haley looked with her plain white shirt suctioned to her cerulean one-piece. "Thanks again for letting us take this trip to visit her. She was getting all whiny."

"She loves you." Haley smiled. "And it's only fair we spend a little more time on this coast during the summer since we went back home during the holidays."

That had been the first time Ethan had had a prototypical Christmas—the kind you see on TV. There'd been snow on everything and piping hot cocoa, since it was actually chilly enough to enjoy it. Haley had admitted that they rarely got much snow until January, but Mr. Winter must have been showing off for his desert-born guest. When they'd loaded up in her crossover to caravan with Remmy's family to a U-Cut Christmas tree farm, Ethan wasn't sure he hadn't been transplanted directly into a Hallmark movie.

Ethan's vision snapped back to the present when a droplet of saltwater ran down Haley's cheek, and she caught it with her tongue.

He gripped the fiberglass board and forced an even breath into his lungs.

"Yeah, I guess . . ." His voice sounded hoarser than intended as his free hand ran through his chin-length hair. Haley had begged him to grow it out to this length. Since she couldn't keep her fingers out of it, it wasn't such a hardship.

Ethan cleared his throat, drumming his fingers on his knee. He'd been thinking about the right way to do this for months, had had the ring for weeks, but every scenario seemed wrong. Even this didn't quite feel right, bobbing offshore, but Ethan was going to explode if he waited any longer.

It was simple physics. He'd combust.

Her face was tilted toward the sun, eyes closed as a smile ghosted her lips.

A squeezing seized every cell in his chest. "Haley . . ."

When her eyes drifted open and focused on his, Ethan understood that she knew. She'd probably known for months, reading him like the book he was. Her careful gaze never seemed to miss an expression, an emotion. Unexpected heat snaked up his legs and clenched his abs.

He was a fool for waiting this long.

"There's just one problem," Haley said through a small grin. "How are we going to pick a place?"

"We could always have two."

She nodded, bracing her board when a slight swell rose beneath them. "I know I should worry about hurting someone's feelings by trying to balance it equally, but this isn't about them, Ethan. It's about us. We're already living two lives—which I love," she added quickly. "It's a fun adventure, but I want this to be just for us." The corner of her mouth quirked. "Props on finding a remote place with no audience, by the way."

The skin beneath his soaked shirt flushed at her teasing tone. Ethan pressed his lips together, his head shaking on its own.

Haley's smirk deepened. "Seriously, it's an unexpected surprise. I always figured it'd be in bed after . . ."

The way her eyes flashed as that sentence trailed off made Ethan wish he hadn't invited his sister to the beach. He could always say they'd gotten water-logged and needed to head back to their secluded bungalow, that they'd meet her and Julien for dinner later . . .

Focus.

A slow breath left his pursed lips. "Stop trying to distract me."

The mischievous twist of her lips only broadened. "But you feel less anxious now."

Ethan's hand twitched on his thigh. "If you don't stop trying to play me like a fiddle, I'll—"

"You'll what? Make all my wildest dreams come true like you haven't already done that over the last eighteen months? Love me forever? Never let me go?" Haley had the gall to add a little pout to her lips, like what she'd said wasn't exactly what Ethan wanted for the rest of his life.

A growl escaped on its own. "You know that's exactly what I'm trying to do."

For the first time, Ethan realized he couldn't touch Haley while separated on their boards like this. Stupid.

Haley smiled as she flung herself into the water, keeping one arm secured to her surfboard. He immediately followed suit. Floating, Ethan used his free arm to snake around her waist and crush his lips to hers.

Haley's hand bunched the fabric of his rash guard, kneading the muscles of his back as they tasted the salt on each other's tongues. Like every time he kissed Haley, feeling her breathe against him felt absolutely essential, completely necessary to his existence.

"I do," she whispered against his lips.

"I haven't asked yet."

Her forehead pinched, those two perfect lines popping up.

Ethan's heartbeat ricocheted in his chest. "Haley, will you make me the happiest man in this ocean and please drive me crazy for the rest of our lives?"

"Yes." She let go of her board to wrap her legs around his waist, her fingers racing through his hair. "Three million times, yes."

It was a struggle to keep one hand on the surfboard to elevate them above the water as their mouths met again. All he wanted was to twine both arms around Haley.

"We're going to drown ourselves this way." Haley broke away from him and pushed back up on her board. As much as Ethan wanted to complain, she was right. "Catch the next one in?"

"Do you want to see the ring first?" he asked after he'd climbed back on his board.

Haley bit the corner of her lip, shaking her head. "Show me tomorrow at the courthouse."

"What?"

She didn't answer, just sprawled herself on the board with a wide grin and paddled away—instantly catching the next swell.

When Ethan finally caught the third wave he attempted and arrived at the shore, Haley was hugging Paige and Julien. Her neck twisted, sharing a private smile with him over her shoulder.

The flawless yellow diamond in a platinum flower setting would stay sealed beneath the plastic zipper of his rash guard for the rest of the day. Tomorrow, after they were officially husband and wife, he'd share and celebrate the news with his sister. Then, they would have to make dozens of calls to notify the rest of their friends and family and probably plan two wedding parties—one in each city.

Paige was going to eviscerate him, but it would be worth it. Whatever Haley threw at him was always worth it. Plus, they'd be married, their souls definitively stitched together.

He only had to wait one more day instead of a year . . . or more.

The second his leash hit the packed sand, Ethan swung Haley in a circle.

"I love you," he rasped as he settled her back on her feet.

Haley's thumb framed his jaw, her eyes lit from within. "I love you."

"Ugh, we get it. You two are too cute for words," Paige teased, as a smile spread across Julien's face.

Ethan pressed his forehead to Haley's with a relieved sigh.

One more day.

Acknowledgements

Tucson locals will note that I minorly adjusted some dates/facts/places to suit my story. I also created new places to rest beside the ones that used to/still do exist in this beloved community.

I'd like to thank my incredible developmental editor and proofreader, Rachel Garber. Every time I get to work with you is time treasured. Thank you to Jenn Lockwood for copy editing this novel, and to Enni Tuomisalo for bringing the characters to life on the cover. Louise Morris and Lisa Wittrock beta read this book, and for that, I am grateful. I'm extremely appreciative of Susanne, Cassandra, and the awesome people in the book community who support and promote my work and my amazing team of ARC readers.

My adorable children helped me come up with some creative words for this book and are always willing to listen to storyline ideas. My supportive husband keeps me sane and grounded while I'm off living in someone else's fictional life. And I'm so fortunate to be bolstered by my marvelous friends, parents, inlaws, and extended family.

As always, I want to end by thanking YOU, the reader. I wouldn't be here without you. I hope this novel tugged at your heartstrings and made you smile. I am forever grateful for the time you spend with me and my characters. Thank you!

About the Author

Laura Langa is an award-winning sweet romance author. She strives to write stories that pull at her readers' heartstrings and create relatable characters you can't help but root for. Laura loves trees and all things green, hates flossing but forces herself to do it every night, drinks tea—not coffee, and believes that salt air can often cure a bad mood.

Visit her website at www.LauraLanga.com
Subscribe to her newsletter for the latest details at www.LauraLanga.com/Newsletter
Follow on Instagram and Facebook @LauraLangaWrites

9 798218 115791